KT-151-331

4721800046761 6

LOVE IN A MIST

LOVE IN A MIST

Sarah Harrison

This first world edition published 2018
in Great Britain and the USA by
SEVERN HOUSE PUBLISHERS LTD of
Eardley House, 4 Uxbridge Street, London W8 7SY
Trade paperback edition first published
in Great Britain and the USA 2018 by
SEVERN HOUSE PUBLISHERS LTD

Copyright © 2018 by Sarah Harrison.

All rights reserved including the right of
reproduction in whole or in part in any form.
The moral right of the author has been asserted.

British Library Cataloguing in Publication Data
A CIP catalogue record for this title is available from the British Library.

ISBN-13: 978-0-7278-8812-9 (cased)
ISBN-13: 978-1-84751-940-5 (trade paper)
ISBN-13: 978-1-78010-992-3 (e-book)

This is a work of fiction. Names, characters, places and incidents
are either the product of the author's imagination or are used fictitiously.
Except where actual historical events and characters are being described
for the storyline of this novel, all situations in this publication are
fictitious and any resemblance to actual persons, living or dead,
business establishments, events or locales is purely coincidental.

All Severn House titles are printed on acid-free paper.

Severn House Publishers support the Forest Stewardship Council™ [FSC™],
the leading international forest certification organisation. All our titles that
are printed on FSC certified paper carry the FSC logo.

MIX
Paper from
responsible sources
FSC® C013056

Typeset by Palimpsest Book Production Ltd.,
Falkirk, Stirlingshire, Scotland.
Printed and bound in Great Britain by
TJ International, Padstow, Cornwall.

ONE

1978

'd just turned nine when this happened. For the first and only time I had been away with a friend's family for a week in Wales, but the friend (I didn't like her all that much) had been taken ill and we'd come home a day early. I sensed my parents were a bit flustered by the change of plan but I didn't care – it was bliss to be back in my own bed.

Midsummer, and the night was stifling hot. Those were the days when summers seemed always to be hot, and there were still so many moths about that you had to keep the curtains tightly drawn when you had the light on. Unless of course you liked moths, which I didn't. Their nasty fluffy bodies and their frantic flittering and bumbling around the lampshade horrified me, and if one blundered against my face I would scream and leap out of bed, arms flailing. Daddy longlegs were nearly as bad, trailing their wobbly, purposeless cotton-thread limbs all over the place.

I was reading one of my many books about a girl with a jolly dog and a sweet old pony. Petunia, my prized birthday cabbage patch doll was tucked in next to me. Zinny (I'd always called my mother by her Christian name) had come upstairs an hour ago to say goodnight but I hadn't been able to sleep, and I soon turned the lamp on again. It was much later when I finished the book. The girl had realized that she was going to have to get another pony if she wanted to win at shows, but that she would never get rid of her faithful old friend, the one who'd taught her to ride. I'd read it many times before but I liked the familiarity, the book's world of gentle tests and healthy challenges sturdily met; the girl's occasional lapses into, and recoveries from, selfish ambition; the cosy anticipation of a happy and improving ending. There were other stories about the same girl – not in real time; she always stayed the same – and I had all of them on my shelf.

I put the book on my bedside table and turned the lamp off. All the internal doors were open to let the air circulate and I could just make out the lowered voices of my parents on the downstairs verandah. No sound of the sea tonight, but I could imagine the smooth, oily waves creeping forward on to the beach, delivering a tiny 'spit', and drawing silkily back over the shiny sand and little stones. During a lull in my parents' conversation I heard something else – a soft rattle and click, like a window or a cupboard door, and a brisk tread – my father's – came to the foot of the stairs and paused for a moment before going back to the verandah. I heard him say 'Nothing . . . out for the count . . .' and thought he meant me.

Our house was a sort of bungalow, but one which crept up the hill, so it was on two levels. The higher, back level consisted of my room and the spare bedroom, with a small bathroom in between. A short flight of stairs led down to the lower floor which was effectively a large flat with my parents' room (they had their own bathroom), the kitchen and cloakroom, and the big living room which ran across the front of the house with a glass door opening on to the verandah. The house was 1920s, and Zinny used to say it looked like a cricket pavilion, a simile I didn't understand as a child, but came to recognize as accurate.

Outside the back rooms a narrow stone-flagged area ran the width of the house, with a parapet, no more than two feet high and topped with coping, on the far side. Beyond that the grassy cliff-top hill rose smoothly to the road half a mile away. What we thought of as 'our' lane, which looped down past us and on over the next headland, was at night like Alfred Noyes' 'ribbon of moonlight', and I often imagined the highwayman riding . . . riding . . . riding . . . on his way to his tryst with Bess.

Picturing this now made the air in the room seem even stuffier. I got out of bed and hauled first one curtain back, then the other. The window was set quite high and I was short for my age: standing on the floor I could only just see the parapet. There was no moon tonight and the moving lights of a single car on the horizon only made it seem darker. I lifted the window latch and pushed it wide, leaving my hands on the ridge between the inner and outer sill.

And then – another hand appeared on top of mine. The hand was spongy and large. It lay heavily on mine, holding my own in place. The back of it was spattered with freckles, the skin slippery and loose, the little finger bent inward at the first joint. It could have been a man's or a woman's, I couldn't tell. The nails were broad, ridged and unkempt and I caught a sour smell in the air.

All of these observations took place in the two seconds before I shrieked and snatched – dragged – my hand away from the sill. The thick fingers clawed ineffectually, trying to hold me back, but terror made me quick and strong.

I flew to the door and down the stairs, my feet barely touching the treads, and out to the verandah. The smell here was of sea and cigarette smoke. They'd heard me coming, because my father's face was already turned towards me, with the smile he'd been wearing for Zinny.

'Floss, what's up?' I hurtled into the protective curve of his outstretched arm. 'Hey, come on!'

'Bad dream I expect,' said Zinny. My mother was always the cooler one.

'What is it?' he asked again, giving me a little shake, trying to see my face. 'Poor old thing, you are in a way.'

'I was frightened!'

He put his hands on my waist and hoisted me on to his knee. 'What of?'

'I thought there was something outside the window.'

'What sort of thing?'

'A person.'

Zinny had already got to her feet. I knew, as I always did, that they were looking at each other over my head.

'How about some hot chocolate?'

I nodded and kept my face hidden in my father's shoulder as she went to the kitchen.

'Now then.' He turned my face towards his. 'Shall I go up and take a look?'

'Yes please.'

'Want to come too?'

'No.'

He stood up and put me in his chair, one of the woven outdoor chairs with cushions; the cushion was warm.

'Don't move a muscle.'

Terror turned to bliss as I sat there, listening to my parents, one upstairs, one in the kitchen, both ministering to me. Just for once, they were apart, and I was the centre of attention. Even after the horrible hand, it was a moment of pure happiness. Zinny turned on the television in the living room and took me through to sit on the sofa. It was boring news, but the flickering picture and the voices were comforting. The newsreader said that a 'miracle baby' had been born. I had no idea what she meant.

My father came back down, but went to the kitchen first and said something to Zinny before turning the sound down and sitting next to me on the sofa, putting Petunia on my lap.

'All well, nothing there. I even went out and had a scout round.' I didn't believe this – either part of it – but that didn't matter for now.

'Can I sleep in your bed?'

'Ooh, not too sure about that . . .' Zinny came back with the hot chocolate in her own big china breakfast cup, with roses on it. 'What do you reckon, darling, can Floss go in our bed for a while?'

I knew they were exchanging looks again so I kept my head down. Then my mother said, 'Alright, just for a while.'

My father fetched his glass from the verandah and settled down next to me again. Zinny closed the verandah door and sat in the wing-back chair she liked. There I was between them, sipping my hot drink, catered and cared for, my fright forgotten, or put in its place.

I fell asleep quickly in their wide, smooth, soft bed that smelt of Zinny. I half-woke once; it was the middle of the night, and neither of them were with me. But I heard muted voices and bumping about . . . the front door opening and closing . . . the car starting up . . .

I sat bolt upright then – were they leaving me on my own?

Zinny came in wearing her green silk dressing gown, her

face pale and clear of make-up. Seeing me wide awake she looked startled but only for a second.

'Come on, you should be asleep.'

'Where's Daddy?' I demanded.

'Oh, a friend of his has had a breakdown on the other side of Salting. He's being very, very kind and going to help.' Even then I realized this was unlikely – my parents didn't have many friends, let alone one for whom my father would make a mercy dash in the small hours – but I knew not to expect more. I lay down, and Zinny took off her dressing gown and lay carefully down next to me in her pale-yellow nightdress. She touched her fingers to her lips, and then tapped them on my cheek.

'Night-night, Flora.'

'Night, Zinny.'

That's what happened. Something – but I didn't know what. Not for a long, long time.

TWO

1998

I may not have landed the best-paid job in the world, but I couldn't have asked for more beautiful surroundings. Edwin Clayborne was squarely in the very English tradition of intellectual humanists who nonetheless love the Anglican church – its books and liturgy, its music, its buildings, most of all its buildings. His house in the cathedral close was itself a Georgian gem, the windows gazing calmly over the green lawns and between the glorious oaks to the leaping spires and buttresses of the minster. The great surges of tourists, and the slighter, more regular flow of clergy and worshippers came and went at an acceptable distance. He had all the beauty and none of the nuisance. I found out that was also true of his church-going. He attended services to soak up the words, both spoken and sung, untrammelled by the need to believe any of them.

I'd not been in the job long. I started in late March, and now it was mid-April and the close was a-flutter with daffodils and narcissi. Pigeons and starlings roosted on the ledges of the minster, but they had to be wary; a pair of falcons was nesting on the east tower, predatory and protected, a camera trained on them day and night. The city was proud of its falcons, even though (the camera and good binoculars revealed) the carved head below their nest was now even more grotesque with thick tears of guano.

The walk to the close from my modern flat on the outskirts of the city took half an hour. If the weather was really bad I drove, but I usually I preferred the walk, which woke me up and meant I arrived ready and firing on all cylinders. This morning was cool and bright, if anything a little too shiny, the bustling high cloud threatening rain before eleven. The first service of the day was over and the coaches had not yet begun arriving. Two clergy – the very tall Dean, and another – were in conversation by the north door. I took a small pride in being part of that select community: people who belonged in the close.

Edwin's house was directly opposite the north prospect of the minster, at the centre of a run of five late-eighteenth-century houses. All of them were fine, but his was the prettiest. Never having been invited to do otherwise I observed the formalities, going in through the shoulder-high iron gate and up the gravel path between the two neat squares of lawn, one with a dryad birdbath, the other with a sundial. These weren't the lightweight imitation statuary you could buy from garden centres but the real thing – heavy, mossy and gnarly. It was too early in the year to identify much else, but there was some sort of fruit tree in one corner, climbing plants over the south-facing wall, and an edging of twiggy lavender along the sides of the path.

I went up the three steps to the dark red door and pulled the iron bell-pull on the left (there was one on the right labelled 'Garden Bell'). The uneven clangour always sounded loud and peremptory, but I was getting to be less embarrassed by that. My employer always answered the door promptly, as if he'd been watching my approach from some vantage point.

'Hello, hello.'

'Good morning.'

We rarely if ever used each other's names. In fact we never called each other anything. Perhaps we were sizing each other up, getting the weight of our working relationship. I had decided to take my tone from him.

He peered out over my shoulder as I entered. 'What's it like? I haven't poked my nose out yet. Hmm . . .' He adopted his faux dotty professor tone. 'We shall have rain.'

'No, we won't.' I patted my shoulder bag. 'Because I brought my brolly.'

'Good thinking.'

We neither of us cared whether it rained or not but these little exchanges about the weather were part of our morning routine, and they seemed to amuse him.

'The kettle is on,' he said as I hung up my parka. 'And the hobnobs are out.'

'Right.'

He followed me through to the kitchen. I sometimes wondered if he fetishised this small ritual, getting everything ready so he could watch me pour the hot water into the mugs and put the biscuits on a plate.

Not that I'd have minded. I liked Edwin, very much. Being in his company was like blood temperature for me. We understood one another. After the interview, back on a snowy afternoon in February, I left feeling optimistic. This wasn't vanity. I quite simply felt at home with him and he, I intuited, with me.

In the interests of due diligence I'd looked up his website. Professor Edwin Clayborne, emeritus professor of English at something-or-other hall Oxford. Now better known as E.J. Clay, author of the bestselling crime novels set in academia, two of which had received the Crime Writers' Association Gold Dagger Award. The profile picture showed him as more E.J. than Prof, the long planes of his face moodily half-lit, his overlong curly hair like live wires. A little intimidating, to be honest. In real life he was lanky and charming-looking, with bright eyes, and hands like paddles. He had slight dyspraxia – I was always having to help him open jars and fit the memory stick into the computer, that sort of thing. Which made it all the more surprising that what he liked to do in his spare time was rock-climbing. There were pictures all over the place of him outlined against one yawning void or another, wearing a harness, a helmet and a mad grin – the one reserved for these circumstances. Strange that someone who couldn't for the life of him untie knots should be happy to entrust his life to a belaying rope. His real-life smile was a shy, retiring thing, only breaking cover occasionally. When it did, it completely changed his face so that he looked ten years younger. From reading his website, and from odd references, I supposed him to be in his early fifties, but the twenty-odd years' disparity in our ages was compensated for by our complementary skill-sets: Edwin could quote from *Beowulf* and write bestselling novels, and I could change the strip light over the cooker.

I wouldn't want to give the impression that he was one of those stereotypical brilliant-but-no-common-sense people. He gave everything the attention that was its due. From what I could tell he was in demand socially (though I suppose being a distinguished professor and bestselling author is a useful entrée), and from time to time I would be despatched to the posher of the local supermarkets to pick up a list of high-end convenience food. He could make an omelette Arnold Bennett, he told me, and when I said I'd never heard of that he made one for lunch, and very nice it was. People came and went, and invitations appeared on the mantlepiece.

So he had friends, but there was no evidence of a marital hinterland – no photographs of children, no telltale rogue possessions, no references to an ex (though come to think of it that wouldn't have been his style); he appeared to be a member of that vanishingly small category, the baggage-free bachelor. No wonder he got asked to dinner parties: he represented a significant catch.

At the very beginning I wondered if he was gay. Not because he showed no interest in me – I neither sought nor at that stage wanted that sort of attention from him – but because his kind of singledom was so rare. Even if I had been looking for something, this wasn't the place to look. I wouldn't have wanted to rock the comfortable boat. What we were, almost from the first, was friends. We fell into friendship not as something surprising, but as though it was something that had always been there, waiting for us to come along. Neither of us would have mentioned the other to anyone else, nor did we make any verbal acknowledgement of friendship between ourselves. And no-one observing us would have thought us chummy. During the working day – the only time we saw each other – we moved, comfortably, in our separate zones.

I poured the boiling water – tea for him, coffee for me – added his milk and my sugar (in spite of repeated Lenten efforts I couldn't wean myself off it), and we picked up our mugs. This was the moment when the day's schedule, if any, would be mentioned. He was an easy, open-minded employer. I was that old-fashioned thing: an amanuensis or general factotum, he felt free to ask me to do more or less anything that was within my powers, and I was equally free to admit if it was beyond me. Today, though, was a departure.

'I wonder if you'd read a couple of chapters for me and let me know what you think.'

I didn't blink. 'Of course.'

'I'd like your views on my female narrator.'

'First person?'

'Well, rather rash you might think, but yes.'

Part of the currency of our conversation was that we affected never to be surprised by each other. We were two autonomous individuals (went our thinking), each with a quiverful of talents and competencies which the other one might not even be able to guess at. The corollary of this was that we had not to be surprised by gaps in the other one's knowledge or skills. I had read and enjoyed a couple of Edwin's books before coming to work for him, but I never expected to be asked for editorial input, and was secretly flattered. I wasn't going to refuse.

'I'd be happy to,' I said.

'Good. I've got to go out in an hour. I'll give it to you before I go.'

'Fine.'

We went our separate ways, he to his pleasant work room in the back garden – 'the potting shed' – and I to my small office, which must once have been a boot room or scullery.

By tacit mutual agreement I had never been into the potting shed; I rang him if I needed to talk to him. If I needed to go over there I knocked and waited.

Edwin must have taken to me, because I didn't have a dazzling CV. I hadn't been to university and never even applied. I have no idea if I'd have got in. After A Levels I just wanted to work, to get my own life and earn my own money. I'd always done holiday jobs – chamber maid, waitress, shop assistant – and saw no reason why I shouldn't do any one of those again while I took an IT course (even I could see that was essential). I worked in Felicity Fine Things in Salting for a year, itself a crash course in the retailer–customer interface. The residents of Salting were unfailingly polite and pleasant but from April to September the 'grockles' came in their hordes and in their funny shorts, mob-handed, off the leash and trailing flotillas of disaffected offspring. Admittedly Salting didn't attract the more fiercely entitled holidaymakers, who went in search of sun and sand, not the pebbles and ozone of the English coast, but the visitors were still a different and more demanding breed.

Fine Things was a gift shop – a superior one, but a gift shop nonetheless. The eponymous Felicity, a tall, hard-bodied blonde, was the business brains and her husband Ian, a retired police officer, was the buyer. He was avuncular and charming; she was scary and demanding. But my year there was useful and when I left I'd learned a lot, about stock-taking, accounting, marketing and how the world worked.

After that, and with the experience and the IT course under my belt, I went on to first a hotel near Lyme Regis, where I was a sort of under-manager, in charge of bookings and day-to-day trouble-shooting, and then to a prep school where I was secretary for five years until I applied for the job with Edwin Clayborne. I was happy at the school, and might have stayed longer but for two things. My first proper, but vaguely unsatisfactory relationship (perhaps it was too proper) ended miserably, and that happened at a time when I was already becoming restless; the two things were probably not unconnected. I spotted Edwin's advertisement in *Private Eye* of all places, it was 'flexible hours' for nearly the same money I was getting at the school. I applied in a spirit of what-the-hell, half expecting it to be some sort of joke or, perhaps, vaguely indecent.

But it was neither, and to my astonishment I beat off extensive competition to land the job. I had only one interview, and he never told me why he chose me. But on those days – and this was one – when I had to pinch myself to believe I was here, I reckoned it was just because of my varied, down-to-earth experience. From my unflashy CV he inferred, correctly, that I could turn my hand to things. I was not a specialist but a generalist and so, in his admittedly more high-powered way, was he.

In the interview, when I mentioned I'd read two of his books, he said, 'Oh, did you? Good effort.' I liked that, the appreciative note that was neither creepily grateful nor prickly. He didn't ask me what I'd thought of them, either, so my carefully prepared response wasn't needed.

Today there was a letter from the Wine Society and a dozen emails, half of them website feedback forms, a pretty standard morning's intake. The cat, Percy, lay on the windowsill gazing at me with slit-eyed disdain. Percy was a long-haired tabby with the slightly tufted ears of a Maine Coon, whose defining characteristic was his enormous size. He was easily the biggest cat in the close, if not the county, and Edwin had one photograph of him hunting (well, strolling around) on the green, which could easily have been passed off as an escaped panther. Like most of his kind he was idle, opportunistic and largely indifferent to those with whom he shared his space. Edwin claimed that Percy had been foisted on him some years ago by a friend who had moved house, but they had shaken down together.

When I'd dealt with the feedback forms, replied to a couple of others and forwarded the rest to Edwin with my comments, I returned to my current ongoing task, trawling the web for sites, books and authorities on radical free-thinking schools over the past hundred years. This was for the next E.J. Clay, presumably the one with the female narrator – he was currently proofreading the one that was due out in the autumn. He was perfectly competent on the internet, but he liked me to get the spade-work done, to sift through for the best places to visit, ones I knew would suit him.

At five to ten I heard the click of the French window, and Edwin appeared in the doorway, making a tapping motion with the knuckle of his forefinger.

'I'm off. I've emailed you something to read.'

I touched the keyboard. 'There it is. Thanks, I'll look forward to that.'

'I'm sure I don't have to say this, but – be frank, won't you?'

'Don't worry.'

'You'll probably be gone by the time I get back, so see you tomorrow.'

'See you then.'

He hesitated as if going to add something but then just smiled without catching my eye and said, 'Right.'

He'd sent me a few thousand words, about forty pages, so I printed them off. I'd always rather read pages than a screen, particularly as I was being asked for a reaction. I wanted to look at this (the working title was *Dead in the Water*) just as if it were my chosen bedtime reading and not an extension of my work. I put the pages in a plastic wallet, and the wallet in my bag. At one o'clock I forwarded the results of my researches to Edwin's email, and left.

I worked four mornings and one full day, the latter a moveable feast according to what was going on. In the afternoon I walked, shopped and did domestic stuff, and in the evenings I had classes, watched TV or met up with a friend. Only one of my real friends, Elsa, actually lived in the city, and she was married. I didn't mind and I wasn't lonely. My life was of my own making and I was happy with it.

Today I had nothing planned, so when I'd eaten my Pret wrap I lay full length on the sofa with two carefully positioned cushions behind my head, and began to read.

I went through the pages once quickly, then made some coffee and read them again slowly. When I'd finished I put them down on the floor beside me, folded my arms and crossed my ankles and gazed at the Artex ceiling. Elsa couldn't understand how I lived with the Artex, 'sperm mix' as she called it. But I couldn't have cared less – who looked at the ceiling? And if you did, as I was doing now, there was something soothing in the bobbly concentric swirls.

How was I going to tell Edwin that he had got his character, Donna Wheatley, mostly right, but that getting something mostly right, like a watch that is accurate most of the time, is really not much use. The little bits that weren't right sabotaged the rest.

I closed my eyes to concentrate. The point was, I decided, that he was trying too hard to get the 'female' aspect right. Donna was a good character – dry, amusing, vulnerable but competent, and those qualities alone were enough to make her credible. There didn't need to be references to leg-shaving and (God help us) periods; it was enough that we knew she was a woman and liked her. I was rather embarrassed at the clunkiness of these details, but touched by them too, and by the uncertainty which had prompted him to ask for my advice.

There was a nice park near my flat – an open piece of ground landscaped around the foundations of a little Norman castle that had once been there – and I often went there to walk. The pretty changeable light of the morning had turned churning and grey, the April afternoon had turned into the tail end of winter rather than the early spring, but that kept the people away and I had the park to myself. There were a couple of seats inside what remained of the castle keep, and I went in there to sit out of the slapping breeze, to have a think. I felt that I had been given some sort of test. To fail would not be fatal (and anyway I might not know if I had), but I wanted very much to pass, and also to be honest.

When I got back I'd decided to write my comments down. That way I wouldn't be flustered into saying something I didn't mean. I sat with my laptop at the little table in the living-room window. First time out I wrote far too much. When I read it through it sounded jejune and bet-hedging, every observation tempered and qualified. The second time I kept it short, one paragraph, saying how much I liked Donna but suggesting that he didn't need all of the 'female' detail, some of which I itemized. When I'd finished I pressed Send before I could change my mind.

Coincidentally, that evening was the first episode of a new cop show with a female detective. I noticed there were all sorts of things you could do on television, little touches, which in writing would have seemed too heavy handed. I pictured Edwin reading my comments and squirmed.

The next morning he opened the door and we went through to the kitchen as usual. Nothing was said about my email. I thought I had either failed the test or he hadn't read it yet – I wasn't going to ask.

When I went on to the computer I saw with a jolt of anxiety that he had replied.

Thanks so much for that, most useful – noted and appreciated.

THREE

My parents weren't like other people's. Perhaps all children think that about their parents, but in my case my suspicions were confirmed by others. That said, the differences my school friends perceived were different from those I saw.

'You're so *lucky*,' they said. 'They let you do anything!'

This wasn't quite true, but it was true enough to give me a crackle of gratification. Not that licence as a teenager made me into a wild child. And childhood itself was a freer time than it is now. The 'out all day on a bike' thing was still common in the mid-seventies, and mobiles were still in the future so none of us could be checked up on.

Other kids liked coming to tea at ours because we were allowed free access to the cupboards and fridge and could concoct what we liked – sandwiches made from chocolate digestives and peanut butter, white bread with crisps, custard-in-a-glass cocktails, tinned frankfurters with ketchup and sweet mustard out of a tube . . . even oven 'dampers' made out of white flour, water and sugar, with a hole poked in the middle for jam. Zinny would never have dreamed of eating these things herself, but was prepared to maintain a contingency supply for us.

My friends were also impressed, though more ambivalent, about my calling my mother by her name. I was often asked, 'Doesn't that feel weird?'

'No.' It wasn't weird to me; saying 'Zinny' was like saying 'Mum', because I'd never done any different. From my earliest days, that's what she was.

'Is that her actual name?'

'Her name's Zinnia. It's a flower.'

I got used to the wide-eyed attention. Much later I realized no-one was jealous of me. They were simply glad to have this unusual resource to hand. My situation must have appeared thrillingly bohemian but no-one wanted to swap places – they were glad to go back to their more ordinary homes where food was cooked and house rules applied.

I don't want to give the impression that we primary school kids were on our own when we went back to mine. My father, whom I called Dad, just like everyone else, would be there on these occasions, though not much in evidence. He would manifest himself now and then, not exactly to check up but to show the flag.

'Hi girls!' he'd say. 'How's it going?'

I usually ignored him, but one or two of my friends would blush and say 'Fine thanks' as if he was really enquiring. He'd stand there in his stockinged feet, hands in pockets, hair ruffled, gazing at us.

'Everyone happy? Anything I can do?'

I'd shake my head, but the other person would usually mutter, 'No thanks.' And that was his cue to disappear.

My father's name was Nico. He worked as a sales rep for a well-known confectionery company, criss-crossing the country with a boot full of highly coloured, tooth-rotting merchandise (something else there was always a supply of in our house). The nature of his job meant that he was either away for days on end or at home 'doing paperwork'. Zinny worked odd hours so having friends 'to tea' happened when my father was around. The paperwork happened in their bedroom. He lay propped up against the bed head with stuff strewn around and a biro in his hand; once or twice I went in and he dropped something very quickly over the side of the bed. His huge smile was meant to distract me, but I noticed.

My parents' distinguishing marks – in my friends' eyes anyway – were these: my mother was glamorous, and my father was young. Also, Zinny was older than him and he looked younger than he was, so the difference was striking. It was just as well about the glamour, or his boyish manner and appearance might have made her seem dowdy. As it was you could see what the attraction was, and they made a charismatic couple, something I came to appreciate more as time went by.

My father's boyishness meant that we were like pals. He didn't have the massive presence in my life that some other people's fathers did. I had the distinct impression that far from being chief provider, he worked only because it would have looked bad if he hadn't. He didn't lay down the law, or stand between me and whatever dangers might be out there; he wasn't the person who could sort anything out, fix problems and bicycles and broken chairs. In fact he stood in the same relationship to these things as I did: one of baffled helplessness. We were chums, laughing together at 'the innate hostility of inanimate objects' which were always letting us down. It was as well that Zinny kept a comprehensive list of 'little men' in the back of her diary. We needed them.

My mother wasn't much on the domestic front either, but that was because she had a job she enjoyed, and preferred to be doing that, or anything, than cleaning. We had Mrs March to do that, who treated us all like children in the nicest possible way. If Nico couldn't be there after school or in the holidays, Mrs March filled in. Zinny worked in the box office at the local seaside rep, in the town on the far side of Salting. She and Nico had complementary natures; they suited one another. His underlying indolence did not annoy her, and he wasn't in the least diminished by her need to be busy.

So that was good – for them, anyway. The question I asked myself was, where did I fit in? My parents were a near-perfect couple, but that didn't leave much room for anyone else. I didn't doubt that they loved me in an absent-minded way, and I wasn't neglected, but I certainly wasn't the focus of their attention the way other children were the focus of their parents'. My father was casual and playful and when he was around we often had fun. I was sure that when he was away he didn't think about me at all. Zinny was busy and not around so much day to day – and even when she was she didn't play or take me on outings. What she did do was interrogate. One instance will serve to illustrate this.

'How's school?' she'd ask. This was usually when I'd just been dropped off by one of the other mothers in the lift-share scheme, when all I wanted to do was eat biscuits in my room.

But there was no gainsaying Zinny when she wanted to know.

'OK.'

'I know it's OK. Tell me what you've been doing?'

'Nothing much.'

'But what?'

'Maths, RE . . . We had news assembly.'

'Oh? What was your news?'

'It wasn't our year's turn.'

'Ah, I see.' I thought she sounded rather relieved. 'What sort of thing do people say?'

'Holidays and stuff. What they did at the weekend.'

Zinny frowned. 'What do they do at the weekend?'

'Go to places. Like Harrington House.'

I knew this would go down well: Harrington House was the local stately home where we'd been a couple of times ourselves. 'Really? Do they like it?'

The truth was that most of my schoolmates found the tour of the house boring – 'interesting' and 'very interesting' were the telltale words – but they did like the other stuff.

I waited, hoping to get away and listen to my tranny, but Zinny was pleased with the way things were going.

'Let's see,' she said, 'what did *we* do last weekend?'

We thought about this. My parents had been out on both

Friday and Saturday nights (on the first I went to a friend's house, on the second Mrs March came round), and had slept in the next morning. On Saturday I'd gone to the beach with my father. On Sunday he'd played cricket and because it was sunny we'd gone along, sitting under the tree behind the bowler's arm, my mother reading her book behind dark glasses and me coming and going from the swings where I'd made friends with a girl who'd come with the other team.

'Just a nice family weekend,' suggested Zinny, content to have put a label on it. The slightly dull wastes of daytime had probably seemed restful to them after their late nights.

'Can we have a dog?' I asked. I tried this from time to time when Zinny was in a good mood. If Dad was around he'd say, 'Oh yes, come on darling, do let's!' But he was only teasing and Zinny usually raised an eyebrow and quirked her mouth in disdain at the very idea.

This time she said: 'I suppose we could discuss it.'

Had I heard her right? For the first time the door had been left ajar, admitting the merest thread of light. I was so gobsmacked I didn't even take her up on it in case she changed her mind. I scooted off, but I knew I'd have to make headway with my father at the very next opportunity. He could be relied on to say whatever was easiest for everyone on any given occasion. I would need to make my case so that he'd actually feel able to back me up to Zinny.

Next time he had a weekday at home, we went for our usual walk on the beach after school. A few hundred yards from our house there was a lay-by where people often pulled over to admire the view of the bay. From here there was a precipitous wooden walkway of broad rickety steps with a wobbly handrail that broke off long before you reached the bottom. It wasn't surprising that the walkway was in a poor state of repair: passers-by couldn't be bothered to pick their way down between the brambles and sloes to a beach where there were no facilities and where the sea came in to within yards of the cliff at high tide. Round the headland in Salting there was ample parking and a nice high street, plus beach huts, loos, a tea shop that sold homemade local ice cream, and helpful boards giving the times of tides, which anyway didn't affect the available space the way they did here. Plus, you could walk back to your car without risking a coronary.

Occasionally in the parking spot we'd catch remarks about our house, along the lines of 'Nice place . . . lovely position . . . but honestly would you want to live here in the winter . . .?'

I often thought the same thing myself. I liked the house, and where it was, but in some way I couldn't work out it didn't quite 'go' with my parents.

Today we had the place to ourselves. My father had stuffed a plastic bag in his trouser pocket so we could pick blackberries on the way back. He always looked at the sloes and said he had once made sloe gin and might well do so again, but as far as I know he never did. I once tried a sloe and it made my whole face wince and my tongue pucker. He laughed and said, 'Serves you right.'

The weather that day was soft, grey and blustery, the wind just enough to keep the rain clouds moving along. The waves bustled and rushed, rearing up and flopping down on the shiny stones and patches of silky grey sand. The bay was no more than half a mile long, with rocks at either end. The rocks to the west were piled up like a ruined castle, good for climbing on; the eastern ones were a long low tumble covered in slimy green weed and bladder wrack, where you could find crabs, anemones and sometimes little fish in the pools at low tide. We turned right, to the west. Because not many people could be bothered to come here the beach should have been clean, but stuff still got washed up by the tide, and blown about from the over-full bin in the lay-by; my father and I would pick up the more egregious items like cans and bottles, and either hide them or, if we could be bothered, carry them to the top and dispose of them. Today everything was pristine apart from a very dead gull, its feathers shimmering with microscopic scavengers.

I came at the topic obliquely. 'Did you have any pets when you were young?'

'Umm . . .' He paused and kicked at a clump of seaweed. 'Let's see . . .'

'You had that rabbit,' I reminded him. This was not a new conversation.

'Oh yes.' He stooped to pick up a shell, studied it and discarded it. 'Correct.'

'Thumper.'

'You've got a good memory, Floss.' We both knew I didn't have a particularly good memory, it was just that we were on familiar territory.

'Did you look after him?'

'Not if I could help it.'

'Why not?'

'I told you, because he was a vicious brute.'

'But he was a rabbit!'

'Rabbits aren't all fluffy cuddly bunnies. Ask any vet.'

We'd been through all this before. 'How did he die?'

'He met a sticky one."

'Were you sad?'

'Stop it, Floss.'

'What?'

He continued to walk but put his hand on the top of my head and rubbed gently back and forth as if erasing my thoughts. 'You know jolly well what. No dog. Your mother's not keen and it's not fair to keep on about it.'

'But she's *not* not keen. Not so much as she was. She said we could all think about it.'

'Did she?' He pulled a face. 'Well, now we have.'

I remember we had nearly reached the castle of rocks. Even on completely calm days there would be spouts of spray around its base, and you could hear the fierce hissing and sucking of the sea; in the gullies between the rocks the trapped water banged and smacked around, trying to get out. What usually happened was that I ran on ahead and climbed up as far as I could – at ten years old I was still in the 'Look at me!' phase when all that was required of my father was to stand at the bottom and wave admiringly.

But just as we reached that point, a dog appeared.

I mean it *literally* appeared, manifested itself, materialized out of some concealed alley through the rocks about halfway up and hurtled dangerously down the uneven sprawl towards us. We scarcely had time to react before it was upon us, a medium-sized, brown and black wire-haired dog with sticky-out eyebrows and a beard and a pointed tail that went round and round like a propeller as it greeted us.

'Hey, what's all this, who are you, where's your collar?' enquired my father pointlessly and amiably as the dog leapt around us, grinning and panting and planting its wet gritty paws on our legs.

I knew exactly what it was all about. The collarless dog had been sent in answer to my prayers.

'Where's your owner?' asked my father, tousling the dog's head; the dog didn't answer. 'Be here soon I expect, eh?'

I climbed up the rocks, and the dog followed, then tore back to my father, then up again, barking enthusiastically. It was an indefatigable animal, full of beans and the joys of spring.

'Careful he doesn't knock you over!' called my father. 'Floss – hear me? Be careful!'

I knew he wouldn't knock me over. He was as surefooted as a goat and wanted only to keep me company.

'Can you see anyone over there?'

I pulled myself up on to my best vantage point, where I could see the narrower strip of beach on the far side. It was completely empty as I knew it would be.

'No! Nobody here!'

The dog stood next to me, gazing in the same direction and panting happily. Then suddenly he rushed down on to the other beach and charged crazily back and forth, picking up a stick on the way and shaking it.

'Right!' called my father from behind me. 'He'll know his way home. Come on.'

Hearing my father's voice the dog dropped the stick, looked up with his head cocked and then charged back up to where I was standing.

'Damn, did you call him? You're not encouraging him, Floss, are you?'

'No!' I shouted back happily. Something told me I didn't need to do any encouraging.

'Come on down now. If we set off in the opposite direction he'll soon lose interest and go back where he belongs.'

He didn't, of course; I knew he wouldn't. We went all the way to the far end of the beach, alternately ignoring him and, in my father's case, shooing him away, but to no avail. I was careful not to say anything, though at one point my father looked down at me with a comical frown and said, 'Floss, you don't *know* this dog, do you?'

'No!' I said, hoping I sounded aggrieved.

'OK.'

He picked up a stick and hurled it as far as he could into the sea. He was a cricketer: he could throw miles.

'Come on.' He grabbed my hand and towed me towards the steps – I could hardly keep up. I glanced back and saw the dog's head bobbing on the surface of the waves, a long way out. My father tugged. 'Don't worry about him, he's fine!'

We were only a short way up when the dog overtook us, dropped the stick on the next step and had a massive shake, spraying us with sea water. My father first yelped in outrage, then roared with laughter. It was an absolutely delicious moment.

'Right,' said my father, still chortling. 'Point taken, I give up.'

He was wearing a soft, frayed webbing belt, and he took this off and threaded it round the dog's neck. It made a very short lead, but the dog became docile and walked nicely, so my father handed the end of the belt to me. The dog seemed content, as if the makeshift lead were a place of safety. I thought I might die of happiness as the three of us made our way up to the road.

'What are we going to do?' I asked.

'Well he's clearly run away from someone or somewhere; he's well looked after. I'm going to look up the numbers of local vets and ask them to put something on their notice boards. There must be a system for lost dogs.'

I wondered what Zinny would say, but decided not to mention her. This had been my father's decision and his only; I'd had nothing to do with it. When we got home we dried the dog with an old tea towel, and put down a bowl of water in the kitchen. I petted him (it was a him: he had a willy with a sprout of hair like a jaunty feather) while my father sat at the table with the handset and the yellow pages, looking up vets and making calls. It was clear from his end of the conversation that they didn't hold out a lot of hope. The very first one asked what breed the dog was, and of course we didn't know, so my father said it was a mongrel, and described the colour as black and tan, which was near enough. Not having a collar was a problem; I suppose if he had had one we'd have been able to contact the owner ourselves. Dad left our name and phone number, and after three calls he put the handset back and lit a cigarette while he gazed at the dog. This was a sure sign of discombobulation: Zinny was very against his smoking and was trying to make him give up. He flapped his hand in front of his face, and I opened the window.

'OK,' said my father, 'here's what I suggest. We leave Towser here for half an hour and pop over to Salting. We can put a postcard in the post office window, and the newsagent's, and I suppose we'd better pick up some dog food and some sort of collar from somewhere.'

All this made my heart leap, but I stayed poker-faced.

Or so I thought. 'Don't get any ideas,' said my father. 'I wonder if we have time for me to dig out the Polaroid and take a photograph . . .'

I knew what he meant: he meant did we have time before Zinny got back. Of course we couldn't find the Polaroid to begin with, until he slapped his hand to his forehead and went to rummage in his bedside drawer.

Something about the camera in front of my father's face made the dog jump about excitedly, but I got hold of his scruff and kneeled down next to him and made him sit.

We waited for the damp print to scroll out of the camera.

'Not a bad mug shot,' said my father. 'For a dog.'

We put the folded picnic rug down on the floor as a bed, but the dog just stood there, gazing glumly at us, tail swinging, as we closed the kitchen door.

'Would it be better to take him?' I asked.

'Absolutely not; we don't know how he'd behave in the car. We shan't be long.'

We weren't. My father bought a packet of postcards in the post office, asked the girl to stick the photo on and scribbled a few lines including our phone number. Then we dashed into the Co-op and bought four tins of dog food. Four! No joy with collars and no time to look.

'We'll have to improvise,' said my father.

We jumped back in the car and whizzed back out of town, forking left on to the coast road that led to our house.

'Oh no,' said my father. 'Damn.'

Zinny's green mini was in the drive.

The kitchen door was still closed, and the house was quiet. I closed the door behind us.

'Zinny!'

While my father waited, I took the bag of dog food through to the kitchen. The dog was standing exactly where we'd left him, and leapt for joy, tail thrashing, nearly knocking me over. I put the tins on the table and went back into the hall, careful to shut the door again behind me. My father was fiddling about outside with the car; it occurred to me that he felt just as unsure of himself as I did. This struck me as encouraging – he and I were together in this situation which made it two against one.

'So.' Zinny came out of their bedroom. She had changed out of her work clothes, and was wearing a yellow shirt that tied at the waist, and black trousers. 'Who's going to tell me what's going on?'

'He was lost and he wouldn't leave us alone.' I was inspired, I knew what to say. 'And he's got no collar so we brought him back. We thought he might cause an accident,' I added. We had thought no such thing, but it was the kind of thing adults said.

'I see.'

Nico came in, looking rather sheepish. I could tell from his face that unlike me, he was not inspired.

'Hi darling, sorry about the visitor.'

'Flora's been explaining.'

'He was very wet and very lost, we didn't have much option . . . We've put out notices, haven't we, Floss?'

I nodded furiously. 'That's what we were just doing.'

'Oh well,' said Zinny, 'good. He seems a perfectly nice animal, I don't suppose it'll be long. Just so long as I don't have to have anything to do with him.'

'I'll make tea, shall I?' said my father, going into the kitchen and closing the door after him. I knew he'd feed the dog; I was a bit jealous but didn't give in to it.

Instead I followed Zinny into the living room. She picked up the paper, kicked off her shoes and sat on one end of the sofa with her long legs curled up next to her. I couldn't quite believe it. Was that it? What had she said?

Oh well . . . a perfectly nice animal . . .

Did that mean everything was all right? That if no-one claimed the dog he could stay? I wasn't going to ask.

'Do watch telly if you want to,' said Zinny.

'It's OK thanks.'

She looked at me over the paper. 'What?'

'I said it's OK. Thanks. I don't want to.'

'Really?'

'Yes.'

'Why don't you go and help Daddy bring the tea through?'

'OK.'

I could feel her watching me as I went. In the kitchen the dog was noisily wolfing down his food (still can-shaped, he hadn't mashed it up) out of a plastic mixing bowl which wasn't up to the job, so food was going all over the place.

'Don't worry,' said my father, 'I'll clear it up.'

'I will.' I peeled off several squares of kitchen towel and knelt down by the dog, wiping and pinching to collect the bits. To my surprise, he growled. I saw the white of his eye, and his top lip curled back threateningly.

'Best not to disturb him when he's eating,' said my father unnecessarily as I jumped up in alarm. Seconds later the bowl was empty and the dog was hoovering up the stuff on the floor, tail wagging happily enough. We stared at him. My father pursed his lips.

'I suppose he should go out.'

'I'll take him.'

My father re-attached the belt. 'Be careful of the road.'

The small garden of our house was at the front, laid to grass with a shingle path and a single wind-twisted Scots pine. A low wall made of pebbles mixed with cement separated it from the road – there was no footpath. As the dog and I stood there, gazing at each other expectantly, I was conscious of my parents' faces turned my way. The window that was on the latch was opened further and my father leaned out.

'Why not take him up the hill a little way? But don't for heaven's sake let go of him, will you?'

I was already on my way. Let go of Towser? That was never going to happen, never!

FOUR
1989

When I was twenty I was working at the Dorset Arms Hotel in Lyme, living in as a junior housekeeper. I say junior, but actually I was doing rather well, moving up on the inside of the full housekeeper Mrs Collings. Fortunately she was nice, and encouraging. It was tacitly acknowledged between us that I was better at dealing with the guests (whom she regarded as a necessary evil, always messing up the beds, complaining about the TVs and leaving unmentionables in the bathroom bins), but there was nothing you could teach her about readying a room. Her half-hour induction course was a swift, economical exemplar of time-and-motion put into practice, after which the place would be fully functional and spotless.

'Everyone who comes into a hotel room,' she would say, 'wants to feel that they're the first person ever to have used it. One tiny thing that reminds them they're not, that's spoilt it for them.'

She was old-school though. Queries about pillows and herbal tea were met with her most blankly benign expression as if a child had said something crude without realizing its implications. It was left to me to deal with those, and to update the Dorset Arms' marketing. The owners were a jolly, prosperous couple who had made a lot of money in high-end boats, and for whom the hotel was really no more than a hobby. They were prepared to put money into getting it right, but then they wanted it to float, like a well-appointed yacht, without much effort from them. The arrangement worked quite well, and they recognized in me someone who might have good ideas to help them pick up a more youthful clientele.

On the day, a Friday, that I was promoted to PR and publicity duties – an arrangement which left me and Mrs Collings still good friends – I rang home to tell my parents. I'd been given the weekend off, and wanted to go home and share my success. This, surely, would be grounds for a celebration.

The phone rang three times before the answer phone kicked in. I'd suggested they set it to ring longer for everyone's sake, but this was the way Zinny liked it – she wanted to vet calls before picking up.

'Hello,' I said, 'it's me. Are you there?'

Apparently they weren't. At least I hoped they weren't, and that I hadn't fallen foul of Zinny's vetting.

'Just to say I'll be coming back tomorrow morning, I've got till Sunday evening off. And I've got some good news. OK?' I paused in case they had just walked in and were rushing to the phone. 'OK. See—' That was it, out of time.

That night I went down to the Jolly Sailor with Conor, one of the waiters. As we were leaving the 'downstairs' phone rang, and it was Zinny.

'Look, we're in Bath for the weekend but there's every chance we'll be back in time to see you on Sunday, so why don't you go down anyway? There's plenty of food about the place.'

'Well,' I said, 'I might.'

'So what's the good news?'

I was cast down. 'Oh, nothing.'

'All right.' It was so like Zinny not to press me. 'See you Sunday with a bit of luck.'

I rang off. 'Problem?' asked Conor.

'Not really.'

I didn't want to hang about in Lyme on my days off, so I allowed myself a lie-in and set off along the westward coast road to Salting at twelve in my metallic-grey Micra. The car, still on the never-never, was my pride and joy, taken through the giant rotating scrubbing brushes once a week on the basis that a clean car runs better. The radio was playing Kylie and

Jason as I got into top gear and hummed along. I entertained a sudden gratifying picture of myself – the vibrant young freewheeling professional moving out and moving up . . .

My euphoria was short lived. The weather was muggy and grey and the coast road on an early September Saturday was no place to be, clogged as it was with caravans and family cars with harassed drivers at the wheel. On top of which I was going to an empty house, which reminded me how limited were my social options. I didn't have a boyfriend, 'proper' or otherwise (interesting that 'proper' in this context meant the opposite), and few friends to speak of in the area. I hadn't bothered to keep up with people from school, and since then I'd not had those useful university years when traditionally a girl might forge relationships with like-minded fellow students. Most of the time this lack of a social circle didn't bother me – I wasn't interested in clubbing or pubbing; I was happiest working and when I wasn't doing that I was generally content with my own company. But today was different: there was something to celebrate. I'd hoped to be welcomed and, well, cherished. *Why* I allowed myself to hope for these things was a mystery. Experience showed that my parents weren't much interested. They (especially my father) seemed happy enough in my company when there was no alternative. But I always had the sense, which grew more distinct as the years went by, that if I had been spirited away in the night I wouldn't have been missed. Their lives would have continued serenely enough without me.

I suppose I just continued to think, from time to time, that they'd shape up. They weren't *bad*; they weren't *cruel*; they were – when it came to me, their daughter, their only child – heedless. I should have been used to it, but I wasn't.

I remember once reading a saying: *A child may hear what you say, it may see what you do, but it always knows who you are.* I knew who Zinny and Nico were. They were a couple sufficient unto themselves, to whom I was a mildly inconvenient adjunct, accepted and catered for but not celebrated.

I turned off the radio because they were doing golden oldies and Bonnie Tyler was rasping away about her 'Total Eclipse of the Heart'.

* * *

I turned off the main road for Salting, taking the loop by the tennis club and the (now defunct) station, and continuing out of town in the direction of our bay. I drove past the familiar landmarks – the scout hut, the common, the beech wood and the beacon path – and then left at Keeper's Cottage and along the winding lane that led to the sea and over the cliffs. The main road didn't come near here; it shot past Salting and this stretch of coast to the fleshpots of Deremouth with its golden sands, donkeys and funfair.

The road trickled along by the sea for a while and then began to climb up the broad bluff which was the easterly arm of our bay. Everything about this journey was Proustian, freighted with memories and half-submerged feelings. Later, I came to see that most other people took home for granted – home was like a second womb to them, the source of life-support systems, a haven of security from which to set out and make one's way in the world. Home for me was a restless place, not unhappy but full of uncertainty, where I was always trying, always seeking, never quite sure of where I stood.

On the brow of the hill I pulled over. I was looking down over the left shoulder of our house; I could see the upstairs windows with the stone terrace built into the hillside, and the corner of the arched wooden verandah. From here you couldn't make out the walkway down to the beach – the road below me that ran past the house looked as if it were on the lip of a precipice. Standing there on its own the house appeared secretive. Standoffish might be a better word. Not welcoming.

There was a parking area on the far side of the house in front of the garage, and with my parents away I left the car there and let myself in. The place was, as usual, immaculate. I haven't described the interior and I really should because Zinny had good taste and everything was down to her. The predominant colour in the large, light living room was a dusty pink, with soft greys and blues; a pretty, feminine room, but ample and comfortable too. There were always flowers – today there were pink and blue stocks in a tall white pottery jug on the hearth, and a little vase of smaller flowers (love-in-a-mist – she grew them each year in a pot) on the table by her chair. The bookshelves on the back wall were full, but Zinny

left gaps and put things in the gaps – shells and funny orna-
ments and vases, a framed photograph of me and my father
when I was (they told me) three. There was a big Turkish rug
on the wooden floor, patterned in red and grey, but so faded
that it too looked pink. Over the fireplace was a watercolour
seascape, not of this coast but one of long level dunes running
almost to the horizon, a blurry shimmer of sea in the distance.
I'd always liked the picture with its great expanse of light and
air, the sense it gave of space and possibilities.

You would never have guessed, from the slightly frowning
and austere outside of our house, how pretty it was in here.
This relaxed, sensuous, sweetly coloured room was, like so
much of my parents' life, a sort of secret.

And quiet. So utterly quiet. Is there anywhere more silent
than someone else's house when they're not there? None of
one's own atmosphere, one's personal vibrations, the reflection
of oneself sent back by one's own belongings.

And this was someone else's house. Theirs, my parents'. It
always had been. For the first sixteen years of my life I'd
resided here, but made very little impression on the place.

I left my weekend bag on the sofa and went looking for
something to eat. They'd never been rich enough to put in a
modern kitchen, so apart from the cooker this was pre-war,
but under Zinny's supervision my father had scrubbed and
painted it so that the old-fashioned wooden cupboards and
shelves and the pulley hanging from the ceiling looked like
the most chic retro accessories. They'd put in brass taps
over the butler's sink, and lifted the lino to reveal the tiled
floor. So it had a certain style, but anyone over eighty would
have felt right at home here.

Not that we had many visitors. Another defining aspect of
our family life was its separateness. My parents liked to go
out and enjoy themselves, they had acquaintances connected
with the rep and the cricket club, but they didn't have people
round – there were no dinner parties or sociable Sunday
lunches. They were sufficient unto themselves.

I discovered early on that I had no grandparents, or none
that I'd met. My father's mother was dead, and he described
his father as a 'complete wastrel', who had taken off long

since and with whom he'd lost contact. Zinny was even less forthcoming, saying only with a cool smile that she had 'cut the traces long ago', and had no intention of going back.

As a child you accept how things are unquestioningly. Only gradually did it dawn on me that my home life was different, and strange. And even then I coasted on the admiration and envy that my parents attracted. I wasn't unhappy, but over the years I began to see us through others' eyes.

I opened the fridge more in hope than expectation. Now that I wasn't in residence there was no need for an array of convenience food. Four cans of lager, a bottle of sauvignon, some scarily organic yoghurt, salad and eggs. It was a waste of time looking for cake or biscuits, but I disinterred a loaf of sliced bread from the freezer, and tuna and mayonnaise from the cupboard. I'd get fish and chips in Salting this evening. I could already feel that tomorrow I'd have a lie-in and head back to Lyme.

Being here on my own reminded me of the dog, who'd found us and loved us. Me especially. Down there near the fridge was where we'd put the picnic rug for him. A lump swam up into my throat and my eyes oozed tears. I ripped off some kitchen towel and sat down at the table so I could cry properly, and noisily. I sobbed and gulped and wailed and gasped. I rarely cried, and the relief was intense. I gave myself up to it, like an orgasm (the orgasm I imagined and looked forward to: I had never had one). The tears weren't only for Towser, they were for me.

Everything had gone so well with Towser to begin with. School holidays began and I was not just willing but desperate to take on dog-care duties. They were just what I needed, solitary, conscientious child that I was. My parents were impressed, especially Zinny, who I think suddenly saw both how good I was at it, and how good it was for me.

'I must say, sweetie,' she remarked in her light, laconic way one evening, 'you're really getting into this.'

Sweetie! This was her only term of endearment, and reserved for the most specialized occasions. My heart leapt, my cheeks burned, I positively glowed with gratification. A 'sweetie', and for doing what I liked best in the world – what I felt, at the time, might be my vocation! My school friend Alice (the one with whom I'd gone to Wales) had a black Labrador and a Jack Russell at home. She had quite liked Towser, but got rather sick of the brushing, feeding, training and walks, which in her house were undertaken by others, and which she took for granted. She wanted to play upstairs and chat and do hairstyles on Girl's World. But looking after the dog was what I liked best. He took precedence over Alice and our always-fragile friendship. When I was asked over to hers in Salting for the day I made up an excuse. My father thought this rather a poor show.

'Come on, Floss, you should go.'

'I don't particularly want to.'

'But she's a friend of yours, *she* wants you. She's asked you.'

'I know but I'm not in the mood.'

'You like old Alice, don't you?'

'Yes.'

'I thought you and she were thick as thieves.'

I shrugged and mumbled. He sighed.

'It seems a pity not to go for no reason.'

No reason. No reason? I closed the door behind me and led Towser across the road in the direction of the cliff walkway. *I know what it is,* I thought complacently. *They want me to see Alice so they won't be embarrassed by me. So that I'm out of the house. They want me to have friends because they don't have any.*

There was some justification for my childish arrogance. My father in particular did want me to have friends, but for my own sake – he was always more intuitive than Zinny (though not necessarily any better at showing it) and with hindsight I can see that he didn't want me to be isolated. And he liked Alice, who was a bouncy, uncomplicated girl. But hey, it made me feel good to look down on them for a change, just a little. I was being more grown-up than they'd expected. I hadn't begged for the dog, he'd arrived out of nowhere and I'd had no part in his semi-adoption, but I was still taking responsibility.

Again, looking back I can see their dilemma. There were no messages from the vets or the post office, and no posters up anywhere about a lost dog. There was a Blue Cross place but it was twenty miles away, and the nearest animal shelter was even further. Also, there was my involvement which reflected well on them: their ten-year-old daughter actually looking after an animal, when you were always hearing about children begging for a pet and then leaving all the work to someone else.

More food was bought, rubber-soled dishes that wouldn't clank and slip, a collar and lead (though my father balked at an identity tag), and a plastic dog bed.

'They can all be sold later,' said Zinny airily, but nothing could conceal the fact that things were drifting my way. And I kept them on course by not making too much of it, not asking questions, fulfilling my self-appointed role as inconspicuously as possible and with iron reliability. Even when supplies of food needed replenishing I would try to catch a moment when one of them was going into Salting and ask if I could come along and make the purchase. The only thing I didn't have was the cash, and that wasn't a problem.

What I didn't do was look too far ahead. My plan, insofar as I had one, was to keep things running so smoothly that when term started nothing would change except the timing of our walks.

Happily, Towser was a model pet. Content in his adopted home, his natural bounciness calmed down and he was affable but not intrusively so. He seemed instinctively to know that when it came to tolerance I was top of the list, Zinny at the bottom. He gave her a wide berth, confining his attentions to a shuffle of the shoulders and a thump of the tail. My father he approached more directly, inviting some patting and ear-ruffling. I, as wielder of the tin opener, brandisher of the lead, and owner of the ever-open bedroom door, got the full five-star treatment. But I worked on training him; I didn't want to be seen as spoiling Towser for selfish reasons, to ingratiate myself but make life worse for everyone else. I wanted everyone to love him. We went into the front garden every day for fifteen minutes, armed with a bag of treats, and did sitting, lying down, staying, and walking to heel. He thought it was a game, beaming throughout, though the walking to heel tended to go by the board when we were through the gate – he knew that the cliff top or the beach meant freedom, and pulled like a train against the moment of release. He always came when called, hurtling at full pelt, though that might have been the treats.

Still, there was no doubt he was a smart dog. You could see it in his bright eyes and the way he cocked his head sagaciously, ears pricked, as he listened. The way he had our respective numbers and understood how far he could go with each of us, how clever was that? He was brilliant, adorable – a canine paragon. And I was pretty sure he was working (I won't say worming) his way into Zinny's and Dad's good books. Their attitude was shifting daily from mere tolerance to something very like a baffled affection, especially in my father's case.

The end of the holidays was two weeks away, and I knew that was going to be a turning point. Arrangements would have to be made, and I didn't believe they had – presumably my parents thought that to do so would be to accept Towser as a fixture. They were going to see what happened, but I was less inclined to leave things to chance. Mrs March had taken to him, so I picked my moment and asked her if she would be able to keep an eye on him and let him out when she was here in the morning.

'Of course, bless him,' she said, adding, 'if he's still here.'

I ignored the second element and thanked her profusely.

'You could put his food down before you go?'

'I should think I can manage that.'

This was all very satisfactory, but I didn't tell my parents. The situation had to progress smoothly, without too much discussion.

The day in question was a Friday. Term was due to start on the following Monday. In spite of my arrangement with Mrs March I was dreading going back. My life had taken a different turn. Home life was happy; not that it had exactly been unhappy before, but everything and everyone seemed more relaxed. Towser had sorted us out by sheer force of personality.

I had been at Alice's, for form's sake. My father picked me

up on his way back from a sales trip to Bristol. When we got
home he went into the bedroom to change into 'mufti', as he
called it, while I put down Towser's food, watched as he ate,
and went to get his lead.

'Where are you taking him?'

'On the beach.'

'I'll come.'

'OK.'

He smiled. 'That's all right, is it?'

I hesitated. The truth was that where easy companionship
was concerned the dog had almost succeeded in replacing my
father.

'Hmm?' He cocked his head on one side; the dog did the
same.

'Yes.'

'Thanks.' I didn't know if he was being serious. Sometimes
he behaved like another, older, child. Poker-faced, I put on the
lead. Before we got to the gate, my father held out his hand.

'May I?'

'What?'

'May I hold the lead?'

He could never have guessed how much I did not want to
relinquish that little loop of leather. But in the interests of
peace, I did.

Seconds later, peace was over and my dog was dead.

The woman cried and cried as if she wanted us to feel sorry
for her for what had happened. I just wanted her to go away.
Sobbing, she helped my father scoop up Towser in a rug
and put him in the back of our car to take to the vet while
I looked on stony-faced, petrified by shock and grief. My
father's face was white and he kept saying little single words,
with lots of breaths in between: 'There . . . right . . . OK
. . . now . . . there . . .' When he'd slammed the boot he
asked the woman if she wanted a cup of tea or 'something
stronger', but she just flapped her hands at him as if that
were ridiculous, which it was. My father went inside and
got a pen and notepad, and when he came out they had a
huddled conversation and he wrote things down and tore off

a page and gave it to her. We watched her drive away, with Towser lying dead in the boot just feet away. My father turned to me.

'I'm so sorry, Pet. Pet . . .?'

'It doesn't matter.' Why did I say that? This was the worst thing that had ever happened to me and I was dismissing it as if it were no more than a broken cup.

'He just jerked away from me at the very moment . . . She was right, there was nothing she could do, poor woman.'

Poor woman!

'We should take him to the vet.'

'Why?' I asked. 'He's dead.'

My father's face twisted in a strange, miserable way. 'Not quite, I don't think . . .'

I knew that any second I was going to cry and wouldn't be able to stop. My whole body – my head, my stomach, my arms and legs – was full of a heaving grey sadness, the very worst thing I'd ever felt, uncontainable and that would go on forever.

'Anyway,' said my father. He came towards me, he was going to put his arm round me and kiss me, I couldn't bear that. 'Pet . . .?'

'No,' I said.

'All right, but . . .' He put his hands in his pockets and glanced wretchedly towards the car. 'Do you want to come?'

'No.' It seemed to be the only word I could say. Deny it. Say it isn't so. Refuse.

'Right.' Then he added, as I knew he would, 'I'll phone Zinny.'

He went into the house, and stood in the hall with the door open, dialling firmly. I stayed outside, near the car; near my dog. I could tell the moment Zinny answered, because he turned his back and took a couple of steps away, and his hand went up to his face. The conversation seemed to go on for ages, minutes. How long could it take to explain what had happened? When finally he returned the handset and came back, he looked rather better for having shared the trouble.

'She'll be here in a few minutes.' We stood awkwardly. 'Why don't we go inside?'

I shook my head. By admitting that we could wait a few minutes he was conceding that Towser was dead. I knew it anyway, but there was something feeble about his earlier pretence, and this acceptance.

'Anyway, I could do with some tea.'

He went back in, and I continued to stand there. My legs felt locked, like a couple of sticks. I couldn't have sat down even if I wanted to. I was like a soldier on duty, showing respect. In a moment my father came back with his mug, and sat down on the wooden bench below the verandah. The slats were bleached and flaky, they would scratch my bare summer legs. I think he felt bad about sitting, he sat hunched forward with his forearms on his knees, gazing down into the mug. After a moment he put the mug down on the grass and morosely fished out his cigarettes. I was bitterly glad he was stressed.

We didn't talk any more, and my father had finished the cigarette and thrown the stub into the hedge by the time we heard the harsh roar of a car coming down the road at speed. As he got up he didn't even notice that he'd knocked the mug on to the ground, but it was empty and didn't break.

Zinny swung across and pulled up by the wall.

'Oh dear,' she said as she walked towards me. And then again, 'Oh dear, oh dear . . .' over my head, over her firm, light embrace. She was looking at my father, wondering how on earth they were going to deal with this.

She released me, but placed a firm hand on my shoulder, taking charge.

'You get going,' she said to my father. She glanced down at me. 'Are you sure you don't want to?'

'No.'

'You mean yes, you're sure.' I nodded. She knew very well what I meant. 'Go on, Nico.'

He came over and opened the car door. As he started the engine my leaping, fluttering heart felt as though it were in my head. I hadn't touched my dog since I'd put the lead on him, and now he was going to be taken away – soiled, broken and cold – to be disposed of by a stranger.

'Are you all right?' asked Zinny, smoothing the back of my hair. I didn't answer, and I felt her gesture with her other hand, telling my father to hurry up. The car backed out into the road, turned, moved off. Was gone.

Zinny steered me inside and sat down on the sofa next to me. The pain was beginning to stir in earnest now; I wouldn't be able to contain it much longer. Even so it was harder to escape from Zinny, such was her dominion over me.

'What an awful thing to happen,' she said. 'Awful.'

She took my hand in both of hers – her long, perfectly manicured fingers enfolded my little paw. She wore a silver bracelet on her right wrist, but no rings except a wedding ring, and that was the thinnest, plainest ring imaginable, and always looked a little loose.

Now she sighed. 'And we never found out where he belonged.'

I wanted to scream: *Here! He belonged here!* Instead I carefully withdrew my hand and rubbed it over my eyes, not because I was crying, but to stop myself.

'I couldn't believe it when Nico called.' She seemed to be talking to herself now. 'That woman must have been driving far too fast. They do go too fast along here, they don't think. It should be a forty.'

She was turning the conversation into something else: a question of bad driving, of culpability, when who cared? When beautiful, bouncy, loving Towser was dead, and gone, never to return, carted off in the boot like rubbish for the dump.

I stood up. 'I'm going upstairs.'

'Are you?' She looked at me quizzically. 'Why not stay down here with me, and when Daddy gets back—'

But I was already on my way. I heard her sigh again as I left. When the bedroom door was closed behind me I grabbed my pillow and sat on the floor with my face buried in it, husbanding the storm, keeping my grief close, all to myself.

They were worried about me, and I don't blame them. An hour later my father returned and I heard their lowered voices in the hall, then a pause (in my mind's eye I could see Zinny pointing up the stairs), before the living-room door closed, and the voices became only the merest murmur. I didn't catch any of what they said then, and I didn't want to.

Later in life I heard, and agreed with, the view that some events and occasions provide us with an excuse to cry; a reason to feel sorrow for ourselves, and to express that sorrow freely. I may have felt a little queasy, on the occasion of Diana's death, at the sickly smell rising off that sea of rotting flowers in Kensington Gardens, the clumsily expressed declarations of undying love for 'the people's princess', the incontinent weeping and embracing . . . but I recognized and understood it. Here was a shocking, technicolour national tragedy with built-in beauty, and we buttoned-up Brits were going to make the most of it, not just through sentimentality, but because we all had something to cry about – some regret, or guilt, or loss, or remorse, some loss or failing – and now we could. I did. I was dry-eyed until I saw the princes walking like soldiers behind their mother's coffin, and then the tears came and didn't stop.

A lot of people will tell you that the death of a dog brings a particularly sharp pain, that they wept more over the passing of their pet than their parent. Perhaps this is because the loss of a dog is simpler, less complicated; the dog is 'ours' in a way even the closest relative can never be. There is less to process; the dog is with us, and then it's not. And in my case I was still in the honeymoon period. But looking back there was no doubt I was also grieving for myself; mourning those ill-defined, unnameable things I didn't have and which I was just beginning to see through the mist.

A little later my father came up and tapped on my door. I didn't answer but the door opened and a hand appeared holding a plate with a sandwich and a carton of juice on it, and then his head appeared a bit above that.

'Hey, Floss. Brought you some supper. Egg mayonnaise, think you could manage a mouthful?'

By this time I was lying on the bed, hugging the pillow. 'Thanks.'

'I'll leave it here, unless of course you'd like to come down and have supper with us.'

'No thanks.'

He put the plate on the bedside table and perched on the edge of the mattress, his hands on his knees.

'The vet was awfully nice. He'll look after him.'

I nodded. I didn't even want to think about what that might involve.

'Have a go, won't you? Do you good, make you feel better . . .' He looked at me for a moment, then slapped his knees and got up. 'We're just going to have something ourselves, then I'll come up again.'

He went out, leaving the door slightly ajar.

It was Zinny who came up later, and encouraged me to undress, clean my teeth and get under the covers. As she popped a kiss on my cheek she said, 'It'll all seem better in the morning.'

I might have forgiven her that, which was a typically stupid grown-up thing to say. But I couldn't sleep, and later I heard them go out on the verandah as they often did after supper, leaving the house door open. I crept out and sat on the stairs. My father was smoking – he must have been upset for Zinny to allow that in front of her, even outside. I was glad about that, glad someone else was just a little sad.

'Oh!' Zinny leaned her head on the back of her chair and put her hands over her eyes, 'What a perfectly ghastly day . . .'

My father said, 'I do feel bad about my part in it.'

'Don't.' Zinny raised her head again and picked up her glass. 'From everything you've told me it couldn't have been avoided.'

'No . . .'

'Really, Nico.'

'No.' He had wanted to be persuaded, and now I could tell he was. 'Actually you're right.'

'And I'll tell you something else.' Zinny's voice lifted and became lighter as if she had decided that the time for restraint was over. 'Horrible though it was, it may be a blessing in disguise.'

There followed a pause. Then my father said in the same easily persuaded tone he'd used before: 'Hate to say it, but I agree.'

They say eavesdroppers never hear good of themselves, so maybe I deserved it. But I think it would have hurt me less if I had caught them criticizing me. Instead, their self-satisfied, treacherous sneakiness was about Towser, who'd done no-one any harm and had now been dealt with by the kind vet – got out of the way before any tricky decisions had to be made. They'd been relieved of those, and oh! Were they relieved. The atmosphere out there on the softly lit verandah had become almost festive because another awkward problem (the first being me) had gone from their lives.

That was the moment I truly realized that my parents had never – nor would they ever – care half as much for me as they did for each other.

FIVE

The memories wouldn't have affected me so much if I hadn't been there on my own. I wouldn't have been able to indulge in them and wallow in self-pity. I hadn't shed a tear since the night of Towser's death more than a decade ago. Now, I let rip.

When I eventually calmed down I took a bottle of beer from the fridge and went out to the verandah. The day was overcast, the sea flat. There were no cars in the lay-by: Saturday was often quiet as the holidaymakers changed over. I decided to go down to the beach. I didn't use the beach at Lyme much – one end was always so busy and the other was the fossil-hunters' territory.

I left the empty bottle on the verandah table and went upstairs, where I dug an old swimming costume out of the chest of drawers in my room and put it on under my long cotton dress. There was always a pile of scratchy beach towels in the airing cupboard. I rolled one up round my house key and set off.

The sea may have been calm, but it was breathtakingly cold. The icy line of the surface moved up my body in a shock wave, leaving everything below it numb until I acclimatized and began swimming. I went straight out for fifty yards, then turned and swam parallel to the shore in the direction of Salting. I was a strong swimmer, and having learnt in the sea it held no fears for me. In docile, civilized Salting there was a wicked west–east current of which unsuspecting swimmers often fell foul, and where the river bustled out between the crab rocks and the beach you were advised not to try crossing at high tide. But here in our steep, round bay the sea formed a kind of lagoon, and was by and large good-natured. After five minutes I felt better. The air, the exercise, the cold salty pressure of the water, the different view of the land – they all helped to restore a sense of perspective. I kept going back and forth for about half an hour, doing twenty strokes crawl, fifty breaststroke, until I was thoroughly in the zone, and felt as if I could have swum to France. That was the point at which I turned back towards the beach: experience showed that this sensation was rapidly followed by tiredness, and I was some way out. When I finally emerged, trudging through the shallows, I could feel that peculiar sensation of airy weightlessness after the hug of the water.

There was no-one about, but a habit of modesty made me careful as I wriggled out of my cozzie and tugged my dress back over my head with the aid of laborious towel-work. My father was a great one for what he called the 'blink-and-you'll-miss-it' school of changing – whipping his trunks off and his shorts on with what amounted to sleight of hand – but I had neither his speed nor his chutzpah. Now that I was dry my thin cotton dress made me completely warm. I spread the towel on the sand and sat down with my skirt wrapped over my knees. I faced away from the sea, and could just hear the tiny spit of its edge advancing and retreating behind me, like the game grandmother's footsteps.

From here I could see only the top half of our house and the effect was rather like a boat on the horizon, with the rough lip of the cliff forming the wake, and the smooth spread of the green cliff top like a huge wave looming over it from behind. Again I realized how isolated the house was – and how isolated we were in it, cut adrift, floating in space.

It was as I sat there, relaxed after my swim, contemplating the house, that I remembered something I hadn't thought of for twenty years. And no, I didn't just remember; I *experienced* it – felt the heat of the summer night, the weight of that hand on mine, saw the freckles, the nails . . .

Had my parents believed me? Had they even known something that I didn't? Their air of breezy certainty had succeeded in persuading me it was a dream, or that I had imagined it. There had been an oddness about that night that was not all to do with me. But at that age, before their fall from grace with Towser, I had been, like all children, only too willing to believe them. For a week or so I'd resisted going to bed and once there had difficulty going to sleep, but that wore off and I never experienced anything like it again. So the memory faded, and was consigned to whatever mental box room contains those moments too powerful to discard but too unpleasant to revisit.

Now, though, I had been ambushed by that long-ago happening – ambushed and shocked. The memory was so vivid that I felt vulnerable sitting on the sand, and got to my feet. The top of our house peeped over the cliff at me. I could see the slope of the roof, the chimney, and the single dormer window over the stairs where Zinny sometimes put a candle 'to warn the sailors' – an uncharacteristic gesture of whimsy.

Carrying my shoes and towel I set off towards the walkway with a steady, measured pace though I still felt shaky. At the top I wiped the soles of my feet on the grass and put my shoes on. My empty beer bottle still stood defiantly on the verandah.

I unlocked the door, leaving it open behind me. Draping the towel over the newel post I went up the stairs and into my room. The window was still securely closed, but now I opened it and leaned out. There was the paved area where I used to sit, and beyond it the low wall, matching the one at the front of the house, made up of beach pebbles set in concrete. I lifted the window latch off its housing and pushed it back flat against the wall. I hitched up my skirt and with very little difficulty got one leg over the windowsill, swung the other round, and lowered myself on to the narrow patio. With my hands behind my back against the parapet I faced the way I'd come. Here was another angle on the house, the two large bedroom windows glaring at waist height, with the small bathroom window like a frown line in between them.

To my left was the spare room, dull and plain, always empty. Even as a child I'd wondered what – and who – it was for,

since no-one ever came to stay. We had no friends or relations
that I knew of. My parents' social circle was a mystery, and
on those rare occasions when Alice stayed overnight, she'd
top and tail in my bed with me. About twice a year Mrs March
went in to 'do a whizz-round', an exercise that took all of five
minutes.

I had hardly ever been into the spare room: there was no
reason to. But now, in my capacity as a spy in my own house,
I was overcome with curiosity to see it from this new angle.
With one hand on the parapet I moved along and looked in.

Or would have done, but the curtains were closed. There
was not so much as a chink or a wrinkle in the thick, grey
lining; they were as flat and opaque as an extension of the
wall. Why? I found myself running my hand over the window,
as if I could move the fabric aside from out here. I felt like a
fly, creeping over the skin of the house.

A moment ago, I'd been prompted by no more than idle
curiosity. Now, there was nothing I wanted more than to see
inside.

I climbed back into my own room and replaced the window
on the latch. I went on to the landing and along to the spare
room. The brass door knob, like everything in the house, was
polished.

But I could only turn it half an inch: the door was locked.

I frowned down at the knob and tried it again, giving it a
rattle as if I might have been mistaken. For the first time I
noticed the brass finger plate and keyhole beneath the handle.
I glanced back at the other doors on the landing – my own
had no keyhole, and the bathroom had the usual latch on the
inside.

There are things you can only do when you are completely
alone and unobserved, some of them trivial, some unmention-
able, some downright shifty. What I did next came under the
third heading. My curiosity induced an extraordinary clear-
headedness. Perhaps this was how burglars felt when they had
to be in and out of somewhere quickly. Some sort of mental
filing system came into play. I could see the cards riffling at
speed, almost quicker than the mind's eye could grasp. Wait
. . . wait . . . Yes! There was a drawer downstairs somewhere

– one of those drawers with a jumble of miscellaneous items, including keys.

I ran downstairs and paused in the hall. In my head I could see the open drawer and its contents, but where was it? I went into the living room: no drawers in here, nor in the hall. The kitchen . . . I pulled open all the drawers beneath the work surface, but found only the usual array of cutlery, kitchen implements, tea towels and food wrap. I sat down at the kitchen table, eyes closed and fingers thrust into my hair, for a think.

When I opened my eyes I saw at once the long, shallow drawer that sat just below the rim of the table. I pulled the wooden handle. The drawer was old and warped, it stuck before jerking out. There were the lengths of string, the tubes of super glue, the plug adapters and the curtain hooks – and a plastic wallet full of keys.

I took the wallet upstairs and kneeled down by the door. There must have been at least twenty keys. I intended systematically to try all the non-Yale ones, but key number six slid in and turned with buttery ease. Childishly pleased with myself, I replaced the other keys in the wallet and ran my hand along the seal, before propping it against the wall and pushing open the door.

I didn't draw the curtains, but I did turn on the light. I'd forgotten how big the room was – it must at one time have been the master bedroom, the largest in the house, but it was signally lacking in Zinny's stylish touch. The double bed was covered in a mushroom-coloured candlewick bedspread below which hung a valance; the side tables were cream-painted repro; the lamps bulbous china things with pleated nylon shades. There was a safe, greetings-card landscape over the quilted headboard, and a narrow white wardrobe in the corner by the window. The only other items of furniture were a bow-legged stool in front of a kidney-shaped dressing table – a 'vanity unit' it would have been called in its day – with a glass top, a triptych mirror and a flouncy pink fabric skirt. The beige fitted carpet was threadbare by the door and next to the bed. Not exactly Bluebeard's chamber, then.

I moved into the centre of the room. I still didn't draw the curtains, because I felt like an intruder – why else would the door have been locked?

I thought I'd never been in such a dead place. An unhealthy, faded fragrance hung in the stuffy air; old clothes and talcum powder. There was a small drawer in the centre of the dressing table, and in each of the bedside tables. All of them were empty, except for flower-patterned lining paper – the only bright thing in the room.

I drew back the corner of the bedspread. The bed was neatly made, with pale pink sheets and cream, satin-edged cellular blankets. Again that faint crackle of synthetic fibres, when Zinny was so keen on her cotton and linen and pure wool . . .

The whole place was vaguely unpleasant, and not solely due to its being dated and unused. The atmosphere was both sterile and, curiously, toxic. This wasn't a room kept clean and orderly to welcome a friend; it was abandoned and sealed up.

I went to the wardrobe and tried the door. For a moment it stuck and I thought that, too, was locked. But then it gave with a jerk. More flowered lining paper on the floor; half a dozen metal hangers rattling like bones, and a couple of those shiny padded ones with bows – what, ever, was the point of them? There was another smell in here, from the mothballs that hung from the necks of some of the hangers.

Above the rail was a shelf. I reached up and felt around the near edge of it with my hand. Just the now-familiar paper again. I don't know what I expected to find, but now I'd begun to explore I needed to finish. I pulled over the bow-legged dressing-table stool and put one foot on it, pulling myself up via the wardrobe rail to test its strength. I planted a foot care-fully either side of the seat: it held my weight without wobbling. But I'm not tall and the stool, though stable, was not very high. Even standing on it I could only see the front half of the shelf. I stretched an arm and swept my hand from side to side. Nothing at first, but then my fingers brushed something soft and unpleasantly yielding, with a texture I couldn't identify.

A mouse? A spider's nest? The chrysalis of some weird giant moth . . .?

I gave an involuntary shriek of disgust and fright, and my own voice made me jump. I just managed to prevent myself from falling by grabbing the edge of the shelf. The wardrobe, a jerry-built thing like the rest of the furniture, tottered danger-ously. I let go and sprang down backwards, taking the stool with me.

The musty silence closed round me again. Heart galloping, I righted the stool and stood there feeling stupid. When I'd collected myself I took out one of the wire hangers, unwound the neck and stretched it out to form an ad-hoc probe. My knees were shaking so I didn't get back on the stool, but reached up with the hanger into the corner of the shelf. The end bumped the nasty, fluffy thing. I prodded to get a purchase and drew the wire back towards me, standing well back.

The object appeared, quivering slightly on the end of the wire, and then fell soundlessly to the floor. Fluffy, trem-bling, weightless . . . What it most reminded me of was one of those moths I had so hated. I poked it again, tasting bile in my mouth.

It was a hairnet, one of those very fine ones that women used to wear to keep rigidly maintained styles in place. And it was clogged with hair, iron grey with some black strands. Someone had cleared an alarmingly large amount of loose hair out of a brush, rolled it up in the old net and . . . what? What exactly had they done? Thrown it in the top of the wardrobe rather than in the wastepaper basket? Put it there to hide it?

Squeamishly I picked up the tangled mess, nipping it fastidi-ously between the nails of my thumb and middle finger. There was something about the hair, as if these dead fibres – dead, like all hair, long before they were discarded – might come to life and cling to me parasitically. Holding the horrible thing at arm's length, I felt through the closed curtains, opened the window and dropped it outside. I closed the window again and went straight to the bathroom to wash my hands, pressing my nails into the soap and lathering vigorously before rinsing. Back in the spare bedroom I had the queasy sensation, in spite of its eerie passivity, of being watched.

I closed the wardrobe and came out, shutting the door behind me. I was halfway down the stairs before I remembered some-thing. I ran back up, turned the key in the lock, and went down to return the key to the kitchen table drawer.

* * *

I didn't spend the night. I went back into Salting that evening, had a glass of white wine and fish and chips in the Hat and Feathers, then drove back to Lyme. I had the following day off anyway, and I planned to have a lie-in, and read, and walk along the Cob in the afternoon.

My parents may or may not have been surprised to find me gone on their return. I don't know, because they didn't get in touch.

SIX
1981

When I was a young teenager – thirteen or fourteen – I sometimes went with my father on his sales trips in the school holidays. These were always character-ized as 'fun' and 'a bit of an adventure' by my parents, though I suspect they were a way of getting me out from under Zinny's feet, and away from home. We did go on an annual holiday, to a hotel in Crete where my parents were greeted like the second coming, but though I liked the swimming pool, the motherly owner and the historic chips, it was, as with every-thing, much more their holiday than mine. I had usually finished all my books by the end of the first week, and soon grew tired of the Greek sitcoms and soap operas on television. Like most only children I was well behaved; I didn't whine. My father's indulgence was to hire a sports car and we always had a few days out, whizzing round mountain passes and along the coast road, with me feeling rather sick in the rear tip seat. The beach was quite nice, but Zinny wasn't good in the ferocious sunshine, so that was limited to short stints in the early evening. Anyway, we had a beach at home, and ours was better.

So the summer-holiday jaunts with my father were intended to be a little extra, just for me. And actually, whatever the ulterior motive, I have to admit I did quite enjoy them. I sat in the front seat so there was no danger of car-sickness, and we always had a stash of sweets in the glove compartment. Because this was his job, my father drove smoothly and steadily: there were no death-defying stunts or hairy over-takings. We chatted a little and played Radio 2 a lot. There was a pleasant security in the car, a sense of doing-something-while-doing-nothing, for me in particular a kind of purposeful idleness. My father may not have been an especially proactive parent, but he was easy company, especially on what was effectively his home turf.

His beat was the south-west, as far east as Bridport and as far north as Bristol – a huge area. We always went to the furthest point first, and I had grown to recognize some of the outlets and their managers. On the occasion in question we were actu-ally going to drive all the way to Birmingham before working our way back down. My father showed me where this was on the map.

'That's miles away!'

'Not so very far, and it's nearly all motorway.'

'Why are we going there?'

'I've got to drop in on head office. They like to run the rule over me from time to time.'

At that age I still thought of my father's job as glamorous. I perceived him as a kind of commercial cowboy, out there riding the range, a free spirit and a law unto himself. The idea of anyone, let alone the denizens of some distant faceless grey office, 'running the rule over him' (it sounded like a head lice inspection) didn't accord with this image at all. This was some years before I realized just how starkly my father was under-achieving, though perhaps one can't use that phrase of someone with no drive or ambition. Can a person be said to be under-achieving if achievement doesn't interest them? It was simply that I sensed, in a childish, intuitive way, that my father was a clever as well as a charming person. He was handsome and good at jokes, he could do quick, cartoonish drawings, and imitate other people with hilarious accuracy. For a long time I thought his free-wheeling work required these qualities and made use of them; that he was some sort of star. Only much later did the scales fall from my eyes. My father was a lowly sales rep, covering hundreds of miles in his modest workhorse of a car, with his jacket and ready-tied tie on a hanger in the back, his samples in the boot, his fags and complimentary bon-bons in the glove compartment. This job provided a modest income, something to do and lots of freedom.

We set off early, at seven a.m. on the Monday morning. Zinny had packed for my three nights away, as she always did – she was good at packing, and we were both happy that I was going away for a while. I didn't mind that she was happy. I understood that she was not an especially maternal character, and that her abstractedness wasn't personal.

Before leaving we sat on the verandah and had tea, mine accompanied by a digestive biscuit, my father's by a cigarette. Zinny, with black coffee, kept us company in her elegant kimono. Then we loaded our bags on to the back seat of the Sierra, and she waved us off, holding aloft the rolled newspaper, with her sleeve falling back like the Statue of Liberty.

Tradition dictated that at nine o'clock we would stop at the Gordano Services on the M5 near Bristol and have a full English, which in my experience was about as close to heaven as food got: sausage, bacon, beans, and little triangular hash browns, accompanied by buttered toast and hot chocolate. The only thing I wasn't keen on was the fried eggs with their dried-up yokes. My father did like the eggs and usually had two, with bacon, beans, and black pudding, which I'd never tried but didn't like the sound of. He also had an enormous cappuccino in a cup with handles on either side and a cinnamon heart done with a plastic stencil on top of the swirly foam. You could have a flower or a heart, but the girl always gave him a heart without asking and he'd give her one of his specially smiley thank-yous. I was beginning to see that women did flirt with him, and though it embarrassed me it made me quite proud too.

People sometimes said I looked like my father, but it didn't work to my advantage. I never went through that budding, blossoming stage of girlish loveliness. I was stocky and homely with awkward straight hair, the kind with a tendency to stick out rather than hang sleekly. Zinny was firm about the necessity of a good cut, but what was meant to be a neat bob came out perilously close to a pudding basin. My father's was sticky-out straight as well, but on him it looked boyish and rumpled. Probably the ages between twelve and sixteen aren't much fun for anyone, but I was particularly ill at ease with myself.

After breakfast we topped up the tank and sped on up the M5. We began to see Birmingham on the signs, and there was that sense of the badlands, the sprawl that surrounded the approaching city. I was a little disappointed that we didn't have to go right into the centre – head office turned out to be on an industrial estate on the edge of town. We followed the road grid between rows of buildings that were like large metal boxes, or cubes of brick with square windows and doors with lists of bells: HO turned out to be one of these. It was in almost the furthest corner of the estate, and there was actually a patch of grass next to the parking area, and a couple of cautious trees.

My father pressed the bell: a buzzer sounded and the door opened. You went through another door almost immediately, and then you were into the reception area, which was surprisingly nice – much nicer than you'd have guessed from the outside. There were fitted carpets, framed posters for Hopgood's confectionery over the years, and a table with a hot drinks machine, polystyrene cups, a basket of sugars and tubs of milk, and another of fun-size Hopgood products. Facing us was a reception desk with a glass sphere containing shiny coloured stones. The glamorous girl behind the desk beamed when she saw my father.

'Mr Mayfield, good to see you!'

'Hi Sandy. I know we're a bit early.' He glanced down at me. 'We made good time, didn't we?'

I nodded. 'Yes, even with a stop.' I'd heard him say this.

'Breakfast en route, did you?'

'We did.'

'I'll just let them know you're here.' Still smiling, but at me now, Sandy picked up the phone. 'Mr Mayfield is here.' She replaced it. 'You can go on up.'

'By the way, Sandy, this is my daughter, Flora.'

Sandy got up and came round from behind the desk. She wore a white shirt with the collar slightly turned up, and a fitted black skirt; her hair was dark with a swoopy fringe and flicked up at the back (it was the age of the flick and the fringe). Everything about her was sleek and crisp and her waist looked tiny where the shirt tucked into the skirt. When she held out her hand I was caught in a haze of some light, fresh scent.

'Pleased to meet you, Flora.'

'Hello.' I felt both dazzled and frumpy. But as if beauty weren't enough – and I was learning that it very often was – Sandy was lovely.

'Would you like to keep me company while your Dad's in his meeting?'

'Thank you.' I didn't have much option, but it was still a good offer.

'Have fun, girls,' said my father. 'Perhaps you can make yourself useful, Floss.'

I must have looked doubtful, because Sandy laughed. 'There's no need for that. Come and sit round here, why don't you?"

I spent the next couple of hours very happily in Sandy's neat little compound. From her (now my) perspective, we sat at a table with a shelf unit in front of it, the top of which formed the reception 'desk' which held the sweets, the sphere with the stones and the signing-in book. Sandy had a swivel chair, and there was another ordinary chair which she must have moved in for me. Her wide-shouldered raspberry-pink jacket hung over the back of the swivel chair, and her black bag sat on the floor with a packet of sandwiches sticking out of it. A paperback book was tucked into one of the cubbyholes. The small space felt cosy, feminine and pleasant. I thought what a perfect job it must be to sit here and greet people and be nice to them all day long, but perhaps it required one to look like Sandy, and that was a tall order.

I was a polite child. 'Is there something I can do?'

'Well if there is, I'll tell you. But for now, you know what? My job for the moment is talking to you.'

I think I may have blushed. She took a handful of fun-size bars out of the bowl and put them on the work table between us.

'Help yourself. I'll need to spit mine out if someone comes.'

Only a handful of people did: a couple of men in suits who

passed straight through to the office with a 'hi' to Sandy; a girl with a brisk, bossy walk who did the same but without the 'hi'; and a motorbike courier delivering a plastic jiffy bag requiring Sandy's signature. She explained to me that there was more to it than just greeting people and sending them through, that she had to take and transfer calls, look after collections and deliveries and make sure the reception space looked good at all times. I wondered if she ever got bored, and fortunately she answered the question I was too embarrassed to ask.

'I do get a bit bored some days,' she said. 'I'm never exactly rushed off my feet but believe it or not it can be busy. It's quiet today which is why it's nice to have you to chat to.'

She got us hot drinks from the machine – milky coffee for her, hot chocolate for me, my second of the day. It wasn't as nice as the one at the motorway services, but Sandy gave me permission to complain.

'Machine drinks, yeeuch,' she said, stirring in sweeteners, 'but beggars can't be choosers.'

After she'd told me about work, which didn't take long, she asked me about school, and friends, and we discussed what music we liked and the stars of *Neighbours*. She fancied Simon Le Bon, but not Rick Astley even though he had a good voice. She had been engaged, she told me, but got cold feet and called it off. She'd done the decent thing and given Steve his ring back. There was nothing the matter with Steve; she just wasn't ready for marriage and neither was he though he wouldn't admit it. They were still friends – here she sighed – maybe that was all they'd ever been really, and we both agreed that you needed a bit of electricity, didn't you?

At the end of the bit about Steve she asked me, with what I thought was a slightly different look in her eye, 'What about your dad?'

'What about him?'

'Oh, I don't know . . . He's really nice, he must be a fun father to have.'

I'd heard this before, often, but not from someone as pretty as Sandy. 'He is.'

'I bet you have some laughs, the two of you, out on the road together.'

I wasn't sure whether we 'had laughs' exactly, but neither did I want to complicate things. 'Yes – yes, we do.'

'I thought so . . .' Sandy smiled, shaking her head enviously. 'What about your mum, does she work?'

'She works for the local rep.'

'Wow, that sounds interesting.'

'She really likes it.'

'What does she do there?'

'She helps in the box office.'

'Lovely.' Sandy gazed at me. 'What busy parents.'

'They are.'

There was another little pause during which I could feel her covertly studying me.

'He looks incredibly young, doesn't he?'

'I don't know, does he?'

'Well of course you wouldn't, he's your dad.'

'People say he does,' I admitted.

Why did they? Why did people always wind up talking about my parents?

The phone rang. 'Well,' said Sandy, swivelling round to answer it, 'we all think he's lovely.'

I picked up on that 'we all'. So apparently there was a whole group of people who were fans of my father's.

In due course he emerged smiling broadly through the double door. My peripheral vision caught a microscopic change of manner in Sandy. I recognized it as the look on a classmate's face when she slammed her desk lid down on some contraband item as a teacher entered the room – a moment of swift, pleasurable guilt.

He leaned on the front of the desk, looking down on us, this young-looking man who was my father.

'How are you, ladies?'

'We've had a good time, haven't we?' said Sandy. 'I wish I could have such nice company every day; she cheered things up no end.'

'Glad to hear it.'

'Would you like a horrible coffee before you hit the road?'

He laughed. 'You make it sound so tempting, but I'm full of the decent stuff they serve through there.'

Sandy looked at me, eyebrows raised. 'Spurned!'

'I'll sneak a few of these though, new line . . .' He took a handful of sweets from the bowl and slipped them into his jacket pocket. 'Come on then, Floss, better get going.'

I stood up, and Sandy came round with me.

'Safe journey.'

'Thank you,' I said.

'My pleasure, love.' To my surprise she leaned forward and deposited a quick kiss on each cheek. 'I hope your dad brings you again.'

'Well,' said my father, just loud enough for Sandy to hear as we headed for the door, 'some people get all the luck.'

We drove out of the city and into a world of picture-perfect green fields, dotted with large smart houses with smooth lawns, white fences and metal gates. The villages we passed through were pretty and (even I could tell) exuberantly prosperous.

'All very nice,' commented my father, 'but I'd hate to live here. What if you don't keep your door knocker polished?'

This made us both giggle. I was reminded of what Sandy had said, and realized *We're having some laughs.*

We stopped at a pub for lunch, and sat at a table in the leafy garden with our sandwiches: 'lots of cress and no crusts, there's posh'. Back in the car, I asked where we were going next.

'Actually,' said my father, 'we're going to drop in on someone, not to do with work. While we're in this area.'

'Who?'

'She's an old auntie of mine – well, friend of the family. Bit of a duty for me I'm afraid, you don't know her.'

I was quite excited. Auntie? Friend of the family? These were things other people had, not us – but now it appeared we did!

'What's her name?'

'Jessie.' He glanced at me. 'You're fine to call her Jessie.'

'OK.'

He seemed to think for a moment before adding: 'To be honest, Floss, she's not all there these days. Not at all actually, a bit doolally. She's in a home. Do you mind?'

Mind? First Sandy, now this – things were getting inter- esting. I shook my head. 'No, of course not.'

'You're a good sport, Floss. I don't suppose she gets any visitors, so even though she won't know who we are it's good to show the flag.'

We got to another town, not a massive one like Birmingham but scruffier than the manicured villages, and stopped at a newsagent's for sweets to take to Jessie. My father scanned the plastic jars on shelves behind the counter and chose a bag of iced caramels and another of liquorice allsorts, old-fashioned sweets. The woman in her blue checked overall smiled at me as she twirled the bags so the corners looked like ears. 'Good choice, lucky you.'

'Oh, they're not for us,' said my father. 'We've got plenty of our own; I work for Hopgood's.'

'Do you?' She seemed delighted. 'We stock loads of theirs.'

'Pleased to hear it.'

She wrinkled her brow. 'It's not you that usually comes in.'

'No, this isn't my patch. Probably Keith – Keith Morris?'

'Mr Morris, that's him.' She handed him his change. 'So where are you from?'

'The west country, east Devon.'

'Very nice.' She looked at me. 'By the seaside?'

'Yes.'

'Golly, I envy you,' she said. 'We're about as far from the sea as you can get here. Bang slap in the middle.'

'Better dash,' said my father, 'we're on a double yellow.'

We drove down the high street and along a busy road through endless sets of traffic lights, me with the bags of sweets on my lap. At a big junction we turned left and were soon in a residential area with big grey houses on either side, most of which had the air of no longer being people's homes – some had signs up advertising firms of solicitors, dentists or estate agents, with front gardens which had been made into parking lots, and others had the telltale console of apartment doorbells next to the front door. We took another side road and turned in through a gate with a sign saying 'Oak View Residential Care' with a row of four stars and various names and numbers underneath.

'Here we are,' said my father. 'One hour, OK?'

He seemed a little worried, but he didn't need to be; that

was fine with me. I was bursting with curiosity. A white notice by the door told us to ring and enter, which we did.

I'd never been in an old folks' home before, so the smell of old cooking and bleach was new to me. There were some suspiciously perfect apricot-coloured roses in a vase, and a small table with leaflets laid out in fans. A woman in a navy blue uniform came bustling into the hall, the first one that day not to appear overjoyed at the sight of my father.

'By a process of elimination, Mr Mayfield I presume? I'm Hilary Taylor, the matron.'

'That's right, we've spoken but not met, how do you do.'

'And this is Flora.'

'Hello Flora. Well – I may as well take you along right away then, unless you need anything . . .?' She cast me a look.

'Want to spend a penny or anything, Floss?'

I could have died of embarrassment. 'No.'

We followed her from the hall and through a door that opened with a pressed button and closed with a sigh and a thump behind us. Up a flight of stairs, past a lift, labelled 'Staff only' and through another such door, to the third door along. The matron paused with her hand on the handle.

'Can I bring you all some tea?'

'Yes, why not,' said my father, 'that would be nice.'

'Right.' She pushed open the door and stood against it as we entered. 'Here we are then.'

I'd imagined an old lady sitting down, probably by a window, but she was standing in the middle of the room with her back to us, a tall figure who might just as easily have been a man, with roughly cut short hair, a sleeveless fleece over a floral shirt, saggy tracksuit trousers and trainers.

'Jessie,' said the matron, 'here are your visitors.'

There was no reply, though I did think I saw the broad, raw-boned shoulders twitch.

'Jessie . . .?'

Still no response. Hilary turned to us. 'Not having such a good day, so all the better that you're here.'

My father looked doubtful, and said in a lowered voice, 'Are you sure?'

'Oh yes.' Hilary went further into the room so that she was

facing the forbidding figure. 'Your visitors are here, Jessie, all right? I'm going to arrange for some tea. Would you like some tea? Why don't you sit down?'

Looking at us to do the same, she cupped Jessie's elbow with her hand and steered her to one of the upholstered chairs near the window (the one in which I had imagined her sitting), giving us a meaningful look as she did so.

Jessie sat down and my father bent over and kissed her cheek before taking the seat opposite. There wasn't another chair, so I perched on the side of the bed. It was high – I had to hoist myself up and once there my feet didn't touch the floor which made me feel childish and stupid. Between my father and Jessie was a low oval table with a lace runner, and two pink carnations in a specimen vase.

'Now then,' said my father, with his most winning smile, which on this occasion seemed a bit forced. 'I've brought Flora along to meet you.'

I would have felt even more stupid flopping down off the bed, and anyway I didn't want to kiss her, so I stayed where I was. 'Hello.'

Jessie looked at me. I'd heard the expression 'like a graven image' but had never before seen a face that it so accurately described. Hers was long and wide, with a heavy, rather bulging brow and wiry untrimmed eyebrows beneath which were her deep-set eyes of no particular colour, like little pale, moist stones underpinned by grey semi-circular pouches. Her mouth was long and thin, almost lipless, with a downward curve like a child's drawing of a sad face; except that hers didn't look sad so much as utterly, monumentally indifferent. Two long grooves ran from the outer corners of her hooked nose to the ends of her mouth, and two more from there to her chin. Her cheeks were a waste of mottled skin, ending in two distinct dewlaps. It was a face that it was particularly hard to imagine in the freshness of youth, like the face of a statue that had been left out in the wind and the rain, impassively suffering the onslaught of the elements.

Past caring is what occurred to me as I sat there. Although there was something, some ghost of handsomeness . . .

My father was telling her about our journey and what we'd

been doing, saying it was 'very pleasant' round here, wasn't it, and how nice Hilary seemed. Jessie sat there expressionless, knees apart, mouth set, her forearms resting on the upholstered arms of the chair. The only bits of her that seemed expressive were her big, freckled hands, which curved over the wooden ends of the chair arms, as if holding on to something more intangible . . . her sanity? Her temper? Whatever it was, I hoped she wouldn't let go of it. She wasn't wearing a ring, but I couldn't help noticing a clear indentation on the third finger of her left hand. I wondered if that was something to do with this place, that you weren't allowed to wear jewellery. Or had she hurled it away in some past fury?

She remained completely silent and my father was beginning to run out of steam by the time the tea arrived and gave us something to do. The tray was brought in not by Hilary, but by a motherly underling in a green overall, one of those people who are unembarrassed by silences because they never allow any to occur. She was talking as she came in, and kept up a stream of affable chat the whole time she was in the room.

'Here we are, here we are . . . tea and chocolate suggestives. How are you doing Jessie? . . . Nice to have visitors, she doesn't get many, not any really, so very nice . . . Have you come a long way? . . . Oh just from Brum, that's not so bad . . . Let's just set these cups out, who's going to be mother? Jessie likes a proper brew, don't you, so you can stand your spoon up in it, that's right, isn't it? And a couple of sugars, saucered and blown . . . Are you all right perched on there, love? Anything else I can do for you? Is it a bit warm, I can open a window . . .?'

When the door closed behind her the room seemed unnaturally still. My father said, 'I'll pour, shall I?' but what came out of the teapot was pale as pee, and he put it down again. 'Not brewed yet – better wait after what the nice lady said.'

'This is a nice room.' It seemed high time I made a contribution, but I was unsure of my audience and so addressed this remark to the place in general.

'Isn't it?' agreed my father. 'Big and light and airy.' He peered out of the window. 'Looks like a pretty good garden, too.'

I could tell he was trying to involve me – to share, if not actually to pass, the buck. Dutifully I flopped off the bed and went over to take a look. The only route was behind Jessie's chair. I sidled round the back of it with excruciating care and stood just in front of the tea table, gazing out and trying to think of something to say. I saw a patio with benches, a shaven lawn, huddles of squat shrubs, a palisade of tall dark trees . . .

'What's that?' I asked, pointing. I had a pretty fair idea, but it did no harm to show interest, and we were desperate.

'Which one?' My father shuffled, peering, to the front of his seat.

'That pipe cleaner one.'

'Ah, yes, yup. A monkey puzzle tree. Isn't it, Jessie – would you call that a monkey puzzle?'

As usual there was no reply, but I did hear something as I continued to look out at the drab, empty garden . . . Breathing. Jessie's breathing, suddenly deep, fierce and intense, a slight whistle on the inhaled breath, the shadow of a growl on the exhale. Though I had my back to her I could tell that her great, harsh face was turned towards me, that I was the cause of the change in her breathing, and the thought terrified me. I needed to move, to put distance between me and her, but in doing so I mustn't look at her, or meet her eye. I didn't know what would happen if I did, but I was certain it wouldn't end well.

Still with my back to her I sidestepped until I was level with the back of her chair, and then whipped round and back to my place on the bed, almost doing a Fosbury Flop in my eagerness to regain higher and safer territory.

For several seconds I kept my head down, still avoiding the Medusa stare. Slowly, the awful breathing subsided. When I heard the sound of the tea being poured I glanced covertly at the others through squinty, narrow eyes as if, ostrich-like, by reducing my field of vision, I could reduce hers and so be less visible. But her head was still turned towards the window.

My father put a cup down in front of her. 'There you go, Jessie, your tea. Floss, want some?' I shook my head. 'Biscuit?'

'Yes please.'

'Catch.'

I caught it and he winked at me, but I could tell he was

uncomfortable too; his cup chinked against the saucer when he started to lift it, but then he put it down again as he remembered something.

'We brought you a little present,' he said. 'If Floss hasn't eaten them all.' Dutifully I slipped down and handed him the two small paper bags of sweets which had been lying next to me. He held both out on his palm, tweaking the tops open with his other hand.

'Iced caramels and allsorts, fancy one?'

This offer acted on her like a whiff of salts. For the very first time she seemed not only to have heard, but to be seeing and noticing too. She reached out and delved with her big, square-tipped fingers in first one bag and then the other, laying out six sweets in a row on the table in front of her and making minute adjustments to their positions so that they were equidistant from each other and in a straight row. Then she selected one – a black and brown striped allsort, second from the right – and put it in her mouth.

I say she put it in her mouth, but that hardly did justice to the ensuing operation. What she actually did was so much more than that. With the sweet held in front of her face between finger and thumb it was as though some subcutaneous earthquake were taking place around the lower half of her face, a shifting of the tectonic plates beneath her mouth and jaws. Her lips trembled and heaved, drew back, reached forward, parted . . . Her teeth (I had plenty of time to notice) were large and uneven and all her own, yellowish grey and shored up with dull metallic fillings. I was transfixed. With downcast eyes and her mouth still wide open, she placed the allsort on her tongue in a way that was almost reverential, and hoisted it back into her wet pink maw before pulling her lips back into position and closing them. Her jaws with their curtains of dewlap rotated and chomped. You almost felt sorry for the poor little sweet. I looked at my father and could tell he was thinking the same thing, but his profile was polite as he picked up his teacup and sipped.

Fifteen seconds and it was time for the next one. And then the next.

'I'm so glad you're enjoying those,' said my father. 'I seemed to remember you liked them.'

Out came the lips, down dropped the jaw, in went another. My father poured himself a second cup; I knew he was concentrating hard on keeping a straight face. If he looked my way we would have burst out laughing, and even if we didn't our faces would have betrayed something, and we weren't going to let that happen. Jessie's silence was weird, but we had no idea what the alternative might be and didn't want to find out.

In went another. Four left on the table. But there was still the remaining contents of the two bags . . . I glanced at my watch: three twenty. We had been here just over twenty minutes and were supposed to be staying for an hour. How were we to survive?

My father soldiered on. 'I hope the food's OK here. No smell of the traditional boiled cabbage in the hall, so perhaps it is. You look well, I must say.' He flashed her another of his winning smiles, but he was wasting his time: she was setting out another row of sweets.

'We stopped at a nice pub for lunch before we got here, didn't we?'

I remembered that a simple 'Yes' was not going to be enough, it was all shoulders to the wheel. 'It was in that village with the pump.'

'That's right!' He clicked his fingers as if the identification of the village had been troubling him for hours. 'There was a cattle trough in the square, and an old-fashioned pump, looked in perfect working order. Very nice place, lots of attractive old buildings. Remind me what you had, Floss?'

Gosh, he was even more desperate than I thought. 'Cheese and cress sandwich and crisps.'

'I had the ham, egg and chips.' He laughed. 'For my sins!'

It was so strange, the two of us having this pretend conversation, exchanging information we already knew, for the benefit of someone who was not just uninterested, but seemed scarcely aware that we were talking at all, or even of our presence. My sudden sense of the ridiculousness made me bold. I slipped back off the high bed and went over to the table, my father watching me.

'Please may I have one?'

I felt rather than saw his eyebrows go up. Jessie paused

with an iced caramel halfway to her mouth. Her outstretched lips, rubbery and seamed like a camel's, quivered and sank back in disappointment. She lowered the caramel. Her eyelids snapped, once, twice.

'Floss,' began my father, 'we brought these for Jessie, I think . . .'

But for better or worse I had her attention. She was looking at me. And not just that, she was seeing me. I had never felt so *seen*. Those pale, deep-set eyes were crawling all over me like flies, taking in every bit of me and not much liking what they saw.

'Please,' I croaked, as much to break the silence as anything, 'could I have a sweet?'

My father didn't intervene this time; I think he was as disconcerted as I was.

To my enormous relief, Jessie looked away again. The sweet was still between the finger and thumb of her left hand, and now slightly squashed – she had been exerting pressure. She raised it and I waited for the long and elaborate consumption process to begin again. Instead, she held out her hand, with the sweet, to me, but without looking at me – her eyes were now firmly fixed on the sweet as if it might take flight and escape.

I took it with my own finger and thumb, angling them so as not to touch hers. Taking it required a small exercise of strength; she didn't simply relinquish it, it had to be removed.

'That's kind, Jessie,' said father. 'How very kind.'

I took the cue. 'Thank you.'

Now that I had the sweet I didn't want to eat it. The cracked surface, the warmth from her fingers were repellent. Fortunately she looked away again and I was able to slip it into my pocket. Hopping back up on the bed was difficult because my legs were shaking.

My father began another monologue, this time about his work, the new lines of confectionery that Hopgood's were 'bringing on stream', others that the public had apparently gone off, a complete mystery to the marketing department . . . He was doing pretty well but I was surprised, when she was such an old friend that he called her 'Auntie' and he'd taken the trouble to bring us here, that nothing he said was at all personal. And any questions he asked her were just rhetorical tags, more about filling the silence than anything else. I felt quite proud of myself for requesting, and receiving, the sweet. Slightly frightening though the exchange had been, I recognized it as a moment of real communication, whereas my father was, well, just prattling.

A few minutes (which felt like an hour) later, we were presented with a natural break by the return of the pleasant orderly, coming to see whether we wanted more hot water for the teapot.

'Oh, no, thanks very much,' said my father, rising to his feet. 'Actually, we should be making tracks, we have a way to go.'

'Where's that then?' asked the orderly. 'Back home?'

'No, as a matter of fact I'm on a little work trip and Flora's come along to keep me company.'

'Ah, that's nice, keeping your dad in order, are you?'

I knew she didn't require or need an answer, she was tidying the tray preparatory to taking it away. No-one was going to detain us – not her, and least of all Jessie.

'. . . sweeties is it, they look nice, let me just put them there so I can . . . there we are. Can I ask you to open the door for me, love, thank you . . . see you next time . . .'

She went, and we prepared to make our farewells. But as my father stepped round the table to offer a dutiful kiss, Jessie stood up. She did so smoothly, without effort, there was nothing the matter with her joints. One moment she was sitting there, legs akimbo, in front of her line of sweets, the next she was towering over us. She must have been six feet tall. Bravely, my father put his hands on her arms and kissed her impassive cheek – he almost had to reach up. I had already decided that I wasn't going to attempt any such thing.

'Goodbye,' I said, adding, 'thank you,' for good measure though I wasn't sure for what.

In the next few seconds two things happened that I was never going to forget. I can experience them again any time, in a heartbeat.

We were almost at the door when she spoke. Her voice was eerily light and girlish; my scalp and skin prickled at the strangeness of it.

'The children,' she said.

Not a question, nor properly a statement. Simply words uttered in space, in a void. And then again, in exactly the same tone: 'The children . . .'

Odder still, my father pretended he hadn't heard, that nothing had happened. He didn't look round, but opened the door and was out in the corridor, slapping his pockets, affecting to look for the car key. But I looked over my shoulder and saw the expression on Jessie's face.

For the first time she was completely animated, and her face was alight – brilliant, in fact – with a sly, venomous hostility.

SEVEN

I t was a commonplace of childhood in the 1970s that there were areas of knowledge and personal experience that were labelled Adults Only. But gradually I came to see that with us this was not just a routine case of *'pas devant les enfants'*.

The strange touch on my hand on that long-ago summer night was more my secret than theirs. I knew what I'd felt; they hadn't been there. Long before my odd discovery in the empty bedroom I was aware of an undercurrent of secrecy; covert conversations that petered out or stopped abruptly when I appeared; quick, mouthed whispers and glances that were intended to be over my head or behind my back; a general reticence about the past, almost as if we didn't have one, as if our tiny family had sprung complete from nowhere, the product of a kind of tripartite parthenogenesis.

Even so, like all children, I accepted this as one of the elements of my childhood – a given, like the distinctive smell of one's own house which you don't even notice until you've been away, but which then assails you in a Proustian wave on your return. But after the visit to Jessie I was overcome with curiosity. Here was a strange and unsettling experience for which I felt entitled to an explanation.

*   *   *

My father's mood was buoyant as we walked to the car – a spring in his step and a hum on his breath – but I saw him take a nip from his leather hip-flask before he got into the driving seat.

Once we were on the road and heading for the motel (no more business calls till we began heading south again tomorrow), I spoke up.

'She's not very well, is she?'

'I did warn you.' Terry Wogan was on the radio and he didn't turn the sound down. He didn't want the conversation to last.

'How do you know her?'

'Oh . . .' He turned the volume knob. 'I told you, she's a sort of honorary auntie.'

I didn't have one of these, and didn't understand the usage. 'How do you mean?'

'She sort of looked after me when I was young.'

'A nanny?'

'Sort of.'

There were a lot of 'sort ofs' in this conversation. 'What was your mother doing?'

'She wasn't there much.' While I thought about this, he added: 'But I left home when I was quite young, so—'

'How young?'

'Eighteen. So that was that really.'

'Did you like Jessie?'

'Hard to say, I don't know . . . Not much.'

'But she wasn't like that – I mean like she is now?'

'Good lord no!' He frowned and waved a hand. I didn't know what to believe; he was in a funny mood. 'Anyway! Haven't got a clue if she knew we were there, but duty done eh?'

'She did say something, just as we were going.'

'Did she?' His hand was hovering over Wogan. 'Don't think I heard. Goodbye perhaps?'

'No. She said "the children".'

'Did she? Did she really? A ray of light then, maybe she had some idea who I was after all.'

I considered this, and it seemed plausible in the light of what my father had told me. But I continued to truffle for information.

'Was she nice to you as a child?'

'Not very.'

'What did she do?'

'It was more what she didn't do. Not much affection. Not much fun, playing, that kind of thing. She didn't have a clue about kids really, she was in the wrong job.'

'So when did you last see her?'

'Oh God, I don't know, Floss . . .' For the first time his voice betrayed a glint of impatience. 'A year or so? I don't owe her anything. Rather the opposite. But if I'm in the area I try and pop in.'

'Has she always been so – you know, so bad?'

'For ages. Forever. She was starting to be ill when I was still a boy.'

'You must have been scared.'

His hand was no longer near the radio, but back on the wheel. I sensed memory becoming strong, a presence sitting there with us in the car.

'I was sometimes, yes. You've seen her, she's a big woman. Strong.'

'Did she ever hit you?'

He seemed to hesitate. 'Yes.'

I had provoked the answer, prompted it almost, but now I was shocked.

'What did your mother say?'

'She didn't know.'

This was my grandmother we were talking about, but she was a stranger; I felt no connection to her. Just pity for the boy my father had been, struck by that giant of a woman.

'Where is your mother now?' I asked. I still couldn't say 'Grandmother'.

'She's not around.'

'She's dead?'

My father seemed to nod, but we were at a crossroads and he was looking this way and that before pulling out.

'I don't have any grandparents, do I?' I wasn't being plaintive, but expressing a sort of wonder at my unusual situation.

'Well, everyone has them, but you didn't know them. Poor

old Floss . . .' My father patted my knee. 'You've been short-changed in the family department and no mistake.'

I wasn't much further forward, but the little ground I had gained encouraged me to ask my next question.

'What about Zinny?'

'What about her? Parentage, you mean?'

'Yes.'

'Ah . . .' He changed up and accelerated as we hit the motorway. 'Now you're asking.'

He seemed to be making a game of it, but I didn't mind because he'd cheered up. 'Go on then.'

'She is the offspring of a unicorn and a white witch.'

This seemed so entirely plausible, and he knew it, that we both laughed at the thought. But for once I didn't let him get away with the game thing.

'No, really.'

'I told you.' We whooshed into the fast lane past a couple of lorries. 'No, I've no idea. There was a rift, some sort of falling out when she was very young. She's never talked about them all the time I've known her.'

We moved back into the centre lane and hummed along for a while.

'That's sad,' I said.

'I don't think she's particularly sad. She's a tough one, your mother.' We overtook a white estate car and returned to our lane. 'They're probably dead now. She's a tad older than me as you know.'

'How much older?' I asked, though I had a pretty fair idea.

'Fifteen years.'

'Fifteen years?' I squeaked incredulously.

'I know. Imagine – she'd have been a glamorous young woman while I was still a schoolboy in short trousers.'

I mumbled 'Oh' but it came out more like 'Yeeuch'.

'I didn't know that when I first met her. Not that it would have made any difference if I had. She was fantastically beautiful, as you can imagine.'

I could. Oh, I could. But it made my cheeks burn and the inside of my chest squirm to hear him say it, and I couldn't answer.

'Your mama the cradle-snatcher, eh?' My father glanced at me and chuckled. I sensed he was much more comfortable with this line of conversation. 'Sorry, Floss.'

All these little titbits of information I kept close and husbanded, poring over them like a witch doctor casting stones. In a small way they helped me recover from the trauma (and I don't use the word lightly) of Towser's death and their response to it. Nico and Zinny were *officially* strange, and different. If they were there more for each other than for me, if I often felt left out, well, there were reasons for that. My father was only half joking when he said Zinny was part unicorn; having them as parents was like owning a couple of strange, quasi-mythical creatures. They could never be what they weren't, and I could never change them nor be like them.

But law unto themselves though they were, they still had a profound influence on me and the way I lived my life later on, in a way more hands-on parents never could have done. And there was, inevitably, collateral damage.

EIGHT

Gus was a teacher at Holland House, the prep school I worked at when I left Lyme. He taught a whole rake of subjects to the younger boys (heartbreakingly young to be away from home), and took sport as well: football in winter and cricket in summer.

Professionally speaking, my years at the school were my happiest. It was a lovely place. Prep schools often get a bad press (the middle classes banishing their tender young; eccentric and morally dodgy teachers; unfriendly dormitories and horrible food) but apart from the first – in which tradition and geography were important factors – none of that was true in the case of Holland House. Built by a 1930s industrialist, a manufacturer of flash motor car interiors for petrol-heads of that era, it sat in its grounds with an air of ample ease and confidence, and the modern additions of pool and gym were well designed and blended in.

The job of secretary was only marginally better paid than the one at the hotel, and I had no accommodation in the area, but luckily for me the matron, a pleasant Aussie called Meg Ingles, had a flat in the school with a room which she let to stray young members of staff, and it came free at the right moment. My modest salary was suddenly worth a lot more as I became nearly 'all found' – three square meals a day and homely digs for a peppercorn rent.

I had no experience with children but Meg had more than enough for both of us and I surprised myself by taking to it. The boys, like the staff, were a mixed bunch but they were mostly sweet, funny and very often homesick. My secretarial duties weren't arduous and I found myself helping out in various capacities like mealtimes and games – Mr Fairday the Head told me early on, 'We're an all-hands-to-the-pumps outfit here.' This was how I got to know Gus Farr.

At twenty-one I'd never had a boyfriend. You couldn't count Conor, the waiter at the Dorset Arms. He was one of those pleasant lazy, easy young men, who won't make any effort but will take something if it's handed to them on a plate. I never handed him anything, so we stayed friendly workmates and content to be so.

I wasn't bothered by this state of affairs (lack of affairs more like), and I certainly didn't want to get engaged – the very idea gave me shortness of breath. But I recognized that there was something out there which I had yet to experience; something that my parents, for instance, had in spades, the thing which would always leave me on the outside looking in. My curiosity was piqued, I wouldn't put it any stronger than that.

Gus was a year older than me, an open-faced, simple-hearted, trusting and trustworthy young man who fully expected life to be good. He wasn't complacent, but sanguine, and that made him good company. He was one of those rare people who one never heard say a bad word about someone else, and that may have been because he brought out the best in people, so from his point of view there was nothing bad to say. Unlike me he had gone to university but dropped out, in order to travel, which I thought pretty dashing. He'd embarked on a sort of extended gap year building orphanages, teaching in Thailand (especially swimming, which apparently the Thais were no good at), trekking in Nepal and boating up the Amazon. You could almost see in Gus's eyes the same clear, bright light that must have shone in the faces of the early explorers, their boundless optimism and confidence.

We liked each other at once – well, it was impossible not to like Gus, but as the youngest members of staff we immediately had something extra in common. The problem was that because he was handsome, sweet and interested in me, I didn't realize that I didn't find him attractive. If that sounds odd – well, I was naive in lots of ways.

We began 'seeing' each other – that's the common expression, but the trouble was that I didn't see Gus, not properly. We went to the cinema, and the pub, ate inexpensive ethnic meals, played tennis and took long walks on the beach, the cliffs and around Maiden Castle. I learnt a bit about him. His family were in Norfolk, he had an older sister who was a nurse and a younger brother at Wellington. His plan was to complete a year or two at Holland House and then take off travelling again. Conservation and ecology were his things, but he was a practical idealist. He had been saving and had also applied for a grant to help with a long-term project in Borneo to do with orangutans and deforestation.

With Gus, I occasionally had an out-of-body experience, like a scene from a film, when I seemed to be watching the two of us, a nice, energetic young couple having fun, discussing plans, possibly with a shared future ahead of them. I had to admit I found these fleeting mind's-eye pictures unsettling. I was completely inexperienced, both romantically and sexually, but I was also independent-minded and self-sufficient and secretly relieved that he would be off to the other side of the world next August so our relationship had a natural arc.

I suppose I assumed that Gus felt much the same – that we'd been thrown together by circumstance, easy come, easy go – and it was in this spirit that I had sex with him. I badly needed to cross that one off my list and, thus grown-up and freed up, move on. The earth remained resolutely unmoved, although the relaxed intimacy afterwards was nice. So it was disconcerting to discover after the third time that he and I had apparently had two completely different experiences.

'Would you be shocked to learn,' he asked in bed in his room in the staff house, 'that there's a real danger I'm falling in love with you, Flo?'

His tone was that typically British, circuitous, half-joking one that left me unsure about exactly what he was telling me.

Not for the first time in my life, all I could think of to say was 'No' – meaning *No*, I wouldn't be shocked, but also a more emphatic *No* to the falling-in-love thing. The second implication shot straight past him.

'Well that's good,' he said. 'Because I am.'

He put his arm across me, took hold of my shoulder and rolled me towards him on my side, so that our faces were mere inches apart. I could see the tracery on his pupils and a stray eyelash on his cheek.

'Because you are just the most wonderful woman I've ever met.'

He kissed me so there was no need for me to respond to this. But two things occurred to me while we kissed. One was that he had called me a woman which, while correct, was not something I thought of myself as. A girl, maybe. A 'latency girl', certainly. The other was the implication that he had met lots of women and I had won some kind of competition which I had never entered. But hey, I had been handed a compliment and was happy to receive it. I didn't return it and he seemed not to mind.

Almost unprecedentedly, Zinny took an interest in me at this time. Some instinct – I'd call it 'maternal' but that word never suited her – prompted her to question me about my colleagues at Holland House.

'Are they all like Mr Chips?'

'No, actually.'

'But mostly men.'

'Well, yes, apart from Matron.'

Zinny laughed. It was autumn half-term, Nico was out

having off-season drinks at the cricket club and we were having a rare moment *à deux*, sitting in the living room at four o'clock with the pale sun melting into the sea as our backdrop. I was more at ease with Zinny these days, now that I had my own life.

'And there are several wives,' I added.

'Are there?' asked Zinny, as though this was a particularly striking fact.

'They're not monks, or eccentrics. It's just a normal job.'

A pause stretched, sank, and became a silence, but not an uncomfortable one. Zinny sat with her stockinged feet curled up beside her on the sofa; she wore loose, high-waisted trousers and a pale cable-knit sweater, her reddish-brown hair slicked back from her high forehead. She must have been in her mid-fifties. She didn't so much look young for her age – her style of beauty had always been grown-up and sophisticated – but that she looked like Katherine Hepburn, timeless. I may have inherited (or perhaps learnt) my self-possession from her, but nothing in the way of looks. Any physical family traits – my scrubby hair which I now successfully wore short and spiky, my square-tipped hands, my slightly downward-sloping eyelids – were all from my father and looked better on him than on me.

'Is there anybody young there?' Zinny asked. 'I mean apart from the boys.'

'Quite a few.'

She looked at me directly. Her arms were folded. 'Anyone to be friends with?'

'They're a friendly bunch.'

'All right. Good.'

She dropped this line of enquiry for the time being, but at Christmas it resurfaced. I stayed on at Holland House for a couple of days, ostensibly to get some paperwork done but mainly to be with Gus. We exchanged presents – I gave him a book about the people and ecology of Borneo (coals to Newcastle you might think, but I wanted to show I'd been paying attention) which he opened right away, and he gave me a tiny, clumsily wrapped parcel with instructions to 'keep it till the day'.

'You opened yours,' I pointed out.

'I know, but I want to imagine you seeing mine for the first time.'

'If I open it now, you won't have to imagine.'

'I want to be there at your family Christmas.'

I thought about this as I drove home on a grey, damp day, the one before Christmas Eve. I pictured Gus's Christmas in Norfolk as the full seasonal monty – stockings, church, champagne cocktails, blazing fires, chestnuts, turkey – no, goose, they'd have goose – and a spherical, holly-topped pudding blazing merrily . . . They would probably be amongst those who still watched the Queen, and then there'd be a long muddy walk with a couple of Labradors, followed by games, and tea with cake . . . an evening round the fire with tumblers of scotch and crusty sandwiches. They probably had a seven-foot tree in the hall, real greenery garlands festooning the pictures, the mantlepiece and the banisters, and more Christmas cards than we had people we knew . . .

I wasn't envious; I could never have hacked it. I liked our small, elegant Christmas. It suited us and it was what I was used to. I was looking forward to a few days of quiet with no demands on me of any kind. There would be silver branches by the verandah windows, candles in the fireplace, and a side of smoked salmon with the Cava in the fridge. Tomorrow my father would make the only thing he was good at – rare fillet of beef with baked potatoes and petits pois. Zinny would do her lemon syllabub. We would get up late, I a little earlier than my parents, and I'd take a walk on the beach. We'd eat at four o'clock. Like all households, we had our way of doing things – we would never have used the term 'traditions'.

When I got home, Zinny was still at work, and my father was in the living room watching horse racing on the television. He often had a flutter, and now he greeted me with studied absent-mindedness, proffering his cheek with his eyes fixed on the screen.

'Hold on, this bloody horse could be about to do us an enormous favour!'

Dutifully I stood beside him, watching. 'Which one?'

'That one in the front – yes! Come on you little darling!

One last heave – watch out – aargh! Hell and damnation, bastard! Broke away too early, you see?'

'What a shame.'

'You don't get it, do you?' He got up. 'Like Zinny. I haven't lost much, but if it weren't for a couple of whiskers on that thing's nose I might have made us a Christmas bonus.'

'Try not to think about it.'

'Easier said than done. Let me give you a hand.'

He went up the stairs ahead of me. I may have imagined it, but he seemed to pause for a split second at the top, as if he'd forgotten which room was mine. What I did notice was that there had been some redecorating up here – all the woodwork, including the doors, was a fresh white.

He opened my bedroom door, and it was the same in there, with new gloss on the window frame and sill, the skirting boards and the cornice.

'Everything's looking very nice,' I said.

'Well, about time. Downstairs is always up to scratch but it's easy to forget about this floor. When you're away Zinny and I never come up here.'

'Thank you, it's lovely.'

'Not too smelly? We left the window open.'

I sniffed. 'No, not at all.'

I was on the verge of asking if anything in particular had prompted them to come up now, and who had stayed in the spare room over the years. I watched as my father put my bag down by the bed and went to the window.

'Want me to close this now?'

'No thanks, it's good to have the fresh air.'

He remained standing there, looking out. 'It's pleasant up here, isn't it – to feel halfway up the hill but still at ground level. More or less.'

'I always liked it.'

'I bet.' He turned to me with a grin. For the first time I felt that I was closing on him. That the time was approaching when I might discover the secrets.

'Did you ever go out and lark about out there? I mean on the grass – at night when we were downstairs, when you should have been asleep?'

'Actually no.'

That wasn't true. I had once used my chair to climb out, and slipped over the parapet on to the hard slope with its thin covering of grass. I'd walked about a hundred yards up the hill until our house was below me, the two back windows looking back at me like eyes over a fan. I remembered how weird it was to think of my parents even further below, sitting out on the verandah, not knowing I was here. But that we could all three of us see the same sea, a wrinkled grey fretted with dabs of white. Suddenly shocked at myself I hurtled back down the hill, only to discover I couldn't get back over the parapet. A three-foot drop was nothing, but to get back over the stone wall was beyond me. I had to skulk down to the road and run, crouched over, up the alley to the kitchen door praying that it would be still unlocked (it was) and there would be no-one in there. They were still out on the verandah and didn't hear me, but moments after I was back in bed I heard Zinny's long, soft, barefoot stride come in and cross the hall, pausing for a second at the foot of the stairs before moving on to the kitchen.

There was no real reason to deny this childish outing, except for my impulse to have a secret from my father.

'I don't believe you,' he said cheerfully, patting my arm. 'I'm sure I would have done. Anyway, I'll leave you to it. Come on down when you're ready and we can have a sharpener. Zinny will be back soon.'

He left, leaving the door open, and trotted down the stairs. I closed the door quietly and put my bag on the bed. It didn't take me long to unpack my few things, including my ready-wrapped presents for my parents: a hand-painted glass tray for Zinny and a notoriously uninhibited cricket autobiography for my father. They were easy people to buy for; we didn't set a lot of store by presents and generally expressed astonishment that I should have bought them anything at all. It was the same with birthdays: they were cagey about dates and made nothing of them except for mine which was always properly if simply acknowledged.

I came to Gus's little package, tucked in amongst my under-wear, and undid it at once, in spite of his admonition. I could still tell him that I'd opened it at home and a white lie wouldn't hurt him. The blue leather-trimmed box provoked something I told myself was excitement, but which was really trepidation. There was a small card accompanying it – he had cut it from a larger gift tag, to fit the box. His loose, generous handwriting started large and grew cramped and crooked to fit the tiny space.

To my darling Flora, to wear at Christmas, for happiness always, all my love Gxxx

He had given me a necklace – or more accurately a pendant – and I'm ashamed to say that my first reaction was relief that it wasn't a ring. On the fine thread of a chain hung a tiny silver bird – a bluebird – in flight. It was quite different from anything else I owned, for the good reason that I owned almost no jewellery, and no necklaces at all. Hadn't Gus noticed that I never wore them? Or had he perhaps thought that I was deprived, and secretly longing for one to wear?

I laid it on the bed, and turned my attention to the card, studying the message. 'Darling' was nice, in an old-fashioned kind of way, and 'all my love' was how people often signed off – relatives, or even just good friends. Nothing special could be read into either of those. To wish me happiness was also unexceptionable. It was the 'always' that bothered me ever so slightly. Was that an 'always' that involved both of us, or a sort of send-off? For some reason I felt a thump of sadness, worse for being hard to interpret.

Poor Gus. Poor me. When it came to self-knowledge I was living my life armoured in a sort of exoskeleton that helped me to go through the moves but insulated me from authentic feelings. This lack of understanding wasn't my, or anybody's, fault, but there were reasons for it, which I had yet to identify.

I wasn't wearing the right clothes (I was by no means sure I even owned them, whatever they were) but I put the pendant on right away. The clasp was horribly fiddly but I managed by doing it up in front with the aid of the mirror, and dropped the little bird inside the collar of my crew-neck. I didn't want to let Gus down; on the other hand to put it on for the first time on Christmas Day would be to draw attention to it.

My father would never have noticed, such things simply weren't on his radar, but I'd reckoned without Zinny. We were putting plates away after supper and she wasn't even looking at me when she remarked casually, 'That's pretty.'

'What?'

She closed the cupboard door, still not looking. 'The little bird.'

I glanced down. The bird must have popped out of the neck of my jumper when I was bending down. 'Thank you.'

'Not your usual thing.'

'I suppose not.' I fingered it and slipped it back inside.

'Is it new?'

'Yes.'

She leaned back on the worktop, arms folded. 'A present?'

'Actually yes.'

'M-hm.' To my surprise she didn't immediately pick up on this, and we went back into the living room. But when they went to bed – I was going to sit up a little longer – she came over and I thought she was going to give me one of her vanishingly rare kisses, not always a good sign. Instead she sat down next to me on the sofa, but on the edge and facing towards me. I couldn't remember when I'd last been so unmistakably and entirely the focus of her attention.

'A word of advice . . .?'

If this was some sort of mother–daughter moment, it was unprecedented. I couldn't begin to imagine what she might say.

'Go ahead. By all means.'

'"By all means" – you are funny sometimes.' She must have seen me bristle slightly because she added, 'I just mean about your necklace.'

'OK.'

'Can you take it off so I can show you something?'

'All right.' I fiddled rather crossly with the catch, and handed it over.

'Oh, isn't that sweet.' She held it up admiringly between her fingers and thumbs. '*But* you probably noticed, it's not quite the right length.'

So there was a right length?

'I hadn't noticed, no.'

'Well, in that case you may not agree of course, but if you were to try . . .' She was wearing a black shirt, and now she held the necklace in place so that the bluebird hung in the hollow of her throat, just above her collarbones. 'A squeak shorter and it would be here . . .' She turned her head this way and that. 'Yes?'

'Perhaps.'

'*Or* it needs to be a little longer, so . . .' She brought her hands to the front of her neck and let the bird dive into the shallow valley just below the top button of her shirt. 'See what I mean?'

'Not really.' I did, but I was disabled by embarrassment and awkwardness. I had never felt so thoroughly put in my place. On reflection, I don't think she meant to have this effect; it was just that she couldn't help it. Zinny was suddenly in her element, as I was out of mine.

'Anyway . . .' She handed the necklace back. 'Obviously it doesn't matter, and it's none of my business. But if you did want to get it altered it wouldn't be a big job. That rather strange man in the jeweller's in Salting could take out a few links or put a few more in as easy as anything.'

I could see that she was probably right, but I couldn't concede. 'To be honest I'm happy with it as it is. And I don't want to . . .'

I stopped there but she said as she got up, 'You don't want to offend whoever gave it to you.'

'No.'

'I'm sure he wouldn't be offended.' There was no hesitation about the 'he'. 'He'll be flattered that you want it to be right.' She made a kissing face. 'Good night, sleep well.'

I closed the door and turned on the television, but not because I wanted to watch. I simply needed the distraction, the flickering coloured light and the chatter of voices. The necklace lay next to me on the side table. Any special significance it had held for me was spoiled. At least before, whatever my gut reaction, the story had been mine, to make what I would of, and to process as I wished. In a couple of minutes Zinny had unintentionally robbed me of all that. She had put her finger unerringly on all my insecurities – about myself, my taste, my instincts, about Gus. I was once again the child, the outsider. Not in on the secret.

The blast of the phone made me jump, and I broke out in goose bumps. I turned down the television. I answered cautiously: my parents had an extension next to their bed.

'Hello?'

'Flora? It's me.'

I waited for a second, but there was no telltale click, or the whisper of another person on the line.

'Darling?'

'Hi.'

'You all right?'

'I'm fine.'

'Good. Good – you sounded a bit out of it.'

'Sorry.'

'No apology needed. I just wanted to hear your voice . . .' His own voice had the warm, furry quality I associated with a few drinks having been taken. 'I miss you.'

'It's not for long.'

'It's a pretty fair old shambles here, relatives round every corner. Perfectly jolly so long as you keep the alcohol levels up, which I fully intend to do.'

'I can tell.'

'That obvious, eh?' He chuckled. 'The old man's cracked open the single malt. How are things your end?'

'Oh fine. Quieter than you, no extras.'

I wasn't going to mention the necklace, on the grounds that I wasn't supposed to have mentioned it, but now he asked.

'Have you sneaked a peek?'

'Of course not.'

'Liar.'

'Alright, I have. It's absolutely lovely, thank you.'

'I do hope so. I mean, I liked it but is it, you know, right?'

'It's perfect,' I said, 'but I'm thinking of perhaps having it made a tiny bit shorter.'

'Really? Good idea. Obviously I don't have a clue, but it needs to be right. We could go somewhere together and get that sorted.'

Annoyingly, Zinny had been right in her assessment; he sounded happy. I felt I'd expressed too much interest, too great a commitment to his present.

'That's all right,' I said, 'there's a chap in our nearby town.'

'Not over Christmas. We'll do it when we're back. I'd like to be there anyway, not just to pay, to sort of get the idea.'

'Fine. You're right.'

'Only thing is I suppose this means you won't be wearing it at the festive board.'

'No, I will, I promise.'

'Excellent.' There was a pause during which I heard him taking a swallow of the single malt. 'God, I'd like to be going upstairs with you.'

I knew he meant it and I felt flattered and comforted. But the thought of my newly painted childhood bedroom, airy and austere and most importantly empty, was overwhelmingly more attractive.

'Sleep well,' I said. 'And thanks again, Gus, for my beautiful present.'

'Nothing's too beautiful for you.'

'Shucks . . . Good-night.'

'Night, darling—'

'Night.' I put the phone down gently but firmly. I suppose it could be said that I'd just had quite significant conversations with my mother and my boyfriend, but the combined effect of both was to leave me feeling even more alone. There was too much concealment and evasion in my life and it hung over me like a net, pinning me down and restricting movement.

That Christmas proved two things to me. One was that three had finally become a crowd at home. The second was that I couldn't return the compliment where Gus was concerned, and found the courage to tell him so. The two things were not unconnected. Two days of watching my parents with a slightly adjusted perspective showed me with painful clarity what they had and we – or at any rate I – did not. Why Zinny, in her sixth decade, knew exactly where a pendant should hang for maximum effect and why my father, fifteen years her junior, still had that smile, those shining eyes that were all and only for her.

Whatever Gus and I were up to, we couldn't hold a candle to them.

But when I made my speech about not being sure (I had never been surer, but my courage didn't extend to that), and about it being me, not him, all the usual double-speak, I wasn't prepared for his reaction. He went mad, and not in the way I might have expected – not so much hurt as coldly furious. What did I mean? What was I thinking of? Had I just been stringing him along all this time?

I explained as best I could in the face of this interrogation that I had been guilty only of not knowing my own mind, and that I still didn't, but that to continue our relationship with these doubts and uncertainties in the background *would* be to string him along, and I wasn't going to do that. I knew as I spoke that nothing was going to do any good. I had not realized he was capable of such cutting anger and disdain. His eyes were flinty and small; there was an aureole of white round his mouth.

'How big of you. How bloody condescending.'

'If it's any consolation I'm not happy either.'

'You're all heart, Flora.'

I dreaded giving way to tears, but my voice still broke slightly. 'What would you want me to do?'

'I don't know . . .' For a moment I'd caught him off balance. 'Be true to yourself? Hang in there? Not go back on everything you've said?'

That was it – the moment when I glimpsed the reality of what had gone on. Because I had said nothing. My behaviour may not have been completely honest, but at least some sort of deep-rooted honesty had prevented me from traducing myself in words.

'I never said anything!' But this was no good either.

'No, come to think of it you didn't, did you?' I'd never have believed Gus capable of sneering, but that's what he did. 'But you didn't have to; you were only too happy to soak up the attention and let me believe we had—'

He broke off abruptly.

'What?' I asked. 'That we had what?'

'Something,' he muttered. 'A good thing. A future.'

I did feel sorry for him then. I remembered his voice on the phone at Christmas and the picture I had of him with his family – the adored son, brother, grandson, nephew – the fireside, the tree, the warm inclusive atmosphere of approval in which I was sure he had been raised. If I had been guilty of ticking a box with Gus, then he had done the same with me. And now I'd spoilt it.

'I'm sorry,' I said, and I meant it. 'You don't know how sorry I am.'

'You're doing it again! Patting me on the head, patronizing me.'

'That's not what I was doing.'

'Oh, I'm sure it's *unintentional* . . .' His voice dripped sarcasm. 'It just comes naturally.'

That did it. 'Stop this!' I said. 'Stop behaving like a child!'

His face was a study. I remember thinking he was either going to hit me (which only an hour ago would have been unthinkable) or burst into tears. I was horrified at the havoc I'd wrought in this nice, handsome, otherwise admirable bloke. This chap who had shot rapids, scaled cliff walls, hacked through jungle and penetrated fathomless caves had been completely unmanned by my stab at fearless honesty.

In the end neither the blow nor the tears happened. He grabbed hold of what was left of his composure, turned on his heel and stomped off. It would almost have been funny if it hadn't been so sad. And the stomping didn't end at the door. He handed in his notice and was gone the next day, leaving Holland House with a gap in its curriculum which everyone else had to fill.

The whole thing was horrifying. But it proved that I'd been right. I shed many tears for my own foolishness, and his, and swore that from now on I'd keep my distance. I was no longer a virgin; I had nothing to prove.

I put the necklace away, and Zinny, either through discretion or lack of interest, never raised the topic again.

Eighteen months later I heard via another member of staff that Gus had got engaged to a girl called Sophie Something-or-other whom he'd met on the Borneo project.

NINE

S ometimes, events that seemed inconsequential at the time become emblematic of something that follows much later. For this reason a particular vignette from this time sticks in my mind.

In the spring of the following year, after Gus had left Holland House and people had stopped asking me how I was, I spent the Easter break in Paris. I went alone, through choice. I'd found this much out about myself, that I was quite content with my own company, and not a nervous traveller. I positively liked the odd hitch; my coping mechanism kicked in and I got a little adrenaline high from sorting the problem. Because I hadn't been to university I'd never taken the gap year which was just beginning to be *de rigueur* (there were whole companies springing up that were devoted to it) but if anything this omission had whetted my appetite for travel. I wasn't a completely free spirit; I did like to be organized and enjoyed time in advance spent researching, truffling for bargains and places of interest. Zinny and Nico had an almost proprietary attitude towards Paris and were keen to give me advice, but I politely put them off and said I wanted to find out for myself – if I could successfully manage in Prague, Istanbul and (as a woman alone my proudest boast) Marrakesh, three nights in Paris would be a piece of cake.

I travelled by ferry and train, and stayed in a small, modern hotel near the station, where everything was easily accessible. For the first forty-eight hours I positively inhaled the boulevards, the museums, the art and the atmosphere, and because I walked everywhere I made enchanting discoveries – brilliant tucked-away churches, and painters' houses, and bookshops, tiny bijou parks and cafes. Low cloud and intermittent drizzle didn't put me off – I wore my parka and walking boots with pride; no-one knew me here and I had nothing to prove.

On Easter Saturday I took the metro to Montmartre, which was not at all the vibrant, welcoming place of my imagination. I'd pictured somewhere bohemian but cosy – cobbles, cupolas and balconies outside, warm candlelight shining on glasses, a haze of Disque Bleu cigarette smoke in the bars and cafés, a burble of spirited conversation, a sense of artistic history at my shoulder.

The drizzle had intensified to stair rods, but I don't believe it was only the rain that made it seem different. The day began badly when I nearly had my shoulder bag stolen. The metro carriage was crowded and I was strap-hanging. A thin girl with pinkish-red hair and a peeling plastic jacket was standing near me; I noticed her from the corner of my eye because she was one of the few standing passengers not holding on to anything. She just seemed to ride the movement of the train, her thumbs tucked in her pockets, flinty-eyed and expressionless. I wasn't clueless – I had survived Marrakesh – and kept my hand on top of the bag. When we stopped at an intermediate station there was that bounce and lurch before the doors opened, so everyone standing had to catch their balance, and I felt someone bump into me from behind. I knew at once what had happened – the pink-haired girl and her accomplice (the bumper) had gone, and so had my bag. But if they were a crack team, the locals were a match for them. The man next to me blocked the sliding door, a couple on the platform grabbed at the swinging strap of my bag and snatched it back, and the two girls ran like hares down the staircase, one of them barefoot. The woman threw my bag back, the man gave a thumbs-up and we were on our way.

'*Merci, merci beaucoup!*' I gasped, too late for the kind people on the platform. Everyone else was blank-faced, as though nothing unusual had happened. The man who had held the door for me tipped his head forward.

'*Prenez garde, hein?* Careful!'

'I will. *Merci.*'

'Are you going to Montmartre?'

'Yes.'

'Careful there too.'

My traveller's confidence was a little bruised by this, but it was obviously a common occurrence and at least the locals' instinct had kicked in and saved my life-support systems. Thank goodness I'd got in the habit of leaving my passport, credit card and most of my travellers' cheques in the hotel safe. I did check, just in case the girls' sleight of hand extended to removing cash while still in flight, but everything was still there.

A steady rain was still falling as I left the station with a stream of other tourists, and it was colder up here. I zipped up my parka, having first taken it off and put it on again over my bag. With my short hair *en brosse* and my frayed jeans I reckoned I looked almost like a street urchin myself, and so might be safe from further attacks. I wasn't going to make the same mistake again.

Oh well, I thought, as I marched, hands in pockets and hood up, through the dingy puddles and drifts of litter past a parade of sex and porn shops, tattoo parlours and strip clubs already open for business, it's all part of life and this is the *quartier* I'm in. I found myself thinking, without rancour, of Gus, who's idea of travelling was so diametrically different. What on earth would he have made of this celebration of sleaze? At least, I supposed, there was some anthropological interest, but it was a far cry from the simple longhouses and dignified ancient traditions of the Dayaks.

I passed the Moulin Rouge with scarcely a second glance – red neon and sequin-encrusted tits at eleven thirty in the morning was plain jarring and seedy. I needed to get up and out of this Gallic Soho (though come to think of it that was unfair to Soho which, based on my one visit, was positively cosy by comparison). A sign for Sacré-Coeur pointed almost vertically upward, and I promised myself a hot chocolate once I'd made it.

The climb warmed me up a bit, which made the cold wind at the top of the hill all the more of a shock. Handfuls of fine rain blew in my face like ground glass, making my eyes water. I turned into a small square which I thought might be sheltered, and perhaps home to a welcoming café, but that turned out to be a mistake. A group of kids, hard-eyed and wild as hawks, were on me in a flash, waving a dog-eared piece of card for me 'to sign', waving it in my face and babbling 'lady' and 'miss' and 'for poor!' I began by shaking my head benignly, even smiling, but when the pushing began alarms sounded – my bag must have been detectable under my coat – and I said 'No!' rather too firmly. Instantly the chatter became sharp, the pats and pushes rough. I realized there was no-one but me in the square. I walked as fast as I could without breaking into a run, with my flotilla of black-clad tormentors pecking and screeching like crows until they fell away, like magic, when I reached the street.

At least in Marrakesh there was sunshine. The steamed-up windows of the nearest café were like the gates of heaven. On this foul day it was packed, but I got a stool at the counter, undid my parka and ordered hot chocolate and a pastry. Goodwill towards Paris flooded back as I took the first sip. I was pleased after all to be here on this famous windy hill and who knew – this was an old place, maybe Renoir and Degas had sat in here and discussed techniques over Gauloises and absinthe . . .

'Not very nice out there, is it?'

I'd assumed the elderly man sitting next to me was French, but the voice was unmistakably English, with the slightest quirk of camp.

'No, it is not,' I agreed.

'Do you know this area?'

'No. First time.'

'I bet it's not what you were expecting.'

'Right.'

'Let me say it.' He inclined his head as if about to confide something vaguely risqué. 'A dump, *n'est-ce pas*?'

'Well . . .'

'Known for it.'

He reminded me a little of the art master at Holland House, except this man was probably in his seventies, or even older. He had the sort of looks that must once have been raffishly charming – indeed the charm was still there in the eyes, the voice and the slightly wolfish grin. But he had not, as they say, looked after himself. He was dreadfully thin, his dark grey hair was rather too long, and his complexion had the dull, suffused appearance of the lifelong smoker and drinker. His pinstripe suit was the worse for wear, and he'd sought to make a statement of this by adding a black T-shirt and a neckerchief knotted at the throat; worse-for-wear two-tone shoes completed the outfit.

'. . . can't go wrong with Paris though,' he was saying. 'It's our default option for a short escape.'

Before I could stop myself, I asked, 'Are you here with someone?'

'I am, unfortunately.'

Oh hell, did he think I was being flirtatious? It occurred to me that with today's luck I had washed up next to a bona fide dirty old man. Perhaps he saw something in my face because he added, 'No, I'm here with my other half. She's gone to buy a hat – there's a place round the corner, you should take a look. Stuffed with amusing little *chapeaux*.'

I couldn't tell whether this suggestion was serious, or if I was being teased. I didn't think of myself as an amusing *chapeaux* kind of person.

'I'm not dressed for trying things on.'

He looked at me with narrowed eyes. 'Oh I don't know.'

Within five minutes I'd already noticed a repertoire of small verbal and physical mannerisms designed both to charm and ever so slightly disconcert.

I said, 'I'm dressed for sightseeing in atrocious weather.'

'You are, aren't you, good for you.'

Throughout this exchange he'd been holding a lighted cigarette, occasionally tapping it on the side of the large glass ashtray that stood on the bar by his elbow. His index and middle fingers were yellowed by nicotine. Now he stubbed out the cigarette and raised a beckoning finger to the girl behind the bar.

'*Encore calvados s'il vous plait.*' His accent was execrable, but she seemed to like it. '*Attendez . . .*' He turned to me. 'Would you care to join me in something stronger?'

I was about to decline and then thought *Why not?* This was Montmartre in the rain, a stranger, a little bar . . . 'OK. Thank you.'

'*Deux calvados.*'

Brandy wouldn't have been my choice, but I didn't care enough to intervene. He fished a crumpled packet of cigarettes out of his breast pocket and wagged it in my direction.

'You? I imagine not.'

'You imagine right.'

He lit up contentedly and blew a stream of smoke into the air above us. 'No-one does these days. No Brits anyway. It's one of the things I like about this lot.'

'They certainly haven't got the message.'

'Or don't care to. *Santé*!'

We clinked glasses. I was warming up nicely under the influence of the steamy fug, the hot chocolate and the first mouthful of calvados. I put my glass down and began shrugging off my parka. He caught the nearest sleeve and helped me loosen it, then he hung it by the collar loop on a hook under the bar.

'Think it's meant for handbags, but if you don't mind the bottom dragging on the ground . . .'

'God no, it's only . . .'

'I see you've kept yours safely out of the way.' He nodded towards my midriff and I found myself involuntarily tightening my muscles. 'Your handbag. Very wise.'

'Only after I was nearly robbed, I'm ashamed to say.'

I explained to him what had happened. While I did so I couldn't escape the feeling that I was being assessed, though I also sensed that this wasn't particular to me. The bar woman, the married ladies eating crêpes, probably every female in the room had been assessed by this confident, raffish old man – I'd say gentleman, but he was no gentleman.

'What about you?' he asked. 'Here on your own?'

'I am, yes. I like my own company,' I added, in case he should infer anything pathetic from my answer.

'Me too!' he exclaimed, as though surprised and delighted by our having so much in common. 'I was always a loner.'

'But now you're married,' I reminded him. There didn't seem to be any of the usual boundaries in place; all bets were off in this conversation.

'Did I say that?'

'I'm not sure – but you implied . . .'

'You assumed.'

'All right.'

'I'm here with someone, but I'm a loner at heart. She knows it too.'

I wondered if she did, and if so what she understood by it. Might that explain one or two things about my companion? He still hadn't introduced himself, so I certainly wasn't going to.

'What about you?' he asked. 'Any love interest?'

It was usually women who got to the nitty-gritty quickly, but he and I had cut to the chase in a single bound. I'd have called him a fast worker if he hadn't been so old. I realized, with surprise, that I was starting to enjoy myself.

'There was,' I said, 'sort of, until quite recently. But it's over now.'

'Yes, yes . . .' He nodded as if this only went to show something or other. 'Sad about that?'

'Relieved. It was me that ended it.'

'Poor bastard.'

'He'll be fine. He's gone to Borneo.'

'Best place for him.' This made me laugh, and he said, 'What?' but he was laughing as well. The laugh turned into a nasty cough and I waited for it to die down.

'Jesus.' He thumped his chest and took another drag on his cigarette. 'So what was the problem exactly? With Mr Borneo?'

'Oh, I don't know . . .'

'Yes you do, you just don't want to say.' This was true, and made me laugh again. 'Go on,' he begged, 'do tell. My lips are sealed, and anyway we'll never see each other again which is the perfect basis for an exchange of confidences.'

So it was going to be an exchange, was it? A sort of game.

'I'll tell if you tell.'

'I've got nothing to tell.'

'Of course you have,' I said. 'Everyone has.' I had a brain-wave. 'Think of what you'd least like anyone to know, and tell me that.'

'God but you're a hard woman.' He sighed dramatically and quirked a finger for more drinks. What the hell. 'All right, you twisted my arm. I'll do it. But it was my idea, so you first.'

I realized I had never done this. I'd never talked about Gus, because no-one had ever asked, and there was a heady exhilaration in the prospect of doing so now with this complete stranger.

'He was a chap I met at work—'

'So far, so dull.'

'Not dull at all. He was very nice, very handsome, very admirable—'

'Admirable? Christ! That bad?'

'And I think he fell in love with me.'

'You think?'

'It's what he believed.'

He covered his eyes with his hand – in spite of the nicotine he had nice hands, long-fingered and strong-looking, with pronounced veins on the back. 'The whole thing was doomed.'

'I wouldn't say that.'

The drinks arrived and he took away his hand. His eyes were bright; he was enjoying this.

'What about you?'

'I wanted to have sex with someone—'

'Now you're talking!' He raised his glass.

'And he was very keen—'

'Of course he was.'

'So we did, and—'

'Hang on, hold hard – is that it?' He made a rewinding gesture. 'I want details.'

'No.'

'You said you were mad to have sex with him—'

'I didn't, I said I wanted to have sex with someone.'

'What, anyone?'

'No!' He'd made me laugh again. 'Not anyone. Someone nice.'

'*Nice*?' He made it sound like leprosy. '*Nice*?'

'Someone attractive then.'

'Wait a minute.' He narrowed his eyes. 'This was your first time.'

'Yes.'

Now he chose not to make fun of me. 'Perfectly sensible. Did the experience come up to scratch?'

'I suppose – yes, it was fine.'

'So this – whatsisname . . .' He clicked his fingers but some instinct of loyalty kicked in and I didn't supply a name. 'He passed muster between the sheets?'

'Yes.'

'But that was it – no flame, nothing extra?'

'No. Not for me, and I think if he was honest not for him either. He was heartbroken when I told him—'

'Good man.'

'He left work and it all ended badly. Which I'm sorry about, because—'

'He was nice.'

'Is it a cliché to say I never wanted to hurt him?'

He shrugged. 'Clichés are clichés because they're a statement of the blindingly bloody obvious. I'm sure you didn't want to. You were being cruel to be kind.'

'I didn't even think I was being cruel.'

'M-hm.' He seemed to be waiting for me to add something, but then went on, 'And now look at you. Free as a bird, in the City of Love.' He pronounced it 'lurv'.

I took a sip of the second calvados which I knew I was going to regret. The pause lengthened, I was being lured into saying something else, which I might also regret. There was, however, no need to be polite.

'Your turn,' I said.

'But we haven't finished!'

'I have.'

'Fair enough I suppose. Well now, let me see. Long, long ago, before you were born, I fell head over heels in love with a beautiful girl I'd never even spoken to – and here she is!'

Saved by the bell, I thought. *Jammy.* A woman was threading her way between the tables and the people standing at the bar. My companion held out his arm and hooked her into him, I saw her close her eyes for a second as he kissed her forehead.

Even now he didn't ask my name; he introduced me as his 'new drinking companion' and her as 'Barbara, my better half'. Her hand was small and slim in mine but her handshake was firm. She smiled and said 'Hello' as if this were an everyday occurrence, which didn't surprise me, and even in old age – she must have been seventy – there was the ghost of a soft, luminous prettiness in her eyes, and her still-full mouth. She wore her grey hair in a loose coil on the nape of her neck, and tendrils of it had come loose in the rain; a plain brown coat, flat boots; what Zinny would have called a 'good bag'; no wedding ring. If I'd been asked to sum her up, I'd have said sweet, and tired – very tired. In response to his question she asked for a coffee. I probably should have left, but I was curious.

'So did you buy a hat?' he asked, looking her up and down as if she might be concealing the purchase.

'Yes, though whether I shall ever wear it . . .' Her voice was gentle and a little plummy – like a shy schoolgirl.

'Wear it now, show us.'

'Oh, Johnny . . .'

I thought, *If I was her I wouldn't like to be told 'show us', when one of the other people is a stranger.* But once again she seemed not to mind the way he spoke to her. She opened her bag and took out a soft package. Inside was a black velvet beret, with a jaunty red embellishment. She pulled it on with quite a flourish, tweaking it on one side and cocking her head. She was such a pretty, charming lady. I warmed to her.

'Aah, yes!' He flicked with his finger the red decoration (I saw now that it was a flower) while she stood quite still, smiling gently. 'I *see*.'

It was as though she was keeping him amused, letting him play. Passive, but not, I thought, helpless.

'That looks lovely,' I said. 'It really suits you.'

She raised her hand hesitantly towards the beret, not quite touching it. 'Thank you. Not mutton dressed as lamb?'

'Not at all,' I said, truthfully.

'How nice of you to say so.'

'Anyway I hate that expression,' he said, and for the first time he sounded a touch out of sorts, almost rattled. 'All of those platitudes about ageing, they're ridiculous.'

I wasn't going to remind him of his own analysis of clichés, especially as that would have worked against her, and she was so nice. Instead I took this as my cue to leave.

'Not going, surely?' he asked, cheerful again as I put on my parka. 'The party's only just started.'

'Oh you know,' I said, 'sights to see and all that. It was really nice meeting you.'

'And you,' she said, 'have a wonderful time.'

'*Au revoir.*' He raised his glass. '*Bon chance!*'

As I left I glanced back. She had taken the beret off and was sitting on the stool I'd vacated, sipping coffee while he said something vastly amusing to the bar girl.

I won't say 'that was it, and I never thought of them again'. That hour spent in the crowded bar in Montmartre remains vivid in my memory to this day, both for the oddness of the conversation, and of the old couple. I had only met them for the shortest time, and yet I felt I'd glimpsed their story. If I'd had longer, the gist of it might have disappeared, fogged by detail. The next, the only other time I saw them was at a distance, and they weren't aware of me.

I'm not religious in any formal sense. Outside school assemblies, I'd never attended services, but I liked churches and here I was in a city with an embarrassment of them. Walking back from the station that evening I passed one or two that were advertising the Easter vigil that night. When I asked the concierge at my hotel, she recommended I go to Notre Dame, where the vigil would be *incroyable* – but I would need to be early to secure a place. Together we consulted her leaflet and established that I'd be wise to leave no later than six thirty.

Back in my room the thought of going out again into the chilly drizzle and schlepping across town to attend a service which I wouldn't understand in respect of an event I didn't believe in became rapidly less enticing. I lay down on the bed and fell asleep for a couple of hours, waking up hungover and out of sorts. Still, I decided I would probably feel better for sticking to Plan A and making the effort. I took a shower in the tiny pod, and the diffuse needles of boiling water woke me up. My concession to changing extended only to dry jeans. I reckoned in a Catholic country that the tone would be democratic, and anyway who would know or care? Downstairs there was a different concierge on duty – she didn't admire my virtue, or even look up as I left.

The chaplain at Holland House, an amusing man, had approved of what he called 'mortification of the flesh' but walking two miles in the continuing rain seemed altogether too much virtue. I grabbed a coffee and a *croque monsieur* at the tiny cafe next to the hotel and caught the metro, arriving soon after seven. Queues stretched from both sides of the cathedral like embracing arms and for the second time I nearly gave up on the project. But people seemed to be moving, and when I joined them, with others arriving behind me, the atmosphere was benign, almost celebratory, with people sharing hot drinks and cake and responding to my schoolgirl French in excellent English.

Just as well, because it was well over an hour before we got inside, and then a further hour in a pew well to the back and side, before the service started. The first concierge had told me that the vigil would last three hours so I'd already decided I wouldn't stay for the whole thing and made sure I sat on the aisle. It was so crowded that I left one arm hanging over the end of the pew, holding the candle I'd been given.

Perhaps being a non-believer, and not much of a linguist, was an advantage. I was completely unprepared for and overwhelmed by the solemn beauty and emotional impact of what followed. The sheer scale of the building, soaring and arching above us, was enough to suggest the possibility of God. The crowded, scented darkness of the huge congregation was like an embrace. A great candle was processed through the church and as it passed so all our candles were lit, a gentle, flickering dawn that crept along the pews and up the aisles, lighting thousands of faces and all the assembled belief, unbelief, and hope. People talk of the soul being soothed – I felt it then. The edges of me seemed to soften and to melt so that I was part of the whole, this great mass of people, this ancient rite of redemption, this movement of darkness into light.

As I stood there with my small flame, peace and, yes, redemption, seemed a distinct possibility. I was glad I'd come.

An hour or so later the flock of priests were well into their, to me, incomprehensible liturgy. This was of course a mass,

the idea of which I'd always struggled with, and I left, slip-
ping out of my pew as everyone knelt to pray, the movement
making a sound like wind moving a vast pile of leaves.

I had never expected to see them, and had actually passed
before I realized, and glanced back to check. They were among
the latecomers, a small group of whom stood near each of the
doors. Actually, she had been provided with a hard chair so
it was him I saw first. His collar was up, his hands were in
his pockets, his face set in an expression of irritable baffle-
ment. She sat with her hands folded on her lap, eyes closed,
in the correct attitude for prayer – I would say childlike, but
because her face wasn't animated she looked older. She was
still wearing the beret with the rose.

I'd passed them in a second. But as the usher closed the
huge door I caught one last glimpse, and saw that, in spite of
the irritation, he had placed one hand on her shoulder.

I thought, *They've been redeemed, too.* From what, I didn't
know, but I walked out into the vast, shiny-wet square with a
light heart. And it had stopped raining.

I'd like to say that the Easter vigil in Notre Dame was a road
to Damascus, that from that point on I became a believer, lived
a better life and attended church for good Christian reasons.
I'd like to, but it wouldn't be true. The real legacy of that
evening was twofold: a lifelong affection for churches, either
completely empty or so full that I could go unnoticed; and a
sense of the protean nature of love, and its unfathomable
oddness.

Zinny used to sing a song, the chorus of which was *I'll be
true to you darling always in my fashion, I'll be true to you
always darling in my way . . .* It might have been the theme
tune of the old roué and his pretty, sweet-natured partner. Who
knew what complications and imbalances had affected their
shared past. Whatever their story, I wasn't going to knock it.
On the face of it they were an odd couple, but they had reached
– not just an accommodation; I sensed it was more than that.
More even than simply an understanding. They had found
balance. Peace.

TEN
1999

I'd been employed by Edwin Clayborne for just over a year. *Dead in the Water*, the novel with the female protagonist, was delivered and due out in the autumn – E.J. Clay was a big enough name to do battle with the seasonal heavyweights. This was the first book to come out, on my watch, and what with that and my own small part in its creation I felt like a proud parent.

One morning in late July, Edwin came into my office with a shiny hardback and put it down on the desk.

'Present for you. Just arrived.'

'Thank you!' Thrilled, I riffled through the pages.

'Don't worry, I shan't quiz you. It's just to say thank you for setting me right on a few things. Important things, incidentally.'

I was mumbling something about that being nothing, when he added, 'Look at the beginning – no, er, the flyleaf.'

I did so, and nearly fell off my chair.

For Flora

That was all, and all that was needed. I was momentarily overcome.

'There were all kinds of things I might have put,' he said, 'but perhaps you'll take them as read.'

'I will. Thank you so, so much.'

He smiled and tapped my desk with his fingers. 'My absolute pleasure.'

When he'd gone I flipped through the pages of the book, returning all the time to the dedication to check it was still there. I think it was the 'for' that I found affecting. That one word sounded as if he hadn't simply dedicated the book to me, but that he had written it with me in mind. Though I knew this couldn't be true, it nonetheless gave the dedication a personal ring and I was more touched than I could say.

After this it was business as usual, and following the publicity round he had a three-week holiday planned in Utah of all places. I had no clear picture of Utah, except for Salt Lake City and the Mormons, but he'd showed me pictures of the swirling desert and the great bridges and arches of red slip-rock, and explained that he was going to be hiking with a couple of American friends before travelling south and going to stay with them in New Mexico.

'That's when it becomes a busman's holiday,' he told me. 'I have to give a couple of talks to the local writers, of whom there are many in that neck of the woods.'

'Do you enjoy that?' I was genuinely curious.

'Yes . . . Yes, I do rather. And Americans are such a good audience. Appreciative. They'll have taken the trouble to read some of my earlier stuff, they'll do me the compliment of asking polite but searching questions, and they'll buy the book in quantities.' He pulled a funny, self-deprecating face. 'Which between ourselves is the object of the exercise.'

I wanted to tell him I loved it when he talked dirty, but instead asked: 'Is there anything in particular you'd like me to take care of while you're away?'

'Nothing in particular, no. Don't feel you have to sit around here twiddling your thumbs but I'd deem it a huge favour if you could maintain a watching brief.'

'"Don't leave town."'

'If that's not an imposition. Just keep the show on the road as only you know how.'

I was getting used to the idea that my role was to keep the show on the road, whatever that entailed at any given moment.

'What about Percy?'

'Well, I don't want you to feel pinned down, especially at weekends, so for a small consideration I've arranged for a friend's teenage son to pop in. He's called Fergal by the way, Fergal Ayre.'

'Are you sure? I don't mind.'

'No, no, that's fine. You might want to go away, or do anything. I could have resorted to the cattery but I can't face the guilt. And fifteen-year-olds can always use some cash.'

A couple of days before he was due to leave he got the news that the first of the E.J. Clays was going to be made into a TV drama. It had been under consideration for some time, and we occasionally amused ourselves by imagining its progress around the Beeb – discussions, feasibility studies, casting issues, reservations and so on – so when the news came through we were almost blasé. But not so blasé that Edwin didn't feel a celebration was in order.

'I think this calls for a glass of something amusing – would you like to come to lunch?'

We walked to a wine bar with a reputation for excellent wine and no-nonsense food – I'd never been there. Edwin ordered a bottle of Malbec.

'I recommend the rare roast beef sandwich, on white, with horseradish or mustard.'

'In that case, let's see . . . I'll have the roast beef on white, with wholegrain mustard.'

'You won't regret it. Except perhaps the wholegrain – filthy stuff.'

I'd learnt to know when he was teasing. He sometimes affected a cod-curmudgeonly persona that went with his appearance but was the opposite of the considerate, kind, and intuitive man I'd come to know.

'Here's to television!'

We clinked glasses. The Malbec was almost black, and alarmingly heady. I wasn't a big drinker, and warned myself of the disinhibiting effects.

'Who would you like to play Donna?'

'God knows. I haven't thought about it.'

'It's going to be strange seeing your characters as someone else sees them.'

'And interesting. I shan't object. I shall be a model author, pocket the cheque and keep my mouth shut.'

'I bet all authors say that.'

'Maybe, but – ah, here we are!'

Our sandwiches arrived – enormous, crusty and delicious and the first few mouthfuls put paid to conversation.

'Good?'

I nodded. 'Good!'

We concentrated on eating for the next five minutes, and he topped up our glasses, which were those tall, elegant chalices beloved of wine bars. I wished my hands weren't so workmanlike, that I had long fingers and a perfect manicure to adorn the slender stem. He tilted his happily in front of his face.

'Do you like this?'

'Too much.'

'I apologize for ordering in what many women would think of as a sexist manner.'

'I'm glad you did; I don't know a thing about wine.'

'But you know what you like.'

'Not always even that. I buy by price in the supermarket.'

'Nothing wrong with that. The democratization of wine selection.' We sipped reflectively, mellowing by the second.

'Tell me, Flora,' he said. 'Are you happy in your work?'

'Very.'

'I do hope so, because I'd be awfully sorry to lose you.'

'You won't,' I said, almost too quickly. 'I mean, I don't have any plans.'

'I realize,' he went on, 'that I may be a rather annoying employer, and don't say "not at all" – I know I am because the turnover in that little office has been fairly rapid.'

'You're not very directional,' I said. 'Some people might not like that, I suppose.'

'Not very directional . . .' He took off his specs and cleaned them on his napkin. His face looked vulnerable without the glasses, and younger. 'Well and tactfully put. No, I'm not.'

'But I'm fine with that. It suits me.'

He put the glasses back on. 'How fortunate then, that we found each other.'

He left on the Saturday, so I wasn't there to observe what kind of traveller he was – whether he was an organized packer and what departure rituals he engaged in. But when I let myself in – the first time I'd done so – on the Monday, the house was tidy and clean and Percy was lying in a pasha-like attitude in

the sun on the drawing-room window seat; he looked at me
as though I were something he'd brought in and discarded. In
the kitchen there was a small amount of cat food and milk in
the saucers by the back door, from which I inferred that Fergal
had been, probably the previous evening if the received view
of teenagers' morning habits was correct.

There was quite a lot to occupy me at the moment – correspondence relating to the TV offer and connected to research
for the next book; responses to readers and to book-related
invitations. Edwin ran an old-fashioned but serviceable filing
system which he'd asked me to 'spring clean' as he put it. He
adopted the perfectly reasonable attitude that if he threw
nothing away he would never lose it, but the paper had reached
critical mass and he had given me authority to 'chuck what's
neither use nor ornament'. I did ask if he'd like me to keep
the 'chuck' pile for him to look at on his return, but he'd said
'No, that would be fatal'.

The filing cabinet in my office wasn't the problem; I was
pretty much on top of that. It was the stuff that had accumu-
lated in his study that he wanted me to be ruthless with. The
motherlode of old paper was apparently to be found in a
wooden chest, and on an armchair. For this purpose I'd been
given special dispensation to go into the shed for which, apparently, I didn't need a key.

By Wednesday I'd got a clear desk, and went with some
trepidation across the garden – the grass needed cutting, it
was like a meadow – and opened the door. I was prepared, I
don't know why, for Beethoven-like chaos, the material tumult
of the creative process. But the inside of the shed was if
anything rather austere. There was a table serving as a desk,
a threadbare swivel chair, a pot-belly stove (repro, it was
discreetly plugged in) and – more surprisingly – a bunch of
roses in a jug. The roses shared the table top with a portable
typewriter, an ancient Bakelite anglepoise lamp and a high-
sided butler's tray containing pens, pencils, sharpeners, paper
clips, a torch, nightlights and matches, and a half-full bag of
mints that were not, I observed from habit, Hopgood's. There
was no carpet (I could see the need for the stove) but a rather
wonderful worn, faded Persian rug covered almost all of the

floor. The door and the single large window were on the garden side of the building, two of the remaining walls were covered by bookcases, the third had a framed picture which I recognized as the original artwork for Edwin's second novel, and a cork noticeboard covered mostly in what I at first took to be reviews but which on closer inspection turned out to be newspaper stories which must have caught his author's eye. A lost child . . . a mercy killing . . . an inexplicable car accident . . . a kidnapping . . . a survivor's account of a house siege . . .

I took the trust placed in me seriously. The last thing I wanted to do was snoop, but the would-be snooper that lurks in all of us could see at a glance that this wasn't the room of a secretive person, but of an almost innocently open one.

The armchair was one of those huge, saggy things that over time have begun to appear almost organic; it seemed to bear the slithery mass of papers in its arms like a fat old woman with a bundle of washing. The wooden chest, which must have started life as a blanket box, stood beneath the noticeboard, and I began with that. To begin with, I was slow and careful, but after five minutes I was discarding old utility bills, letters and brochures at high speed. By the time I'd done the same with the load on the armchair it was nearly two o'clock and I was suddenly famished. I decided to call it a day.

The phone was ringing as I opened the door of my flat.

'Hello? Floss?'

A call from either of my parents, especially mid-week, was almost unprecedented. My father had to ask again, 'That you, Floss?'

'Yes, hello.'

'You all right?'

'Absolutely, I just walked in.'

'Sorry to catch you on the hop, want me to ring back in a bit?'

'No, this is fine.' I sat down, gazing out of the window, adjusting. 'It's nice to hear from you.'

'I'd like to say that I just rang to pass the time of day, catch up and so on, but I'm afraid that wouldn't be exactly true.'

There was some kind of soundscape in the background – voices, a percussion of crockery.

'Where are you?'

'In a motorway cafe.'

'One of your sales trips?'

'Partly. Look, Floss . . . Jessie's not well.'

He sounded stressed, urgent. I remembered that long-ago visit – how could I forget? But his tone was somehow unexpected and I in turn wasn't sure how to react.

'I'm sorry to hear that. But . . . well, she must be a huge age . . .'

'Mid eighties.'

'What's the matter with her?' I realized this sounded curt, and added, 'What's the diagnosis?'

'Stroke.'

'Is she in hospital?'

'Yes, I'm on my way to visit her now.'

I remembered that chilling blankness, the sense of time crawling on its belly, the arthritic clock . . . The final fleeting expression of weaselly hostility in those deep-set little eyes

'Will she know you?'

'That's not the point.'

I hadn't intended to be heartless. 'I'm sorry. Of course you must go, I didn't mean—'

'I just thought that as you met her, you ought to know.'

'Of course. Thanks.'

The new awkwardness between us was excruciating. I wanted to say something, anything, to dispel it.

'Is Zinny coming?'

'No.' A pause. 'She didn't really know her.'

'She'll know how you feel, though. She'll have the G&T on ice when you get back.'

This was a stab at, if not levity, then at least normality, but it didn't work.

'Anyway. Sorry to be the bearer of bad tidings.'

I couldn't tell him that I felt almost nothing. 'Not at all. Thanks for—'

'Better go or I won't catch visiting hours.'

'Say something from me, if you think she'll—'

'Bye, Floss.'

The quietness of my flat flowed back round me as I sat there with the phone dead in my hand. Now, too late, with the conversation over, I prickled all over with apprehension. The hairs on my bare arms stood up. I hadn't known, and still didn't, what the weight of that exchange had been. I sensed there had been a message behind the words, but I was unable to decipher it.

On an impulse I dialled our home number. Why I expected Zinny to be able to shed any light on the situation, I can't imagine. She was not in the business of shedding light, most of all on any kind of emotional complication.

But anyway, that proved academic because, true to form, she wasn't there.

ELEVEN

I didn't bump into Fergal until the end of the week. It was disconcerting to know that until then he and I had been coming and going, each unseen by the other, according to our self-appointed rhythms. There must have been times when we missed each other by moments. I noticed that although he replenished the cat's food and drink he didn't clean the dishes. They were becoming crusty and smelly, and I couldn't blame the fastidious Percy for sniffing and walking away.

It was while I was running hot water into the dishes on the Friday evening that I heard the front door open and close.

I turned the tap off. 'Hello?'

There was no reply and whoever it was had a footstep like a Sioux. As I dried my hands on a tea towel he appeared in the kitchen doorway.

'Fergal?'

'Hi.'

'I'm Flora, I work for Edwin. Nice to meet you.'

'Hi,' he said again. He was very tall and thin with a fuzz

of red hair. His black t-shirt had some writing too small to read from where I stood.

'I was just washing the cat dishes.'

'Right . . .' His voice had a middle-class open-throated timbre overlaid by the democratic twang of the local comprehensive. 'Thanks. Sorry.'

'No need to apologize, I just thought I might as well . . .'

'Yeah, thanks.'

'They're in the sink,' I said. 'So, shall I leave you to it?'

'Cheers.'

As he passed, I read the legend on his T-shirt: *If you can read this, you're too close.* I clenched every muscle in the effort not to overstep the mark.

'You're coming in over the weekend, aren't you?' I asked.

'Should be.'

What did that mean?

'How far do you have to come?' God but I was being boring. The age gap between us was an awkward one, both too narrow and wide enough to be a pain.

'Brides Avenue. Near the Fields?'

He named one of the most salubrious areas in a city that had scarcely any that were not salubrious. The Fields referred to a grassy expanse of several acres that had once been wetlands, now reclaimed and grazed by horses and cows. It was also quite far away.

'I come on my bike,' he said, helping me out. He was moving the washing-up brush around on the encrusted dishes without making much difference.

'That's a lovely neighbourhood.'

'It's not bad.' To my slight surprise he added: 'What about you?' And when I told him, he responded with, 'I wouldn't mind being there, you can walk into town.'

'That's true.'

He placed the still imperfectly washed dishes right way up, on top of each other on the work surface. I decided against intervention at this early stage.

'How do you know Edwin – Professor Clayborne?'

He took the tea towel and began wiping off the water, along

with the residue. 'I don't really. Well, I've met him a couple of times. My dad used to go climbing with him.'

'Ah, right. That's probably your father in some of the pictures around the place.'

'Might be.'

'They don't go anymore?'

'I'm not sure. Mum and Dad split up so . . . Don't know really.'

I seemed to have gone from polite to intrusive in seconds, but he was opening a tin and didn't seem bothered. I got the milk out of the fridge. Percy manifested himself, tail aloft, and opened a heart-shaped red mouth to emit strangulated squeaks of anticipation.

'Right then,' I said. 'I'll be off.'

'See you.'

On the way home I reflected on this meeting, this small point of contact, Fergal and I each trailing our comet's tail of separate, complicated experience. I wondered when his parents had split up, and under what circumstances. And where Edwin stood in the mix – presumably if this arrangement had been made with Fergal's mother he was on her side, broadly speaking. And yet the father had been his friend, his climbing companion, sharing long periods of time, and fun, and presumably danger . . . That would be hard to give up, surely? Perhaps he was one of those rare people who could maintain a foot in either camp. Or maybe Fergal's parents were among the even rarer ones, as I understood it, whose separation was sufficiently amicable that friends weren't obliged to take sides.

These thoughts brought my own parents to mind again, and specifically the recent conversation with my father. I rang, and he answered the phone.

'Floss, what a surprise.'

'How are you?'

'Not so bad.'

'How was Jessie?'

'Oh God. Not good. Awful, to be honest. Completely out of it.'

'I'm so sorry.'

I heard him sigh, and something else – he was lighting a

cigarette, so maybe Zinny wasn't there. 'The trouble is, she could go on for ages like this.'

The obvious question about machines and switches hung in the air, but I didn't ask it. 'Is she . . . I suppose you don't know . . . if she's in pain?'

'They say not. I'm going back at the end of next week.' He sighed again, this time with a little vocalization. 'Oh . . .'

'I thought I might come down this weekend. Edwin's away so there'll be no rush on Monday morning. Would that be all right?'

'Oh, I'm sure, that sounds . . . Hang on, I can hear Zinny, let me just . . .'

This was one of those moments when I hated them. The hand over the receiver, the private exchange about whether it would be OK for me to come. A hot flash of misery.

'Floss? That would be great.'

'I'll be there in time for lunch.'

'We'll look forward to it.'

I noticed it at once – the difference, both in them and between them. My father looked pale and haunted. Zinny was if anything more carefully presented, and harder. Her hair was cut shorter and her nails were a shiny carmine. She was like a woman fighting back, though against what I couldn't imagine. Perhaps it was the prospect of imminent retirement. In any event she wasted no time in announcing that we'd be going out to dinner that night: she didn't feel like cooking and there was a new fish restaurant in Salting that they wanted to try.

It was the change in the air, the shift in balance that was most unsettling. I didn't understand it any more than I understood anything about my parents' relationship, so it didn't alter my status as an outsider, but it was unmistakably there. Zinny had the air of someone keeping a tight rein on anger, and my father's famous charm – or anyway the will to employ it – seemed for the moment to have drained away. He was crestfallen and oppressed. Whatever their current reason for excluding me, it was not the same as before.

But I was not the same, either. I would have liked things to be otherwise, but I wasn't so ready to be cowed by them,

or to feel guilty. The restaurant was on the high street and we
weren't able to park outside, so my father dropped us off and
went to find a space. Once we were sitting at our table, I
asked: 'How is Dad?'

'Nico is fine. Smoking too much, but he knows what to do
about that.'

'He seems so sad.'

Zinny shrugged and took delivery of the menus. I persisted.
'Do you think it's to do with Jessie?'

'It might be . . .' She scanned the choices. 'But after all
he's only seen her what, half a dozen times in the last twenty
years.'

'Maybe that's it. Maybe he feels guilty.'

'He does, a little. God knows there's no need.'

'I suppose,' I began, conscious of venturing into unknown
territory without a map, 'it's not always logical.'

'Oh, for goodness sake.' Zinny looked at me over her narrow,
black-framed glasses. 'She was a terrible woman. *Is* a terrible
woman. You've met her.'

'Only once.'

'I'm sure once was enough.'

At this point my father arrived, Zinny offered to drive
home, and things cheered up considerably under the benign
influence of a nice wine and a good dinner. A couple from
another table even came over to say hello as they left. Later,
when we got home, we sat on the verandah for a while. Zinny
fetched the scotch decanter and glasses. I demurred, but she
said, 'Just a splash, it'll do you good.'

As always, the presence of the sea was calming. There was
no moonlight, but on this still night and with only a hurricane
lamp on the table we could just make out its restless breathing
presence. What with that and the tongue-loosening effects of
the wine and the unaccustomed whisky, I'd had enough
of being cautious.

'I don't know when you're thinking of going to see Jessie
again,' I said, 'but I'd be happy to come along. For moral support.'

If Zinny harboured any guilt about her lack of involvement,
she didn't show it. She raised her eyebrows in my father's
direction.

'There's an offer!'

'That's good of you, Floss. I'm honestly not sure when, or even if, but if I do I'll let you know.'

'Edwin's away at the moment,' I explained, 'so I have fewer time constraints.'

'Thanks, well, I'll bear that in mind.'

The sadness was back. There followed an awkward pause. Zinny glanced from one to the other of us as if checking that was that, before saying, 'So what's the Prof up to?'

I explained, placing emphasis on the writerly aspects of the trip. Zinny liked E.J. Clay so I told her the other news.

'And the first book is going to be on TV.'

'Really? How exciting. Did you hear that, Nico, they're doing one of the Clay books on telly.'

'Good for him.'

'When will that be?' asked Zinny.

I explained about the long lead-in – contracts, casting, locations and so forth. Zinny was alight with interest, she loved this kind of thing. My father nodded but he was on autopilot, fishing out his fags and putting them away again, taking snatched gulps of his drink. It struck me that he must have been at least ten years younger than Edwin, but there were no such exciting developments in his life nor, as far as I could tell, likely to be. Zinny picked up the conversational baton, enthusing about some current drama they were following. My father looked miles away. However humdrum his work, he'd always seemed happy in it – content, anyway – but now I felt uncomfortable about the turn the conversation had taken.

'How's business?' I asked, and at once wished I hadn't.

'Business?' He frowned distractedly. 'Fine, as far as I know – look, I don't mean to be antisocial but I think I'll take a bit of a walk.'

I was about to ask if I could go too, but Zinny got in first.

'Good idea, don't go too far.' She laughed. 'When should we send out a search party?'

'Shan't be long, twenty minutes or so.'

I started to tell him to be careful, but he was already disappearing down the steps and over the road into darkness.

'Will he be all right? It's pitch black out there.'

'He knows his way.'

'And he's had a skinful. Those steps—'

'Honestly, don't fuss. He'll probably just go along the road and back.' She darted me a look and added sharply, 'I worry about him too, you know.'

'Of course,' I said, though I knew no such thing.

Zinny removed some invisible speck from her drink with a glossy red nail. 'It's that bloody woman!'

Not long after that I decided that whatever it was, I had as always to leave them to it. I didn't even wait the allotted twenty minutes; the tension was too hard to bear. Instead, I wished Zinny goodnight, took my glass to the kitchen and went upstairs.

A little later – I was still holding my book, though not taking much in – I heard their voices, so I knew he was back. But they didn't come into the house, and in one way it was just like my childhood: up here, me not wanting to listen, but hoping to hear; down there, the voices, softly coming and going, talking about things that weren't for my ears.

In another way, everything had changed.

TWELVE

I didn't see Fergal again. He was probably avoiding me and I wouldn't have blamed him. On the Wednesday of the second week, Edwin rang just as I was about to leave.

'Good, hoped I'd catch you. I wanted to touch base, see if all was well.'

'All extremely well,' I told him. 'Nothing urgent to report. Percy's in good shape, and I met Fergal.'

'Ah, you did. And did he speak?'

'Yes, actually. He seems a nice boy.'

'He is . . .' I thought something else was coming, but he simply said again, 'Indeed he is,' and then went on, 'Did you manage to get to grips with the mountain of paper?'

'No problem. I put out one massive black bag, and there's

a very small pile you need to cast your eye over when you get back. Where are you, by the way?'

'Good question. I'm in a motel somewhere south of Monument Valley. En route to Albuquerque.'

'How was the hiking?'

'Wonderful!' His voice leapt with enthusiasm. 'A quite extraordinary landscape – unique, not remotely like anything else I've done. I must say I feel enormously energized.'

He sounded so delighted, I found myself feeling envious, and not only because I needed a holiday myself. I envied the friends who were with him, participating both in the adventure, and in Edwin's happiness.

We talked for another couple of minutes, and when I put the phone down I thought, with a slight sense of surprise: *I miss him.*

My father called later the same evening, to say that Jessie had died. In spite of this he was composed – unnaturally so. He cut off my commiserations.

'I hate to ask you, Floss, but would you be able to come to the funeral with me?'

I didn't hesitate. 'Of course.'

'Zinny can't make it and – you know.'

'When?'

'That's the trouble, it's this Friday, the day after tomorrow. A working day and not much notice.'

'Remember Edwin's not here, and I'm well up with work. He'll understand, anyway. It won't be a problem.'

'I ought to warn you, it will be ghastly.'

'That's all right, I wouldn't expect a funeral to be fun.'

He cleared his throat. 'We could be the only ones there.'

'All the more reason for me to come.'

'Thank you. I do appreciate this, Floss.'

The funeral was at two. We arranged to meet in town near the home, and go on to the crematorium together.

I had never been to a funeral, but I was happy to be doing something to help my father. I felt wounded on his behalf that Zinny wasn't making the effort, but I was secretly glad that it would be just me and him.

*   *   *

We met in the cafe of a superstore on the ring road, because it was easy to find and the parking was free. My father looked pale but handsome in a dark suit. He'd had a haircut, which always made him look younger. I had opted for black trousers with a white top and a grey jacket. We ordered coffee and toast.

'Like the old days,' I said, 'remember? But without the full English.'

He stared down at his plate. 'I don't mind telling you, I'm dreading this.'

I remembered something he used to say to me when I was dreading something at school.

'Look at it this way. Three hours from now it'll be all over.' I glanced at my watch. 'Perhaps two, I don't know how long funerals take.'

'Not long,' he said. 'Especially this one. Rent-a-vicar, and no-one with anything to say. I did put a notice in the paper, but I don't expect there to be much take-up, if any. She didn't have any friends, and most of the people who did know her will have forgotten her long since. That is if they're not already dead.'

His gloomy summary would have been almost funny if the picture it painted hadn't been so unremittingly bleak.

'Will you say something?' I asked. He shook his head. I had an idea, which in truth I only mentioned because I knew what the answer would be. 'Would you like me to say anything – on your behalf, I mean? Or, I don't know, read something? We could stop at a bookshop.'

'Good lord, no.' He gave a bitter little laugh. 'Now that would be farce. No—' he picked up his coffee – 'we just need to get the job done.'

My ignorance of funerals didn't stop me from realizing that they needed some organization, and it sounded as if this one had received none. If my father was the sole mover in today's proceedings he had done precious little. The phrase 'a poor show' sprang to mind.

The crematorium was also on the ring road, a little further west. It reminded me of a motorway motel, except with a bigger garden. The car park was surprisingly full. A notice-board informed us that there were two chapels, South and

West, and that Jessie Mae Sanders (the name was made up of letters in a slot) would be in West, the smaller one. As we arrived we saw a huge crowd of mainly black-clad mourners from a previous event emerging from South and milling around in a paved and cloistered area discreetly talking, kissing and admiring an impressive display of flowers and wreaths.

That would explain the cars. We were early, and there was no-one else about outside the door of West Chapel, which was closed. There was a bench beside the path, and we sat down. My father lit a cigarette. Like Zinny I wished he didn't smoke, but I reckoned he was entitled to a fag on this of all occasions. The people from the other funeral were beginning to move in the direction of the car park, ties were loosened and hats removed as the mood lifted and relief kicked in. There was almost a party atmosphere. I supposed they were heading off towards a pleasant wake – wine, sandwiches and cake, jovial memories of the deceased. The contrast between them and us could not have been starker. I promised myself that we would find a stiff drink as soon as this was over.

After fifteen minutes or so, the door was opened by a young man in a sports jacket and dog collar. My father dropped his cigarette (he was well into the second one) on the path, and put his foot on it as he got up. The vicar came over, hand extended.

'Mr Mayfield?'

'Yes. And I can see who you are. This is my daughter, Flora.'

The handshake was brief, and vigorous. 'John Ormsby.'

'Thanks for doing this.'

'I was glad to be asked. You're using Mr Jarvis, they're a good outfit.'

I didn't know to what he was referring, but my father glanced around. 'When will they be here?'

Ormsby looked at his watch. 'Ten minutes or so? And just to check, to be absolutely sure, no special instructions?'

'None, thanks. Whatever you'd normally do.'

Ormsby nodded. 'Simple, succinct, dignified.'

'Right.'

'We have some very nice recorded music for entry and departure.'

'Don't worry.'

'Of course. Silence can be better.' As if for illustration, he allowed one to develop. When my father made no comment he added, 'Excellent. In that case I should go and get ready. Do you want to come in, or stay here, in case, you know, anyone else . . .?'

'We'll stay here.'

'Absolutely fine. I'll see you in there.'

He went in, hooking back the main door, and opening wide the interior glass doors, revealing a bright modern interior, all blond wood, discreet lighting and pale grey carpeting. Six semi-circular rows of chairs faced a lectern, a keyboard, an altar, an ominous plinth . . . For the smaller of the two chapels it looked worryingly large.

'He seems nice,' I said.

'It's his job.'

'Still. He was accommodating and pleasant.'

My father wasn't listening, because the funeral director's car had arrived, and pulled up in the driveway next to us. The driver got out and moved poker-faced to open the back of the car. The man from the passenger seat approached, removing one of his black gloves.

'Mr Mayfield? George Jarvis. We still have some minutes in hand. Can I ask if you would like to accompany the coffin?'

'Where to?'

I was on fire with embarrassment, but there was no indication that Jarvis even noticed my father's appalling bad taste, let alone recognized it as a joke. Probably bland, unshakable courtesy was both a qualification and part of the training.

'Into the chapel.'

We glanced at one another. I said, 'No thank you.'

'In that case,' said Jarvis, 'shall we take the coffin in now, and put it in position? Then you can follow with any other mourners. Or attendees.'

'Thank you.'

His politeness and discretion were watertight. The other man must have been listening, because without speaking to one another he and Jarvis took a folding trolley from the hearse, and slid the plain wooden coffin on to it.

'I said no flowers,' said my father by way of explanation, but just loud enough for them to hear. As if there might otherwise have been an avalanche of blooms. The stark barrenness of everything was getting to us both. Jarvis and his assistant showed no sign of having heard. It was all in a day's work for them; they must have seen it all.

'We'll place the coffin and sit at the back of the chapel,' said Jarvis in his quiet, neutral voice. 'Have you seen Mr Ormsby?'

'Yes, he introduced himself.'

'You're in good hands.'

My father muttered, 'I should hope so.'

They proceeded to wheel Jessie in; that great rawboned giant of a woman, neatly boxed up. Ormsby, now in his surplice, greeted them near the altar and they transferred the coffin to the plinth. My father consulted his watch for the nth time. 'Three minutes. Do you think if we just go in we can kick off early?'

'No!' I said. 'Here are some more people.'

The three women introduced themselves as being from the Home. The smart, personable matron (not Hilary, who must have long since moved on) introduced the other two: the oldest, very overweight and with swollen legs, was now retired, but turned out to be the motherly orderly whom I'd met all those years before. A sad-eyed Indian lady in her fifties had been Jessie's main carer for the past three years. We said how nice it was of them to come, but it was hard to say which was worse, us being the only ones there, or having this tiny group of outsiders to witness the desolate proceedings.

Ormsby came down to tell us it was time, and we all went in together. Jarvis and his henchman were in the back row, and closed the doors after us. Ormsby indicated that we should sit at the front, and the three women sat a few rows behind. I was glad there was no music, for it would have made me cry – not for Jessie, but for us. This. The whole sad charade.

Ormsby was as good as his word. We had each been given a card with the words of the service, and he spoke them with a clear, practised sincerity, and no irritating mannerisms. With no hymns, we were only required to mumble along with the

Lord's prayer, which I remembered from school, and halfway
through which there was some movement behind us as if
someone had had to leave.

I'm ashamed to say that when Ormsby declared 'Dust to
dust, ashes to ashes' and the curtains drew slowly around
Jessie in her box, I felt only an enormous relief. We'd done
it, and it was over. But when I looked at my father his cheeks
were glistening. I felt for his hand, but there was no answering
squeeze.

Mr Jarvis came forward and opened another door, this time
at the front, to the left of the altar, indicating with an outstretched
arm and inclined head that we should leave that way. Ormsby
shook our hands, and we were out in the cloistered area, with
its extravagant display of other people's flowers, their lively
colours welcome after the austerity of the chapel.

We talked for a couple of minutes to the ladies from the
Home – they were good at this (undoubtedly practised hands)
and then Ormsby, who'd been hovering in the doorway, came
over and said something *sotto voce* to my father.

'Excuse me for a moment.'

I glanced after him and saw him re-enter the chapel with
the vicar. Not long after that the ladies left – I felt bad that
we weren't offering them so much as a cup of tea – and then
Jarvis came out to say that he was leaving. I thanked him and
stood on my own, admiring the flowers and feeling the afternoon sun on my face. Through an archway I could see a
procession of cars moving sedately towards the car park – the
next lot, presumably. What did I care, we were all done. I was
suddenly starving, and wanted nothing more than to be in a
pub with a plate of chips. I went back in to gee up my father.

At first I thought there was no-one in the chapel. Where
had the others gone? Then Ormsby appeared, back in mufti
with his surplice over his arm. He wished me goodbye.

'I think your father and the other gentleman are in the lobby.'

He left by the cloister door and now I could see two figures
on the other side of the glass. The implications of this weren't
lost on me: they wanted privacy. I hovered in the aisle,
assuming my father would be back before long – after all, he
knew where I was.

The decision was made for us because now there were all the signs of the other funeral arriving – more figures in the lobby, a woman opening the lid of the keyboard, and another in a dog collar giving me a hard stare. The glass doors were pushed wide again and my father came through, looking flustered, hectic and upset – for the first time that day his cheeks had colour in them. There was another man, much older, and smaller, at his shoulder. I was sure it was the man he'd been talking to. But there was no suggestion from my father that this man should come with him, and I just had time to catch his eye before he turned to leave, moving sideways in between those now arriving in numbers. I caught a glimpse of a hard-bitten face, a high complexion, the merest bristle of hair, rheumy, questing eyes – a fierce and disconcerting presence.

'Who was that?' I asked as my father stalked past me and out of the door.

I caught up with him in the garden and we went out through the archway and along the path to the car park.

'Sorry,' he said. 'I needed to get away.'

'I understand,' I said. 'But who was it?'

'Oh!' The exclamation was both unhappy and impatient. 'That was my father.'

'What?'

'My bloody father. Can we find a pub?'

I didn't speak – I couldn't – until we were sitting in the glum lounge bar of the Peahen, a pub which had clearly benefited from its proximity to the crematorium, and whose decor was rather less cheerful.

I was both stunned and incredulous.

'You never mentioned him – never!'

'Yes. Well. I don't suppose he mentions me a lot, either. We've been estranged for years.'

'But why was he there? Did you expect him to be?'

'Of course I didn't. It was a shock, I can tell you, and a very unwelcome one.'

'So why was he?'

'I told you, I put it in the paper. He must have seen and decided to come.'

'Did he know Jessie?'

'After a fashion.'

What was that supposed to mean? On the heels of the numb disbelief came a positive wildfire of curiosity.

'He's my grandfather!'

'Not really.'

'Yes he is! And you didn't even let me meet him!'

'Voice down, Floss.'

I said more quietly, 'Surely he should be here with us, now. Where is he? Where does he live?'

'God alone knows. I don't care! Scotland I think. I don't know.'

'You must have some idea.'

'No, I don't. I've made it my business not to. We've had nothing to do with each other for most of our lives. Since I was eighteen.'

I shook my head, not in denial, but because there seemed to be a swarm of bees inside it. 'But he's my *grandfather . . .*'

'Don't call him that!' Now it was my father's voice that rose startlingly, making my hair stir. He controlled himself with an effort, downing what remained of his drink. 'Please, just don't. He was no father to me, and no grandfather to you. He ran out on us when we were young and made sure he hasn't been seen since. Insofar as I think about him at all, I loathe and despise him. He's less than nothing to me, and even less to you, so don't use that word again.'

Without asking, he picked up both our glasses and went to the bar. I was shaking, my face and hands were cold and I was fighting tears. My father must have undergone a similar shift in mood, because when he came back he leaned forward as he pushed my gin and tonic towards me, and said, 'I'm sorry, Floss. Truly sorry. For everything, this awful day, him turning up . . . You don't need it.'

All my energy went into not crying. My throat strained; I put a hand over my mouth. He reached for my other hand but I withdrew, which I knew was cruel.

He went on brokenly. 'And I'm so grateful to you for coming; I honestly don't know how I'd have got through it without you.' I shook my head, dumbly. 'It's over now, Floss.'

I couldn't make him understand that for me, something had only just begun.

We said goodbye in the dull, workaday surroundings of the superstore car park. After two large shots of strong drink neither of us should have been driving, but the booze seemed hardly to have touched us, as if all the trapped emotion churning and fizzing round our systems had neutralized the alcohol. We put our arms around each other cautiously – you could hardly have called it a hug.

'Thanks again, Floss,' said my father. 'Safe journey.'

In my confused, exhausted state that sounded like advice not just for the next couple of hours but for life.

'I'll give your love to Zinny.'

'Yes.' I'd almost forgotten about Zinny. 'Do.'

'And don't be a stranger.'

Such an odd saying, that. Particularly for me, particularly now, when I felt more than ever like a stranger in my own life. We turned away from one another wretched but relieved, each with our own preoccupations, unable to receive or offer comfort.

I drove home on autopilot, changing lanes, overtaking, negotiating slip roads, junctions and roundabouts without conscious decision or much care and almost certainly too fast. When I got home I walked into my flat and sat down, without turning the light on and with my coat still on. Some words of my father's pricked at me like a stone in a shoe.

He ran out on us when we were young . . .

Who, I wondered, was 'us'?

THIRTEEN

That day cast a long shadow. I didn't hear anything more from my father, and nor did I contact him. I was shocked, and bruised, and was pleased to be back at work, where I felt increasingly at home. In my flat, and even more so at my parents' house, there were all those unanswered questions crowding round like silent, uninvited guests. I had to shrink into myself to ignore their importunings. In Edwin's house I could set them aside; expand, and breathe – be myself.

Only one more week and he would be back. I was looking forward to seeing him, to hearing his stories of the trip, which I knew he would tell amusingly, and to showing him how smoothly everything had run in his absence. Over our celebration lunch he'd expressed the hope that I wouldn't leave any time soon. I absolutely didn't want to – not soon, and not for the foreseeable future. I was happy here.

Other than man the phone and deal with correspondence there was very little to do in the last week that he was away, but I liked being in the house. And in the garden – I even did a little therapeutic weeding, and cutting back of dead stuff. It was while I was out there one afternoon, unravelling great tangles of bindweed from the hedge beyond the shed, that I saw someone at the kitchen window. A woman was looking out at me, and raised a hand in a wave. I dropped the bindweed and headed in the direction of the house, but she beat me to it, and we met on the patio.

'I'm *so* sorry, did I give you a fright?'

'Well . . . I suppose . . .'

'Oh!' She pulled a humorously apologetic grimace. 'I should have left a note or something. You must be Flora. I'm Rachel Ayre – Fergal's mother? He's laid low, so I'm filling in.'

'Poor Fergal,' I said. 'What's the matter?'

'A fluey thing, but they're a bit worried in case it's glandular fever, so I'm indulging him.'

'Do give him my best.'

'Of course I will, he said he'd met you. Anyway, it falls to me at the moment to see to that monster cat!'

She was wearing faded jeans, well-worn plimsolls and a soft oversized grey jumper. Her hair was well-cut just above shoulder-length, but whether intentionally or not it was tousled, her wispy fringe stopped just short of her unusual pale hazel eyes, and she seemed to be wearing no make-up.

Rachel Ayre was beautiful and charming, and dismayingly free of vanity.

I agreed that Percy was a bit of a monster.

'I prefer dogs anyway,' she confided. 'But I can see cats are easy.' She looked over my shoulder. 'Gosh, you have been working hard. I bet heavy horticultural duties aren't in your job description.'

'No, but I don't have a garden, and weeding's surprisingly therapeutic.'

'That is so true.' She made my trite observation seem dazzlingly perceptive. 'But good for you, anyway. You've clearly made yourself absolutely indispensable round here. Tell you what, fancy a cuppa?'

I murmured 'why not', and followed in her slipstream into the kitchen, where she whisked out mugs, teabags and milk and put the kettle on – she'd done this before.

'I wonder if he's got any biscuits . . .?'

I was about to confirm that he had, but didn't need to because she'd got the Royal Wedding tin off the shelf and had prised the lid off.

'Hooray, knobbly ones. Go on.'

I took one. In every way possible I was on the back foot, or I might not have resorted to one of the lamest of all conversational gambits.

'How do you know Edwin?'

'Gosh, good question, I've known him for ever . . .' Rachel leaned back on the work top with her arms folded. 'Since before I was married. He and Mark, who I have to get used to calling my ex, were good friends, they used to go off on adventurous weekends together.' She laughed. 'Sounds slightly dodgy, doesn't it, but nothing like that I assure you; rock-climbing and real-ale pubs were the main things.'

'There are photos around the place . . .'

'That's right, Mark's in a few of those. Ah . . .' The kettle reached a crescendo and she poured tea. 'Help yourself to the other things. What do you think, warm enough to go back out?'

I followed her into the garden. The table and chairs had been stashed away, but there was a wooden park bench at the side of the lawn and we sat on that, which meant we were a squeak closer together than I would have liked. She sipped, and sighed.

'This is nice, I do like a walled garden. In fact everything about this house is lovely, don't you think?'

I agreed. An awful sadness was seeping through me like dirty water sinking into a lawn.

She put her elbow on the back of the bench, her head resting on her hand, fingers pushed into her hair. Her eyes rested on me.

'He thinks the world of you, do you know that?'

For some reason, this didn't help. I hoped that it was true, and if so it was certainly mutual, but the fact of her saying it meant that she and Edwin had discussed me. I made a gauche demurring noise.

'Oh yes. *And*—' she reached over and tapped my leg with her free hand – 'not even his greatest fans, of which I'm one, would call Edwin easy.'

That surprised me. 'Really?'

She shook her head. 'He's been on his own his whole life, and been very good at it. Been pretty good at everything, actually. He's always suited himself. I don't know whether you realize what a quick turnover of PAs there was till you came on the scene.'

'He did mention something of the sort.'

'Did he?' She tipped her head back and laughed. 'There you are then. You're definitely doing something right.'

'As a matter of fact,' I said primly, 'I find him very nice to work for. I thought he would be intimidating, but he isn't at all.'

'Not—' she was teasing me – 'a bit vague? Difficult to get a straight answer?'

'Not really. I only have to ask a straight question.'

'Oh, Flora!' Again, the laugh. 'You are such good news!'

We sat there for another five minutes, finishing our tea and talking about the E.J. Clay books. Then we took the cups back to the kitchen and Rachel went to the front door. With the door open, she paused and looked me in the eye.

'It was lovely to meet you.'

'And you.'

'I expect Fergal to rise from his bed of pain tomorrow and be back on duty, so I may not bump into you. But I have enjoyed it, and I just want to say that I'm enormously fond of Edwin. He doesn't have many real friends but Mark was certainly one. When Mark and I sadly . . . went our ways, it would have been perfectly understandable if Edwin had decided to be in Mark's camp . . . But amazingly he didn't.'

Not so amazing, I thought.

'I suppose,' she went on, 'I'm simply trying to say that he's an absolute sweetie, but not everyone sees that. You know?' She nodded enthusiastically, eliciting my agreement.

'I believe you.' I felt anything but cool, but cool was what I sounded.

'*Good.*' Another tap on the arm. 'Onwards.'

Under any other circumstances, this encounter would have buoyed me up. Rachel was warm, amusing, delightful, and most of all interested. But she had emerged from the hinterland of Edwin's life to ambush me at a vulnerable moment. She must have liked me, or she wouldn't have confided in me, but the effect was to make me feel once again like an outsider. Everything about her had suggested a prior and unshakeable claim on Edwin's affections. I had to remind myself quite forcibly that I was his secretary, and only his friend within that limited context.

I went to bed that night more determined than ever to stop being an idiot, and to manage my expectations. I was everywhere alone.

I saw Rachel again, though not to speak to. The day before Edwin's return I went over to the cathedral to one of their free lunchtime concerts – a local orchestra was playing the music of George Butterworth. I wasn't knowledgeable but I liked the English composers, especially here in this most English of settings, and Butterworth's own story, which I'd learned while at Holland House, was a moving one. I wasn't religious either, but since that Easter in Paris I shared the impulse to get one's mind on to higher things.

As I walked across the close there was that end-of-summer feeling in the air. I didn't mind. I liked the long, slow turning of the seasons, the changes in the light, the amber-splashed trees and the drifting sky. Edwin had yet to tell me about the concept of the pathetic fallacy, but I just knew that they suited my elegiac mood. There were a lot of people already there, both seated for the concert and drifting respectfully around the aisles, gazing upward, scrutinizing plaques, consulting leaflets. The players were taking their places in the spinney of music stands just below the chancel steps. They were mostly my age or younger, and I wondered what it was like to be embarking on a career like that – something you'd always been good at, and aspired to. I wasn't exactly jealous, but a little wistful.

I sat in a chair in the front row of the back section, on the north–south aisle, from where I had a good view of the orchestra and could slip away if I needed to. The cathedral in all its breathtaking, heedless beauty soared up on all sides. It was calming to have my preoccupations put so emphatically, gloriously, in perspective.

When the first long, sweet, yearning notes of *A Shropshire Lad* unfurled and rose into the air like wood smoke, my spirits unfurled and rose with them and for some minutes I let myself drift. I may even have closed my eyes. I'd never been sure how people prayed, but this felt close – a submitting to the moment, a release.

When I opened my eyes, Rachel was the first thing I saw. She had probably been there all the time, because she was sitting in the south aisle near the book stall, and was wearing glasses, and a pale blue steward's sash over her Guernsey. Like me, she was spellbound by the music. Her legs in black tights were crossed, and she was leaning forward with her chin propped on her hand. She must have sensed my eyes on her because she glanced directly at me. Embarrassed to be caught staring, I lifted my chin in 'hello'. She sent back a smile, briefly closing her eyes and opening her hands as if to say, 'Bliss!'

I left after three-quarters of an hour, during a break in the music, not looking at her as I did so. So much for the release, the letting-go of bad feelings. The truth, of which I was far from proud, was that Rachel's presence had spoiled things for me.

*   *   *

I didn't go back to Edwin's house. I was done for the day and also I thought that Rachel, having seen me, might decide to come over. Instead I did something I hadn't done for ages, and called my friend Elsa.

'Hello, *stranger*!' There was the usual domestic hum in the background; hers was a full life in every sense. 'How *are* you?'

'I'm fine. I wondered if I could come round?'

'Fantastic idea!'

'Are you sure? I know how busy you are.'

'Never too busy for you, girl. Hang on, let me turn this off . . . And anyway you've struck lucky, the kids have gone to a party at the leisure centre, and are even being dropped off later, so get your arse over here and I'll put the kettle on.'

Elsa and I had met in a supermarket queue, she with a toddler on her full trolley, me with my more modest load. The woman ahead of us at the check-out was one of those with an amusing explanation for every purchase, and an elusive purse . . . Our eyes met in mutual infuriation, which turned to uncontrollable mirth once we were both through – Elsa had waited for me.

'Don't know about you, but I need intravenous caffeine after that – want to join me?'

Different as we were, we were kindred spirits, and firm friends from that moment.

Her house was on a new development on my side of the city but a little further out, near the hospital. She was ten years older than me, a graduate nurse who kept her hand in on the wards against the moment when her youngest was in school all day and she could go back full time. Whenever I was with Elsa I thought that if I was ill or injured she'd be exactly the person I'd want ministering to me – tall, cheerful, kind, competent, you could practically see the milk of human kindness coursing through her veins.

Her house would never have featured in a lifestyle magazine but it was nothing if not homely. She moved a pile of ironing so I could sit at what was probably a 'breakfast bar' but was covered in assorted paper, mugs and a jigsaw.

'Tea? Or there's some white in the fridge.'

'Tea's great.'

She retrieved a couple of the mugs and rinsed them under the tap. 'Can I ask what brought this on? It's been ages, it's so brilliant to see you.'

'Does there have to be a reason?'

'Of course not, but knowing you I bet there is one.'

There was no point in flannelling her, but I didn't – not yet anyway – want to get into specifics. 'I've just been feeling a bit low.'

'Shoulders for crying on, speciality of the house. Sugar?'

'Two.'

'Go girl.'

'I don't usually.'

'Wheesht! You don't have to justify yourself to me. Saucered and blown it is . . .' She poured and stirred. 'Don't know about you, but the sofa calls.'

We shifted more clutter and made ourselves comfortable. I asked about the children, and her nice husband Paddy, a stalwart of the Round Table and still a useful rugby player. Her answers were full of her typically cheerfully sardonic humour. Life had been pretty good to Elsa, she'd have been the first to admit it, but she was never even close to smug.

'And what about you?' she asked. 'Boss treating you well?'

'He's just been away for three weeks . . . But yes, he does. Is.'

'Three weeks? Does that mean you've had time off as well?'

I explained the situation, mentioning as I did so the upcoming television series.

'Gosh, I've read that – has it been cast? Will you be hobnobbing with the luvvies?'

'I very much doubt it.'

'I wonder if they'll consult him,' mused Elsa. 'Imagine creating a character and then seeing someone completely wrong in the part. It's bad enough when you've *read* the book, let alone written it.'

'He intends to be a very well-behaved author and not interfere.'

'What's he *like*?' Elsa stretched out her legs in pink joggers and rested her mug on her stomach with both hands. 'You've never really told me. Terrifyingly intellectual? I mean I'm sure I'd be terrified . . .' I gave her a sceptical look. 'OK, not terrified, but aware of my shortcomings.'

'I can honestly say that he's never made me feel like that. Intentionally or otherwise.'

'Good. Mind you, your self-esteem is in pretty good shape. As a general rule.' She took a sip. 'Want to tell me about it? Or a case of MYOB?'

There was no fooling Elsa. 'I don't like myself much at the moment.'

'You're a crap judge of character. I'm a good one, and I've always quite liked you.'

'Thanks.'

'Pleasure. So long as it's not him who's making you feel like that. Because work's work and you can always do it somewhere else.'

'No. It's definitely not him. In fact . . .' I was about to say that he was the one person who never failed to boost my self-esteem, but changed my mind. 'There's been some family stuff going on.'

'Has there? Welcome to my world.' She had no idea. 'Poor you, that's always the worst. With your relations you feel there ought to be some special magic that will see you all through to the other side, but is there? Is there hell. My sister and I can still fight to wound. I shan't ask unless you want to say.'

'It's complicated.'

'Well of course.'

I couldn't explain, even to the empathetic Elsa, about the secrets and silences that characterized my family life. However virulent her spats with her sister, they were the stuff of healthy sibling rivalry, not to be compared with what ailed me.

She waited for a moment, just in case, and then said, 'I tell you what though, Flo. Don't let that grind you down. You have nothing to reproach yourself with.'

Good friend that she was, she phrased this as a statement, not an opinion, and I was happy to accept it for now. We talked for another hour about her work, the idiosyncrasies of patients and their relatives, of colleagues and the hospital system. I told her about the trip to Corsica that I had planned

for the new year, and she expressed admiration that I was
going on my own.

'Now that's brave. I'm not sure I could do it.'

'Of course you could – if you had to.'

'I mean from choice.'

'I like it. No-one to consult, making my own choices, eating
what I want.'

'I suppose. But aren't there times when you want to, you
know, say "Ouch" or "Wow" or something?'

'Well, yes. But I have to save that for when I get back.'

'When you can hit the pub with me.'

'Exactly.'

Elsa's children were due to be returned at five, so at four
thirty I made a move to go. She came out of the front door
with me and gave me a hug.

'Don't leave it so long, please.'

'I won't.'

'Anyway I shan't let you, I shall be on your case.'

As I was getting into the car, she waved and called, 'Be
good to yourself, Flo!'

FOURTEEN

Edwin was due to return on Saturday, when I wouldn't
be there. I found myself thinking about this and regret-
ting it more than was reasonable. I had spent so much
time alone in the house over the past weeks, not just filing
and fielding calls but doing those odd jobs around the place
that I hoped wouldn't seem officious – clearing the bindweed
had encouraged me to further efforts in the garden, and indoors
I'd polished some silver, de-scaled the kettle, replaced the odd
light bulb and scrubbed the red wine mark out of the hall
carpet. The papers in the shed were now immaculate. I hadn't
liked to go in and out once the task was accomplished, but I
occasionally peeped through the window just to remind myself
how calm and orderly it looked and how pleased he would be

when he first walked in. I considered leaving a 'Welcome Home' card, but decided that was over the top. Instead I bought an elegant postcard from the cathedral shop, scribbled *Welcome back! F* and propped it against the kettle. The picture on the card was of the rose window with its dazzling mosaic of colours.

There was no reason why I should have heard from him over the weekend, but I was still a little crestfallen when I didn't. I did my supermarket shop, walked by the river, browsed in the bookshop and did some domestic chores. I very nearly contacted Elsa again, but stopped myself just in time. Sunday seemed even longer, a great yawn of a day to be filled. What, I wondered, would Edwin be doing on his first day home? He'd be jet lagged so would probably be awake early, if he'd slept at all. The morning was one of wind and teasing sunshine, a painter's changeable sharp light. I told myself that a walk would snap me out of it, and set off (from habit or some more complicated impulse) in the direction of the cathedral close.

There was a service in progress, so I didn't go in. This was one of the few times when I regretted my lack of religion – perhaps a real belief in a higher power would have helped to soothe me. I walked right round the close, pausing on the south side to sit on a bench for a while, but the clouds came over and the drop in temperature persuaded me to move on.

The frightening thought occurred to me: *Am I old before my time?* Had self-sufficiency bordering on pigheadedness turned me into a fogey? I couldn't work myself out. But if that was the case, would I be experiencing this nervous excitement as Edwin's house came into view?

I was reminded of one of my parents' favourite songs. Their tastes were not the same, but they both liked the musical *My Fair Lady* and especially the number 'On the Street Where You Live'. I didn't know all the words, but one line came to me: 'All at once am I several storeys high!' And I was, I really was. I stopped for a moment and told myself not to be childish, that it was pathetic to have a crush on my employer, especially when there were no other men in my life; when I could scarcely be said to *have* a life. I needed to get a grip and get out more. To meet people, for God's sake! What was

I doing hanging around outside his house on a Sunday afternoon just in case . . . in case what? I was not the female version of the dashing Freddy Eynsford-Hill; I was in danger of becoming a sad sack.

And then he appeared.

But not from the house – a car drew up in the parking area at the corner of the close, and Edwin got out and went round to open the boot. As he closed the boot and picked up his cases the driver of the car got out, locked it – I saw the lights wink – and accompanied him to the house.

Rachel.

The two of them went up the steps, Edwin put down the cases, fished out his keys and opened the front door, standing aside and touching Rachel's back lightly as she passed. They were smiling. He picked up the bags and went in, heeling the door shut behind him.

They hadn't seen me, though I felt like a pillar of fire standing there.

I couldn't even bear to continue walking that way, to pass the house. I turned and made my way back round the close. The clouds had blown over and the sun was shining, the leaves on the trees flickered and danced. So much for the pathetic fallacy! As far as Mother Nature was concerned, if I'd felt pathetic before, that was nothing to my sense of humiliation now. For three weeks I had taken care of Edwin's work, his house, his garden. I had learned more about him – and myself – while he was away. I had longed for his return, not only for the appreciation I hoped would come my way, but because I wanted to see him and be with him. Was that so stupid? There had been signs – our lunch together, his remark about not wanting me to leave – but had that been no more than expediency? And now Rachel was there, doubtless reporting back on me in glowing terms. I could hear her voice as she did so. She would go into the kitchen before him and see my postcard . . .

Oh look! Isn't that sweet of her?

I didn't realize how fast I was walking, or that I was crying, until I was halfway home and nearly stepped into the path of a car. The driver – a woman – had to brake violently, while leaning on her horn. I held up my hands in apology, but that

wasn't enough. She was enraged and I had given her a terrible
fright. I heard her bellow, and her face as she leaned across
to the window was a twisted, open-mouthed mask of fury.
With justification – there was just time for me to glimpse a
child's seat in the back, a toddler strapped in and happily
oblivious to her close shave.

Back in the flat I gave in completely to a delayed shock
reaction. I was cold and lightheaded, and shivering so convul-
sively that my muscles seemed to go into spasm. I craved a
hot drink, but didn't trust myself to boil a kettle. There was
some cooking sherry in the cupboard and I poured a small
shot into a tumbler, the bottle clinking in my unsteady hand.
I downed it in one, and only just made it to the bedroom. I
think I passed out for a few seconds because I don't remember
lying down, and when I came to I was sprawled across the
corner of the mattress, half-kneeling on the floor. I was still
shivering, but no longer faint. Taking it slowly, I managed to
take off my shoes and outer clothes, put on my dressing gown
and crawl under the duvet.

When I eventually did drop off, it was into a shallow
sleep, churning with dreams. At one point I dreamed of a
roaring city street, with cars, buses and lorries travelling at
speed, a howling ambulance, a yelping police car, horns,
bells, shouts . . .

I woke up stiff and sweaty, with no idea what the time was.
The days were getting shorter and outside the window it was
dusk. My watch said seven o'clock. I dragged myself up against
the bed head. There was a small fist of pain over my right
eye; the cooking sherry had done me no favours. Cautiously
I got out of bed and went to the bathroom, lowering myself
gingerly on to the closed loo seat. I stretched out my arm and
turned on the hot tap. The mere sight of the steam was heart-
ening. After I poured in some bubble bath and swirled the
warm blue fragrance around with my hand, I began undressing
with care. This, I thought, was what it must be like to be old
and on one's own – this fear of falling, of having an accident,
of not having help to hand . . . *Stop it.* Naked, I stood on
tiptoe, and stretched my arms above my head, fingers pointed,
as far as I could reach, until my muscles trembled.

I lay in the bath for half an hour, topping up the hot water, feeling my soft tissues slowly expand and relax. Physical recovery seemed a distinct possibility, but with it came the return of that other pain, for which there was no foreseeable cure. As I climbed out of the cooling water I confronted my reflection in the bathroom mirror. It was a shock. The last few hours had created a different picture in my mind's eye, a picture of a stooped, frightened, unhappy, prematurely aged woman. That was how I'd felt. But looking back was the original me, wet from the tub – sturdy, curvaceous, spiky-haired, wearing the expression which I assumed had become natural to me (because others had sometimes commented on it), one of contained defiance and truculence.

I may have been a wreck on the inside, but at least I didn't look it.

I peered back at myself for a moment. The image in the mirror, especially the eyes, reminded me of someone else but I couldn't think who. Certainly not either of my parents. I could remember, as a small child, Zinny cupping my chin in her hand and observing. 'Look at you – little changeling!' I'd been pleased, both because she'd touched me affectionately, and because she made it sound like a compliment.

In pyjamas, dressing gown and thick socks I went into the kitchen and warmed soup in a giant cup which I carried into the living room. It was now after eight and quite dark, so I drew the curtains and turned on a couple of lamps. I turned on the radio and listened to a Radio Four debate while I drank my soup. The debate concerned the advisability or otherwise of home births, about which I had no particular view and not much interest, but there was something soothing about listening to these ardent experts articulating their opinions. I found myself wondering what Edwin would think, but like me he was single and childless so perhaps he wouldn't care much either.

It wasn't till I turned off the radio and got up to retrieve the remote from the top of the TV that I noticed the light on the answering machine winking. I hadn't heard the phone ring, but perhaps that explained the persistent shrill bell in my traffic dream.

I pressed play. Edwin's voice filled the room.

Bother, I've missed you . . . It was a second before I realized he meant not that he'd been missing me, but that he thought I was out. *My flight was delayed and I only got back at an ungodly hour this morning, fortunately someone was able to pick me up and provide support systems . . . Anyway, I know I'll see you tomorrow, but I didn't want you to think I'd been around for twenty-four hours and not at least said . . . I want to say how much I appreciate the way you've looked after everything. Really, you've gone above and beyond the call of duty. Thank you so much. OK. Well . . . hope you're having a good weekend, and see you soon. Bye Flora . . . Bye.*

I played the message several times, both for the pleasure of hearing his voice, and to try and analyse the pauses and hesitations, and the words themselves.

Fortunately someone was able to pick me up and provide support systems . . .

'Someone' – not 'Rachel', though he must know by now that we'd met each other. And not even 'a friend', which would have been neutral. 'Someone' meant he was being discreet. And what were these 'support systems' that she had provided? All the earlier sulphurous bad feeling began to seep through me again. I closed my eyes, tried once again to see myself as I had seen me in the mirror. That spirited, feisty, square-shouldered young woman – *that* was me. Not this jealous, lonely wimp, replaying a casual message for crumbs of comfort.

I turned on the TV and watched a natural history programme for an hour or so, then went back to bed and read my book, or at least gazed at the print and turned the pages; I felt sorry for the author, whose work I usually lapped up. When I did turn the light out I couldn't sleep: there had been too much of that earlier. I couldn't leave my stupid feelings alone, couldn't stop myself picking over not just what I knew, but what I imagined.

Had Rachel been there, with him, when he made the call? Had she perhaps suggested he make it? Why wouldn't she, I was no threat to her. I could almost hear her charming throaty voice, *No you should – she's done so much, and she's such a nice girl. I think it would be appreciated. Go on . . .* She would have passed him the handset. I hated her for her beauty, her kindness, her bloody niceness.

But not as much as I hated myself.

Next morning I woke up early, wired but exhausted, and arrived for work on time. I rang the bell and there was no answer. It occurred to me that Edwin, under the cosh of jetlag, might still be asleep, and as I still had the key he'd left me, I let myself in. Even before I saw the sheet of paper on the floor I sensed the place was empty. There's a hollowness about an empty house, as I'd discovered over recent weeks.

I picked up the note. My name was in capitals at the top.
FLORA

Television's an imperious master, I'm discovering! Car came for me at seven to whisk me to London, the very last thing I need. Sorry not to welcome you on my first day back, hope you got my message. Look forward to seeing you tomorrow, if I'm spared. E.

There was a chair next to the table in the hall, an old dining chair with a threadbare brocade seat. I sat down on it and listened to the silence.

'Do you think he has *any* idea how you feel?' Elsa asked. She had farmed out the children and we were having tea in the cathedral cafe.

'I don't see how. No, of course not. He's my boss – we don't have that sort of relationship.'

'It doesn't sound as though you know what sort of relationship you have.'

She was right. 'I suppose I thought we were friends.'

'You suppose you thought . . .' She smiled ruefully. 'You're in a bugger's muddle, Flo.'

'Yes.'

'He obviously likes you, and you're invaluable to him—'

'For Christ's sake!'

'Careful!'

'Sorry.' I had torn one sugar envelope to shreds and now started on another. Elsa poured more tea.

'Describe the symptoms.'

'I think about him all the time, I picture him, I obsess about what he's doing – and with who.'

'This Rachel person.'

'Yes.'

'That must be awful. But you absolutely mustn't torture yourself.'

'I can't seem to stop.'

Elsa took a sip, lowered her cup carefully as if coming to a decision. 'May I say something?'

'Anything.'

'Jealousy is hideous.'

'I know it.'

'No, I mean it's unattractive. Ugly. A turn-off.'

This stopped me in my tracks. I felt shocked and, if I was honest, insulted. 'I see.'

'Look, Flo, don't be offended—'

'I'm doing my best.'

'I'm sorry. Oh God.' She raised her hands in a gesture of weary desperation. 'Obviously it's ages since I experienced anything like what you're going through. Mark and I moved out of that phase yonks ago. I kind of envy you.' I snorted. 'I *do*. But you're not doing yourself any favours. For a start you've got too much invested in this chap you hardly know – you *have* – and you need to get a bit of perspective. I don't know, take a holiday or something, don't look at me like that.'

'I can hardly take a holiday when he's only just got back, and anyway I haven't even seen him for over three weeks.'

'That may be part of the trouble, you've been imagining him and thinking about him without any boring old reality to tarnish the fantasy.'

'It's not a fantasy.'

'OK, I agree, that wasn't fair. You know what you feel. For heaven's sake I can see what you're going through. But the first thing you really *must* do is get over this Rachel person. For one thing the green eye may be completely groundless, and for another, even if it is justified, you're not going to win him back by being all bitter and twisted.' I started to protest, but she shook her head and cut me off. 'Because that's what it looks like at the moment. You're better than that, Flo – you're

something special, so get your bloody chin off the ground and
start acting the part. I've said enough. Want a slice of carrot
cake?'

Even the best advice is hard to follow, especially when it
concerns emotions over which you have little control. I knew
that Elsa was right, and just as importantly that everything she
said came out of the sort of doughty, trustworthy friendship
which was beyond price. That didn't stop me smarting, but I
did take her words to heart. Oh, my poor frantic, confused
heart.

She'd conceded she was wrong about 'boring old reality',
and I knew just how wrong when Edwin opened the door next
day (I thought I should resume old habits). His smile was as
wide as all outdoors.

'Flora, I can't tell you how . . . Come in, come in, and
here . . .' He pushed my key away. 'No, no. Now that we have
no secrets you should keep it. You ought to have one anyway,
and it will ease my mind knowing there's someone not too
far away who could get in if there were an emergency.'

As I entered I felt the light touch of his hand on my shoulder,
leaving a hot spot.

'Shall we . . .?' He led the way to the kitchen and I
watched as he made coffee, the reversal of our usual roles.
He'd had a haircut which made him look younger, and had
also put on a little weight and caught the sun. He radiated
warmth and wellbeing.

'I tell you one thing,' he said, 'there's too much food in the
States and I have too little willpower.'

'You did all that hiking,' I reminded him.

'Ah yes, but followed by a week with the most hospitable
people on earth.'

I wanted to tell him he looked handsome but made do with,
'You look really well.'

'Do I?' He patted his midriff doubtfully. 'Good. Thank you.
There you go.'

I took my mug and turned to go to my office, but he said,
'It's absolutely glorious out there this morning – do you want
to come and sit in the garden for a few minutes?'

We went out and sat on the slatted bench, which in spite of its hardness was like sitting on a sofa – we were a squeak too close together. Unlike Rachel he didn't turn sideways, studying me, but sat with his legs loosely apart, mug cradled in his hands, face lifted to the sun, perfectly relaxed.

'Soon be autumn,' he murmured, 'with all that that entails . . .'

'How was yesterday?' I asked. 'The television people?'

He sighed. 'Very wasteful, but from all I hear there's going to be a lot of that.'

'What did they want you for?'

'Honestly?' he chuckled. 'Not much. They told me "where they were at" and bought me lunch. I think they just wanted to reassure me I was wanted.'

Oh, if only he knew. 'It's better than the alternative, surely.'

'Of course, and I don't mean to be ungrateful, but I told them I'm quite happy to let them get on with it. They're the experts now, and I want to write another book.'

'How's publication going?'

'Chugging along. They've cast the bones and read the runes and the auguries are good. The planets are in alignment.' He flashed me a humorous glance. 'They always say that.'

'They seem always to be right.'

He didn't answer this but seemed to have dropped back into a reverie. His eyes were closed. I admired his thin arms where they emerged from turned-back shirtsleeves. And his hands . . . he had good hands, long-fingered but strong-looking. Eyes still shut, he began to say something, or – no, to sing under his breath.

'It's very nice to go travelling, but it's so much nicer, oh it's so much nicer to come home . . . True words. Know that one?'

I shook my head, then realized he couldn't see me and said, 'No.'

'No. A question of years. Nothing marks out generations like the songs of our youth.'

'Oh God!'

He laughed and looked at me. 'Why?'

'My youth. All ra-ra skirts and mullets.'

'What's a mullet?'

'QED.' I used an expression I'd heard him use, which I understood from the context and not because I knew what the letters stood for. I remembered something.

'I like musicals.'

'Yes,' he agreed. 'I do. The stories. On the whole I prefer opera, but a friend introduced me to *West Side Story* and I was dazzled. Actually that was Fergal's mother, Rachel – I think you met her?'

Everything seemed suddenly to turn to stone. 'Yes.'

'She was enormously taken with you.'

'Oh.'

'Her exact words were that I'd be mad to let you go.'

Of course, Rachel knew a 'treasure' when she saw one. I didn't answer.

A butterfly, brown and orange with dark markings, alighted on his knee, the faded knee of his chino. We both looked at it, watching as it slowly fanned its wings and posed with them open, soaking up the sun. The butterfly provided a simple shared focus. When it fluttered off I stood up.

'I'd better get on. Anything in particular?'

I was holding out my hand for his mug, but he didn't give it to me. It was nice out here in the sun and he was resisting going in to work.

'There are some researches that need starting on . . . Oh for goodness sake, isn't it delightful out here?'

'It really is.' I stood awkwardly, waiting to go.

'We – I mean all of us, this generation – are extremely lucky.'

Bruised and wrong-footed, I wasn't prepared for the conversation to take this philosophical turn, but he didn't need prompting to continue.

'At the risk of sounding Pollyanna-ish, we really ought to count our blessings. That we're alive in a time without global war, of unparalleled prosperity and scientific advance, with every expectation of a long and healthy life.'

'I suppose.'

I might have argued – disease, pollution, overcrowding, conflict, terrorism – but the energy was sucked out of me. And besides I didn't want to tarnish his mood. What we had was an exact reversal of age stereotypes – he with his shiny, appreciative optimism, I with my grim cynicism.

He stood up, laughing. 'Not exactly a ringing endorsement!'

I pretended to laugh too, and walked ahead of him into the house.

That evening my father rang.

'We wondered if you were thinking of coming down any time?'

It was typical of them not to extend a direct invitation. Visits had always to be my decision and on my initiative. Perhaps, I thought, it would be a good idea. If I stayed here I was going to torture myself.

I asked, 'Are you there this Saturday?'

'We shall be.'

'See you then.'

'OK. And Floss . . .'

'Yes?'

'I don't know. Nothing. We'll look forward to it.'

FIFTEEN

Retirement didn't suit Zinny. She wasn't seeing any more of Nico, who would remain at work for the foreseeable future, and she wasn't someone disposed to throw herself into local causes and become a pillar of the community. She looked as beautiful and soignée as ever, but I wondered how much of the impeccable toilette was now down to having too much time on her hands. She was not a woman with hobbies; her home-making skills were predicated on a good eye and a list of Little Men. Cooking was a matter of judicious shopping and applying heat, so afternoons of therapeutic baking were not on the agenda. Also, though they had their circle of social acquaintances, she was essentially a loner with no close friends. I lacked the first but at least, in Elsa, I had the second – someone non-judgemental in whom I could confide, something my mother had never bothered, nor wanted, to cultivate.

I sensed my father was worried about her, and that may have been what had prompted his call. I couldn't summon too much sympathy, but when she and I were alone on Saturday afternoon (Nico had gone to meet a fellow rep) it seemed only right to ask how she was finding things.

'Let's put it this way,' she said. 'I shall adjust.' Adding crisply, 'Everyone seems to.'

'Do you have any plans?'

As soon as it was out of my mouth I knew that this question was likely to annoy her, but it was too late.

She quirked an eyebrow. 'Plans?'

'I don't know . . . Things you've always wanted to do. You've worked so hard for so long.'

'What else do people do? Actually, please don't answer that. Honestly, I never realized there were so many hours in the day.'

'And now they're all yours to do what you like with.'

'My God, don't remind me!'

We were sitting on the verandah. There was an autumnal feel to the air and Zinny had her coat on, a camel coat with a big faux-fur collar that she had turned up so that it framed her face like an Elizabethan ruff.

Her face did look a little drawn and I said more gently, 'It's early days, you probably need to take things easy for a while, get used to it. You'll find a different rhythm in due course.'

She put her hands up and tweaked the collar so that it curved round more – defensively, it seemed to me. 'What do *you* think I should do?'

This was completely unprecedented. I couldn't recall her ever having asked for my advice before, and I was a little shocked.

'Me?'

'Yes. If you were me, what would you do?'

'I can't imagine—'

'Exactly.' She pulled a chilly grin. 'You can't.'

'All right,' I said, 'all right. Why don't you go back?'

She shook her head. 'I couldn't, it was my choice. They could do with someone younger . . . that's not an option.'

'Somewhere else then? There must be dozens of things you could do, and I bet you'd be snapped up.'

'Such as?'

'I can't tell you. You have to get out there and look.'

'Study the cards in the newsagent's.'

'No – yes. Anything. Ask around, see what's out there. Think what you'd like . . .'

'What I'd like,' she said, 'is to spend more time with Nico.'

I knew she was telling the truth because her voice sounded completely different. There wasn't much I could say to this, so I waited.

'All we ever wanted to do was to be together.' She had been looking out to sea but now she looked straight at me. 'Really. We never made a plan, we just upped and left. We never needed anyone else.'

Two things in this little speech struck me as strange. One was the 'upped and left'. Where had they left? The words seemed to imply flight, but from what? And then of course, there it was again, the familiar refrain which didn't need repeating:

We never needed anyone else.

'You had me,' I reminded her. My voice was as small as a child's.

'Oh, of course we did, of *course*! And you're part of us!'

'Am I?'

'You know you are.' She leaned across to touch me, but I clenched into myself just enough to avoid her hand. She withdrew it at once – you'd wait a long time to be cajoled by Zinny – and went on as if this little exchange hadn't happened.

'I do want us to have more time together, before, I don't know, before we're past it.'

She meant her, because she was so much older than him.

'Could he give up work? Or maybe arrange things so he didn't have to take the long trips.'

'I'm sure he could, but he enjoys those. As you know.'

'You could go with him.'

This suggestion met with the look of sardonic disbelief that it deserved.

'Well,' I said, a little impatient with her self-pity (I believe

I thought I had a prior claim on that). 'You should talk to him.'

'I have, actually.'

'And?'

'I don't like to whine.'

I thought: *Isn't that what couples do? Discuss things? Work things out?*

The lights of my father's car appeared on the rim of the hill and began winding down towards us, appearing and disappearing with the steep bends.

'I'm sorry,' she said, suddenly brisk. 'None of this is your problem.'

No, I thought. *It never is.*

That evening we went into Exeter to see *Saving Private Ryan* and then had a curry. A modest enough outing, but (once we'd got over the impact of the film) my parents were sparkling company, and we were like three friends on the town. I think they both, for their separate reasons, wanted to lift the mood, theirs and mine. I felt ashamed of my mean-spirited response to Zinny earlier. Hers was a familiar situation – the ageing beauty who knows that time is not on her side, the more so in her case because my father was so much younger. I had seen how he was with other women – or more accurately how they were with him – and I was sure she had nothing to fear. He worshipped her. In hindsight I believe that any reciprocal flirtatiousness on his part was only a way of keeping his end up, of reminding himself that he could if he wanted to.

Of course they asked about Edwin, 'the Prof' as they called him.

'I wish there was someone like that around here,' said Zinny. 'I reckon I'd make an excellent PA.'

I was not, *not*, going to be offended. 'Maybe there is.'

'Don't,' said my father. 'I don't want you closeted with some lecherous genius all day long; I wouldn't have an easy minute.'

'Would you not?' Zinny was enchanted. She turned to me. 'Is yours lecherous?'

'Not at all.'

'He looks quite attractive on his covers.'

'They're good photographs.' I couldn't bring myself to say that he was attractive, that I found him so, and that mere photographs could never capture what I loved about him.

On the way home in the car, they began to sing. As a child I'd found this embarrassing, but tonight I didn't mind. After the conversation with my mother that afternoon I was pleased they were happy. I felt like the adult, sitting quietly in the back seat as they gave their rendition of 'Everyday it's a-gettin' closer' and the Beatles' 'Yesterday'. Zinny knew all the words; my father had to *la* quite a lot but he had a nice voice with a bit of a dance-hall warble.

When we got to the top of our hill my father pulled over. 'Look at that.'

The moon was there to greet us, sitting over the bay with its long gleaming net cast over the water from horizon to beach. Zinny flung open the door and got out.

'Let's walk!'

Nico laughed. 'That's the sauvignon speaking.'

'No, I'd like to walk.'

'What, in heels? Leave the car here?'

'Why not? We can collect it tomorrow.'

'You mean *I* can collect it tomorrow. I can't see you trudging all the way back up here on a Sunday morning!'

'I shall walk then!' She was in a strange mood, capricious and wilful, not like her usual self.

'Zinny!' My father got out. 'You're not walking on your own, it's pitch dark.'

'No it's not, it's a moonlit night.'

'Why don't you walk down together?' I said, opening the door. 'I'll take the car.'

They both looked at me as I got out.

'There you are!' Zinny put her arm through my father's. 'Offer accepted.'

He was still frowning. 'Are you sure?'

'Absolutely. Take care and don't loiter.'

Zinny began towing him away. She was laughing. 'Oh, we can't promise that . . .'

I sat behind the wheel and started the engine. They were laughing as I drove past them, and when I looked in my rear-view mirror I just caught a glimpse of their heads coming together in a kiss.

I often thought that I didn't understand my parents. But for that moment, I did.

From his expression, I thought Edwin was about to deliver bad news, but it was the opposite.

'Could you bear to . . .?'

'I'd love to.'

'I know it's an imposition,' he went on as if I hadn't spoken. 'Taking up your free time . . .'

'No,' I said. 'Thank you. I'd really like to come.'

'Marvellous.' He beamed. 'In that case, consider yourself my Plus One.'

The invitation was to a champagne reception to celebrate the opening of a new wing to the city museum, in about three weeks' time. When it took its place on the mantlepiece in all its engraved vellum glory, I noticed that there was no mention of a plus one.

I dared to believe that, extraordinary though it was, Edwin had invited me because he wanted me to be there. Something in me started to unfurl, responding to the warmth and light of happiness. Or the anticipation of happiness. And I saw in my mirror that this state of mind was a good beauty treatment. I had a shine about me. I liked myself.

I also took Elsa's advice to heart, and refused to think about Rachel. I was elated – which didn't get past my friend.

'What are you going to wear?'

'I haven't thought.'

'Well I'm no style guru, but I think you should get into a dress.'

'I'm not sure I own one – not that sort of one.'

'There are shops, Flo, and you're a woman of substance. Want me to come? I won't interfere, but I will be honest.'

I trusted Elsa – she understood that I wanted to look like myself. In the end it didn't take too long to settle on a green velvet dress with a wide, shallow scoop neck, long sleeves, and a slight swish to the skirt. I intended to wear it with a silver choker and black suede boots.

'Good idea,' agreed Elsa. 'Customize it. Make it your own.'

'You look . . . You look . . . extraordinary.'

He pronounced this quietly and thoughtfully, as though he were in fact still thinking about it, his face warm and alight with a gentle admiration. We were standing in his hall, waiting for a taxi. I felt shy – me, shy! – and looked down at myself to cover this up.

'Thank you. I hope . . .'

'It's lovely, Flora. Really.'

There is an intimacy about sitting with someone in the back of a car, and I'm sure we both felt it. Mindful of the driver, we didn't talk much on the short journey, but at least once I felt his eyes on me. When he'd paid the taxi and we were standing on the steps of the Arthur Coldshaw Building, he said, 'I'm so pleased you're here. I can't tell you.'

'I'm looking forward to it.'

'Are you?' He laughed. 'That's nice of you to say. You may find it rather . . . how shall I put it, stuffed shirt?'

'I don't mind. I don't get out much. A party's a party.'

'That's the spirit. And we shall be the life and soul of it.'

We were certainly the object of attention. I'd expected, and was perfectly happy, to pursue an independent course once we were inside. After all, Edwin would know everyone – he'd have networking to do, flesh to press, appropriate comments to make. I pictured myself as an observer. But that didn't happen; Edwin kept me at his side and introduced me to successive individuals and groups by name only, with no qualifying description. The combination of social status and anonymity boosted my confidence and I enjoyed myself. More than that – I was flying. Every moment I was conscious of his physical presence. The two of us had such different physiques – he tall, lanky, with long hands and feet, a classic ectomorph; I was an endomorph, square-shouldered and short-legged. I couldn't stop imagining what his body would feel like against mine . . .

'. . . how you know Edwin?'

Someone was asking me a question. A cool-looking bearded man in pinstripes with a white T-shirt and trainers.

'Through work,' I said.

'So are you an academic, or a writer?'

'Neither.'

'Publisher?'

'Try again.'

'Can't be bothered. But I do like your necklace.'

'Thank you.'

A tray passed. 'Want another?'

'All right, just juice.'

Edwin was talking to a woman in a long, layered robe with an African comb in her hair, but I could feel the bat-squeak of his attention. My companion removed my empty glass and handed me a fresh one.

'What do you think of this place?'

'I like it. It's stylish. It gives the whole building a much-needed lift.'

'Good.'

Something in his manner alerted me to thin ice. 'Oh my God, hang on – are you the architect?'

'Guilty. Just as well you said the right thing.'

The African-comb lady moved on and Edwin turned to us. 'Alastair – you two have introduced yourselves.'

'Actually no,' said Alastair, 'we were working blind.'

'Flora.' We shook hands and I said to Edwin. 'I'm afraid I didn't realize he was the architect.'

Edwin laughed. 'I'm sure you would have spoken your mind anyway.'

'I like to think so.'

Alastair said, 'I'm being hauled off to say a few words. Nice to see you, hope we bump into each other again.'

We listened to Alastair, who struck the appropriate modest but inspirational note and also contrived to be amusing and brief, but when it became clear that he was to be followed by several other dignitaries with points to make, people to thank and axes to grind, Edwin said softly, 'Shall we slip away?'

There was a cab rank on the corner and mid-evening was not a busy time. As we approached the driver got out and opened the door for me. So it wasn't just that I felt different; I appeared different too. Edwin paused.

'I wonder – can I offer you some supper?'

The fresh air had taken some of the buoyancy from my mood and I hesitated. Was there a protocol here? Was this invitation simply a *quid pro quo* for helping him through a dull do?

'The night is yet young,' he said, 'and we were both doing our social duty in there. It would be good to have an opportunity to talk.'

'All right, that would be nice.'

'Turkish suit you? There's a jolly little spot more or less round the corner.'

I had forgotten the simple pleasure of sitting at a table opposite an attractive man, and Edwin was a perfect host. The restaurant was busy but the proprietor knew him, beamed at me, and showed us to a corner table. Our candle was lit. We ordered mezze and a carafe of the house red. Edwin raised his glass.

'Good health.' We clinked. 'Thank you for keeping me company. I hope you weren't too bored.'

'I wasn't bored at all,' I said truthfully. 'I spoke to lots of interesting people. And anyway my life's much too quiet.'

'Really?' He frowned a little. 'That makes me realize how little I know about it. About you. Whereas you, I fear, know pretty much everything there is to know about me.'

'Not at all . . .'

'You do look beautiful.' He said this in a matter-of-fact tone. 'I took a great deal of simple blokey pleasure in being seen with you this evening. So it really is time I asked you some of those questions that people ask other people as a matter of course. I mean . . .' He raised his hands, fingers spread, palms upward, inviting a question from out of the ether. 'Where do you come from? What's your story? Do you ride a bicycle?'

I must have talked for the best part of an hour – about the hotel, and Holland House, and Salting, and Elsa – even about Gus, whom I found I was able to describe affectionately more in sorrow than in anger. Edwin was an excellent listener,

attentive and interested. But he was no fool and picked up
on the one area I didn't touch on.

'What about family? I'm particularly interested in those
because both my parents are dead and I don't have siblings.'

'Me neither.'

'Another "only" – do you say, like me, that it never did you
any harm?'

'I think we'd be the last to know, wouldn't we?'

'Fair point. And your parents? I imagine you're still lucky
enough to have those.'

'Yes, I do.' We were at the coffee stage and I stirred
unnecessarily.

'Do you see much of them?'

'Not very much these days. They live in the west country.'

'You make it sound like outer Mongolia.'

I didn't say that that was what it felt like sometimes. The
strangeness of our house, combined with its magnetic pull.
And as for Zinny and Nico – he probably imagined a nice
newly retired couple, typical of those on the 'Devon Riviera'
with all the Saga generation trimmings: well-organized holidays to places of interest, membership of the U3A and at least
one reputable wine club, dinner parties, golf . . .

After we paid the bill we waited outside for the taxi he'd
ordered.

'This has been such a pleasure,' he said. 'Perhaps we might
do it again some time. What do you think?'

'I'd like to.'

'I don't mean the corporate entertaining, of course.'

'No!'

'Just supper, conversation. Getting to know one another.'

He was watching me as he spoke, but from my expression
he could never have read how gloriously happy I was. The
habit of secrecy, of keeping poker-faced, dies hard. I couldn't
quite believe that this was happening, or that I deserved it.

'That would be really nice,' I said.

'You won't find it awkward with work, and so on? You'll
have to help me, Flora. You're the modern young woman; I'm
in unknown territory.'

Little does he know, I thought. *We both are.* The taxi came round the corner.

'So,' he said, 'I'm going to walk, it'll do me good.'

'Really? It's miles, surely.'

'Look.' He pointed at the floodlit spires of the cathedral. 'Easy – my guiding light. Not far at all.' He opened the door for me and handed a note to the driver. 'This lady will tell you the address. I'll see you tomorrow.' Briefly, he leaned in and kissed my cheek. 'Goodnight, Flora.'

Incredibly, it seemed that what I most wanted was happening. And I was going to have to shed my armour and deal with it.

SIXTEEN

How fortunate that my Prof was a much, much less stuffy and buttoned-up person than me. Like a Jane Austen suitor, less than a week after that evening of the cautious overture, he declared himself.

The intervening days at his house – I had stopped thinking of it as 'work', though that was still happening – were like a slow, careful dance, a coming together and separating, and turning, and looking and returning, all to the silent music of mutual longing.

I can see how difficult I must have been to read. Like a dog that's been ill-treated I found it hard at first to trust. Even – in fact least of all – myself. And my habitual self-possession worked against me as well. I hung back, unable to believe in what was happening, especially that Edwin, the man I knew beyond doubt I was in love with, might actually be in love with me too.

These days, my heart still beats faster when I think of the risk he took in telling me, when from his perspective I hadn't so much as dropped a glove. I wasn't *playing* hard to get, I was the real thing. Thank God he caught up with me that evening as I was about to leave, striding down the hall (he'd just come in from his office) and stopping me in my tracks.

'Flora!'

I remember I'd already half-opened the door.

'Where are you going?'

'Home . . .' I think I may have looked (God help me) at my watch.

'Don't.' He closed the door, gently but firmly, and took my bag from me, dropping it on the floor. 'Please, please don't.'

I stood there like a statue. Edwin took both my hands – you read of 'nerveless hands' and that was what they were – and pressed them to his lips. His eyes closed and he rocked slightly, as if he were inhaling their scent, their taste. The gesture remains the sexiest I've ever known. I felt myself melt, soften, start to unfurl.

'You must know, Flora,' he said, lowering my hands but still holding them, his voice shaky, 'that I've fallen hopelessly in love with you.'

The most wonderful, unequivocal, open-hearted declaration of love a girl could hope for. And what did I say, in a croaky, broken voice?

'Me too . . .'

Reader, he kissed me.

Gradually I learned to accept the blissful truth, but still I needed to poke it with a stick to check that it was real. Just as well that his delight in us – everything! – was boundless and unshakable. He 'carried me off' (his phrase) to the Welsh borders for a weekend of 'uninterrupted indulgence'. When, one early morning we lay face to face, warm, used up, floating, knowing we could go back to sleep and then do it all again, I felt compelled to remind him of the difference in our ages.

'Disgusting,' he said, sliding an arm beneath me and pulling me against him.

'A quarter of a century.'

'Ah, but look at us.' He tilted my head gently to look at me. 'How easily we close the gap.'

And close it we did, again, before breakfast. And then we walked for miles up the hills of Pilgrim's Pass. We laughed, too, at the same things. Edwin could make me laugh with a look, a turn of phrase, a reference, and the laughter, like the lovemaking, was a release. I realized I hadn't done enough of it – when tears of mirth ran down my cheeks I could feel the tension running out with them.

At home, we picked up the familiar pattern of our lives. What else would we do? We neither of us knew where we were heading and, as Edwin had said on what I now thought of as that first night, we were in 'unknown territory'. I returned to my flat, and turned up at Edwin's house at the appointed hours. There was an enchanted tension in maintaining the structure and semblance of our working lives when everything had changed. I even managed to set aside (not without an effort of will) what my parents would make of all this. Let them wait, and wonder. They had always had secrets from me – now I had mine. Or so I thought until one morning when Edwin had gone to London and the doorbell rang.

Rachel was standing there with her head a little on one side, and a warm, collusive smile on her face.

'Flora!'

'Hello.'

'Is himself in? By which I mean is he in the shed?'

'Actually no, he's seeing the publisher.'

'Hooray, that's what I was hoping!'

I said, 'Sorry?' although I knew perfectly well what she was getting at.

'I know you're busy, but can I come in?'

'Sure – of course.'

She slipped past me into the hall and kept going, saying over her shoulder, 'Can I tempt you to a coffee break . . .?'

I followed her, and watched as she did the business with Italian grounds and the cafetière – Edwin and I usually made do with instant when we were working. She put mugs, coffee and milk on the table and we sat down.

'Well!' She leaned forward on folded arms. 'I've got to tell you, I've never known him like this.'

The proprietary note was hard to ignore. I told myself that she couldn't help herself, and intended nothing by it.

'He's so happy,' she went on. 'And carefree – it's a pleasure to behold. And that's because of you, I hope you realize that.'

'I'm glad.' The kettle roared, and turned itself off. Neither

of us got up to do anything about it. So much had changed
since we had last spoken and I sensed that we both knew we
had to change the terms of engagement.

Carefully I said, 'I don't think either of us saw this coming.'

'Gosh, genuine *coup de foudre*!'

'Not exactly. We got along so well, we were friends—'

'And then, all of a sudden, you weren't?'

'Exactly.'

'How absolutely *great*.'

All this time she'd been gazing at me intently, and something
was happening to her face, behind her eyes. A sad softening,
almost an ageing process – it was like watching one of those
stop-frame films where a landscape moved from summer to
autumn in less than a minute. She propped her chin in her
hands, and fanned her fingers momentarily over her closed
eyelids. Her mouth looked uncertain.

I thought, *Has she been in love with him all this time?*
And the thought came without the smallest taint of
schadenfreude.

What I said was, 'I know how much the two of you care
about each other,' and was instantly appalled by how patronizing I sounded.

But she nodded, swiping her fingers over her eyes, and got
up to make coffee. She needed to do something, to regroup.

'Yes, we do. But perhaps not in the way you think.'

'I don't . . .'

'He was Mark's best friend, and then mine. You're lucky,
you know.' She turned and gave me a wan version of her usual
warm, foxy smile. 'Edwin has a gift for friendship. Perhaps
because he's been single his whole life, he invests a lot in his
friends.'

'I can see that.'

'He's quite simply the kindest and most thoughtful man I've
ever met.' She poured coffee, but picked up her mug and
remained standing. 'And fun! I honestly don't know what I'd
have done without him in the time since Mark left.'

She needed to talk, and I realized that whatever she was
going to say I needed to hear, for both our sakes.

'People probably think I'm over Mark,' she went on. 'And

by the way I'm not sure I ever shall be, or that I want to be. When someone buggers off just because they've had enough of you, it ought to be enough to make you hate them, but in my case it hasn't worked like that.' She gave a thin little laugh. 'My pretty sad case. The bastard was the love of my life. Forget the past tense, *is* the love of my life. Your man is one of the few people who understood that.'

Your man . . . Had she really said that?

'Edwin understood because he loved him too in a way. Mark and I splitting up was a shock to him, but he's never taken sides. Never done that thing of encouraging me to think mean thoughts. Never dissed him, as Fergal would say.'

'That's amazing,' I said. 'Unusual.'

'Unique in my experience.' She sat down. 'He's put up with me and provided the proverbial shoulder. He gives good shoulder, not to mention clean hankie!' She laughed again, this time with more feeling, and I joined in. 'I can't tell you how great it is that you've found each other, and how fucking envious it makes me!'

Still laughing, she burst into tears.

'And now,' she said through her sobs, 'I shall butt out and let you get on with it . . .!'

Rachel hadn't asked me not to tell Edwin about our conversation, but I didn't, and was never going to. By the time she left that day we were friends, which meant I trusted her to do the same.

That was a strange, enchanted autumn. As the world turned towards the solstice Edwin and I both knew we were in one of those times-out-of-mind that exist in parenthesis to real, everyday life. We were heady with love, with discovery and the sweet exhilaration of sex, but nothing in our outward lives changed. Once it did, we would be public knowledge. While the door of our romantic hothouse remained tight shut, we flourished; beyond it lay the inevitable collision of our separate lives and worlds. He still knew almost nothing about the complexity of my relationship with my parents and, whatever he had jokingly said, I intuited that there was plenty he had yet to tell me about his life. Which, however cavalier he chose to be about it, was nearly twice as long as mine.

There are some people you can never fool. When I invited
Elsa round for supper she was on to me before I'd said a thing.

'You're looking good,' she remarked and then, when I glanced
self-deprecatingly down at myself, 'No, no – don't give me that
what-this-old-thing routine, I meant *you*, in yourself. Bright-eyed
and bushy-tailed.'

'Thank you.'

'Let me guess. Life, as we must call him, is treating you
well?'

'He is, yes.' I beamed and she put down her glass and flung
her arms round me.

'Hoo-bloody-ray! Oh, Flo – that's honestly the best news
I've had in I don't know how long. So is it all loving and
dreaming and unfettered bonking?'

'For the moment!' Laughter was coming so much more
easily these days. 'Please don't tell anyone!'

'You dropped it in a hole.' She picked up her glass and
raised it in my direction. We clinked. 'I can imagine there are
those out there who might shake their heads.'

'Exactly. I rather dread going public.'

'The important thing is what the two of you feel about each
other. You're not public property—'

'I'm not, but Edwin is, rather.'

'From all you've said he doesn't sound like a man likely
to be swayed by what other people think. And you certainly
aren't. Oh – what about the dark lady, whatsername . . .?'

'Rachel. That's all fine.'

'No longer feeling unnecessarily threatened?'

My friend probably felt entitled to a bit more detail here,
but I wasn't ready to provide it.

'Not at all.'

'OK, OK, I shan't be nosey.' She chuckled. 'Does he have
scads of relations scattered about the place?'

'No, thank heavens. He's an only child, and his parents are
dead.'

'Flo – you're free as birds!'

In theory, she was right. But there are no shackles as strong
as those we put on ourselves, and I was beginning to worry

about my parents – how they would react, and what Edwin would make of them. So much of my life to date had been conducted on what felt like shifting sands, I was scared of losing my footing and being in some way found out as a fraud. As far as I was concerned, the longer Edwin and I kept our relationship to ourselves, the better.

And then something happened which forced my hand.

Of course it had to have been on the loveliest day, with snow falling in the close, and a bottle of Madeira by the bed. We rarely indulged during the working day, but the softly twirling flakes and the thin covering of quiet had their effect, and we locked the doors and went upstairs without turning any lights on, or even drawing the curtains – let people think we were out. At four o'clock the floodlight in the close came on and from the bed we saw the silvery spires of the cathedral seem to leap heavenwards through the winter dusk. We lay spooned on our sides, with me in front, his thin, strong arms round me, his chin on my head, gazing in delight.

Edwin said, 'That's us, that is.' And I knew what he meant.

Some hours later he said simply, as he had before, 'Stay.'

I wanted to, but I didn't. I can't even remember why not. Something trivial about not having clean clothes for the morning, about wanting to keep up the charade (for entirely notional observers) of a purely working relationship – no, it can't have been any of those things. I put it down even now to what Elsa would have called Forces at Work.

'I'm not going to argue you with you,' he said. ''But I want it minuted that I never wanted to turn you out in the cold and snow; I wanted you here with me, all snug and sexy and available.'

Anyway, I left. He dragged on his terrible old joggers and came down to the hall with me.

'Want to use the back door?'

He was teasing, but that is what I wanted. As we passed through the kitchen he said: 'Sure? I could make you my pasta puttanesca – just the thing for the occasion?'

I'd had it before, and I knew it was delicious. But I still said 'No'. I was already turning the handle when he leaned over me and placed his hand flat on the door, in what was almost a re-run of Declaration Day.

'You don't need to worry, you know.'

'I'm not worried,' I said, but I was lying.

'Nothing bad's going to happen if we stay together. On the contrary.'

'Look,' I said, stretching up to kiss him. 'I'll see you tomorrow.'

He tapped, and then took his hand away. 'Have it your own way. Goodnight, me proud beauty.'

He held the door open so that I had some light as I walked down the narrow path at the side of the house. When I reached the front I turned to wave, but the door was shut. I felt crestfallen: there was no pleasing me.

In the lobby of my block I opened my mailbox and took out the usual handful. Proper letters were a rarity these days, but there was quite a sheaf of envelopes, mostly junk mail and possibly bills. Upstairs the light on the phone was winking and I pressed 'Play'. It was Edwin, wishing me goodnight.

I ran the message twice, while I took my coat off and glanced through the mail. Two catalogues, a credit card statement, a phone bill and – well I never – a handwritten envelope. I binned the catalogue, made myself a mug of tea and sat down with the letter. I didn't recognize the handwriting and I wasn't expecting to hear from anyone. On first reading I scarcely registered a thing, in fact I thought the letter wasn't meant for me at all. But there it was, *Dear Flora* . . . so I made myself start again.

> *Dear Flora,*
>   *I've done a lot of detective work, so I hope this reaches you. I was very angry with Nick for not letting us speak at Jessie's funeral, but that wasn't the time and place for a row so I didn't say. I came because I thought you might be there, no other reason. I don't know what Nick's told you, but even though it's a bit late I've been thinking I want to set the record straight before it's too late. Your*

mother was a hard, sick woman. Long before she went off the rails she wasn't fit to bring up a child. I don't mind saying I ran away from her, and I wasn't sorry when I heard Nick did too. She hurt people and she didn't care, she didn't know how to. But I don't let that be an excuse. She'd be off out doing whatever she liked, she used to leave Nick on his own, she'd have left both of you kids in the end anyway . . .

I lowered the letter and closed my eyes. I was icy cold and my head swam as it did when I'd had too much to drink.

You kids . . .

The words were an echo, of something I couldn't remember. With an effort, I returned to the letter.

. . . and not give you a thought. I'm sorry I wasn't around, Flora, but I had to get out. I knew Nick would do something, he was a good lad then. I don't know how much you know. You'll have to ask him, I'm out of order writing this letter. It was seeing you at the funeral.

There's no address on here so there's no need to write back. I made a new life up north and this is ancient history, but it was seeing you like that. I hope you're all right. Ask Nick if you want to know any more. I'm sorry. With love . . .

He'd signed it with one word. I just made it to the bathroom before throwing up in the basin.

I told Edwin that I wasn't well and needed a couple of days off. He was loving and sympathetic but he didn't press me, and I was glad of that. Any probing and I'd have buckled. I rang my parents' number and they were out, so I left a message saying I was coming. This time I didn't ask, but told them.

After reading the letter I hadn't been able to sleep. An hour into the drive down I had to pull over and close my eyes, and instantly fell into something like a coma. When a little later someone tapped on the window I woke in a blast of shock, with no idea of the time or place. The tapper was an elderly woman wearing a woolly hat and a concerned expression; she must have been even more concerned by my wild-eyed reaction.

'So sorry!' she mouthed, and stepped back warily.

I wound the window down. 'What's the matter?'

'I was going to ask the same of you!' She laughed nervously. She was posh, a good citizen.

'I'm fine, thank you.'

'Good, only you're parked rather—' she waggled a hand – 'you know? A lorry nearly took your wing off, and from his expression I got the distinct impression he considered it your fault.'

'Well I'm going now.'

'Are you sure? You only need to . . .' I started the engine. 'Drive very safely, won't you!'

She was wasting her breath. I drove fast and without much care. If anything had happened, 'reckless driving' would have been cited.

My devastation of the night before had been replaced by white-hot rage. I had no plan except to throw everything – the letter, its contents, its implications, the lies and secrecy – at Nico, and let my fury light a fire under the whole lot. Let him feel the heat – let him struggle, and burn and suffer. I was going to stand there and watch, and wait until I had satisfaction.

That mood didn't last either. By the time I arrived outside the house it was late afternoon and I was almost too exhausted to climb out of the car, and sat there in the gathering dark listening to the small clicks and creaks of the bodywork cooling. When I did get out I didn't bother taking my bag, but picked up the letter from the passenger seat where it had lain the whole way down, slammed the car door and walked stiffly and unsteadily up the path. My father was on the phone in the living room. I saw his face – pale and preoccupied, then more focused as he spotted me, almost scared. I thought: *He has no idea how much he has to be scared about.*

I let myself in just as he came into the hall and for a second we both stood still, as if waiting for the other to speak. My head was so full of what I had to say that I half-wondered if he already knew. Then suddenly his arms were tightly round me, my own arms were pinioned, and he was talking, in a rush, into my shoulder.

'Floss! God, it's good to see you, I can't believe you showed up . . . thank you!'

I was rigid and unresponsive in his embrace, but he didn't seem to notice that, or when I didn't answer. He kissed my cheek fiercely, and took my arm.

'Come on in, have you got a bag? Are you staying? I can't tell you how great this is . . .'

I followed him into the living room. His agitation had moved the initiative from me to him; I had no idea what the cause of it was. I was momentarily wrong-footed. The room was stuffy and untidy, there were papers on the floor and I noticed a smeary glass and a half-full ashtray on the side table by the sofa.

'Bit of a mess, sorry . . .' He began to pick things up in a desultory, distracted way, but then stopped. 'The hell with it. Park yourself, Floss, you're a sight for sore eyes. What brings you down here anyway, telepathy or something?'

I said, 'There's something I want to talk about,' but he seemed not to hear.

'Zinny's not well, she's in hospital right now as a matter of fact while they fire sonic rays at her or something. They tell me they're on top of it, caught early and so on, but I can't help worrying. She's always seemed so bloody indestructible, I've probably taken her for granted. Got to hope for the best and prepare for the worst and all that . . . I'm pretty good at the former and completely crap it turns out at the latter . . . fuck it . . . fuck!'

He looked about to cry. The prospect horrified me and (disgusting but true) flooded me with poisonous resentment. Because, yet again I found myself in the middle of the Zinny and Nico show. I had come all this way to say my once-and-for-all piece and even now they had spiked my guns. I had never, ever, been top of the list, and I still wasn't, even though my life had been turned inside out.

'I'm sorry,' I said. Inadequate words in a small, dull voice.

He'd collected himself, and was lighting a cigarette. 'She'll probably be OK.'

'How long is she in for?'

'Only twenty-four hours. But she'll be in and out, you know . . . They won't be able to zap it in one go.'

'What about – how is she in herself?'

'Bloody fantastic, as always. Rising above it, putting her war paint on. I'm the one that's a mess.' He picked up the empty glass, turned it round in his hand and put it down again. 'I don't suppose you'd like a drink.'

I shook my head. 'Not my time of day.'

'I just meant under the circumstances . . .'

'No thanks.'

He got up, asked, 'Mind if I do?' and when I didn't answer, went to the side and splashed in an unconsidered measure. When he'd sat down again I felt the beam of his attention on me for the first time.

'Poor Floss – I do apologize. You come all this way to see us and have a few home comforts and walk bang into the middle of all this.'

'You could have told me before.'

'We could, but Zinny was agin it. She took the view that with a bit of luck they could sort her out without you ever having to know.'

'Why would that be a good thing?'

'We thought . . .'

'Thought what? Why would I not want to know?'

'I accept we may have got that wrong.'

'You did.'

'Floss . . .'

I said cruelly, 'I'm really sorry about Zinny, but since you didn't think it necessary to tell me, I'm going to take your advice and not worry.'

'I don't want you to—'

'No! I want to show you something.'

Now I saw the anxiety creeping behind his eyes. 'OK.' He tried for a teasing note: 'I think.'

I got up and went to sit next to him, the letter in my hand. 'I got this yesterday. Read it.'

He put down his glass and balanced the half-smoked cigarette on the lip of the ashtray, before taking the piece of paper. His hand shook.

'Terrible writing.'

'But surprisingly easy to read.'

I couldn't bear to look at his face as he read. Instead I sat there with folded arms, staring at my shoes and following the now-familiar words in my mind's eye. Right down to the very last one, that two syllable body-blow.

Dadder.

I heard his intake of breath, and from the corner of my eye I saw him place the letter carefully on the sofa between us and withdraw his hand, as though handling a venomous spider. The silence between us vibrated with shock.

'Well?'

The silence stretched, agonizingly. His breathing became heavy and uneven. I still couldn't look at him, not properly. My hands curled into fists; I would have curled my whole body into a fist if I could. He got up and moved to the window with his back to me. I heard the rustle of the cigarette packet and the staccato rasp as he took four stabs at lighting a match.

'Oh God . . .' He drew on the cigarette and when his voice broke he turned it into a cough. 'We tried so hard not to let this happen.'

'Well it has,' I said. 'So you had better explain.'

'All right,' said this man I no longer knew. 'I will.'

SEVENTEEN
1969: Nico

The headmistress was a pleasant, principled woman well known for her liberal views and steely competence. Fifteen years later she would become a Labour councillor regularly referred to as a 'firebrand'. For now Jacqueline Drew was working thirteen-hour days in an attempt to pull this deadbeat secondary school in the god-forsaken flatlands of east Essex up by its bootstraps. She had even initiated a sixth form and A Levels for the more able students (Jackie didn't like the term 'pupil'). Staff, governors and those parents sufficiently interested accounted her a success, though being a sensible believer in not counting unhatched chickens, she would never have said this of herself.

So it was doubly infuriating when a clever boy, Nick Sanders, announced he was leaving halfway through his A Level course for no good reason that anyone could see. She had summoned him to her office with the intention of finding out more about the background to his decision, and in the hope of dissuading him. With regard to the first, she had a pretty fair idea: chaos at home, no support, no interest, perhaps even pressure of an unpleasant kind. To the second, she wasn't optimistic. In Nicholas's six years at the school she had met the father only a handful of times, and just twice with the mother. The father was voluble with a barking laugh, not without charm, but a bundle of nervous manner-isms and with the dark complexion of a drinker. The mother was a strange, big woman who stared. Jackie didn't like either of them, but of the two she preferred the father, with whom one could at least have an exchange even if she didn't believe a word he said. The mother . . . well, Jackie wasn't easily scared, but that woman scared her. She might actually not be well, but it wasn't her place to voice an opinion on that. She felt sorry for Nicholas, but duty-bound, in his own interests, to motivate him to get his A Levels. And altruism aside, it was important for the school's standing to have more successful sixth-form students and perhaps (Jackie dreamed of this) university entrants.

When she heard the knock on her door, she got up and opened it herself.

'Nick, come in.' She tweaked the chair by the desk and went round to her own on the far side. 'Sit down.'

He was a delightful-looking boy, with the added charm of not knowing that he was. Not quite filled out yet, and not one of those strutting playground show-offs, all swank and mouth. Now he perched on the edge of the seat, hands hanging between his knees, fingers linked, a study in awkwardness. She reminded herself not to ask him a closed question.

'How are things?'

'Not bad, Miss.'

Jackie had long since stopped trying to make them lose the 'Miss'. Even if they agreed, they couldn't stop themselves. She accepted the need for some sort of handle, if only in the opening of an exchange, and had tried for 'Ma'am' but that had never taken off and the staff didn't like it either.

'I hear you're thinking of leaving us.'

'Yes, Miss.'

'May I ask why? When you're doing so well?'

'I want to work. I've got a job at Dawson's.' He named a hardware and electrical shop in the high street.

'Well done you,' said Jackie. 'But I'm just going to ask you to think for a moment. If you get your A Levels, and with the grades expected, you could get a better job. And just think, if you went on to university, an even better one. That may seem a long way off now, but believe me it isn't.'

'But if I work hard I could get a managerial job in that same amount of time.' He was well-spoken too, and articulate. 'And be earning.'

Jackie knew she must tread carefully. 'May I ask – is this all your idea?'

'Yes.'

The hesitation had been so slight it was barely there, but she was alert to it. 'Please don't be too hasty. Everyone's so positive about you, you're doing really good work.'

'Oh, well . . .' He shifted on the chair and swiped his fingers through his hair. 'I just need to, you know, get on with my life.'

Get on with his life. As if education weren't the best way to do that! Sometimes Jackie despaired.

'There's no rush. Why not think some more, discuss it with your teachers. Come and see me again if you want to—'

'That's alright, Miss. I've decided. I'd like to leave now. There's no point my hanging around pretending to be making my mind up when I already have.'

In dismay, she realized she seemed to have accelerated the process she'd hoped to halt.

'What about your parents?'

'They're all for it.' *No surprises there.*

'Would it help if I had a word with them?'

'No!' He coloured up and shook his head vigorously. 'No, Miss, it's all fine.'

'Just so long as you know that it's never too late to change your mind.'

He let this pass, and after a polite pause, said, 'May I go, Miss?'

Jackie didn't bother to conceal a sigh as she got up and opened the door. He wouldn't meet her eye.

'You know where I am, Nick.'

'Thanks.' And he was gone.

Jackie closed the door behind him and stood there, picturing him walking away, out of school, beyond her influence, away from opportunity, and for what? She'd had her chance, as they say, and blown it. As she returned to her desk she swore under her breath, a word she would have taken immediate issue with if she'd heard it elsewhere in the school.

So utterly maddening, and such a criminal waste.

Nicholas walked faster and faster, along one corridor, left down another, then right again into the college's main concourse. The area was crowded with kids buying snacks from the machines, sitting at tables eating, horsing around, jostling and jockeying. He thought he heard his name – 'Hey, Nick!' – but he didn't bother looking round, seeing who was calling. Now that the sticky interview with the Head was over he just wanted to keep his head down and keep walking, to get out of there and never look back.

By the time he burst through the swing doors into the car park he was sweating. He'd left his rucksack in his classroom, but that was too bad. School had once been a sanctuary of sorts, but that was then. Not long and he'd be eighteen and no-one could make him do anything. In a final gesture of defiance he removed his blazer and tossed it into the litter bin on the corner.

Once he was off the school premises there was nowhere to go but back home, so he slowed down. This, after all, was only the first escape. He came out on to the road where his way led past the parade of shops, the statue of a sea captain, obscenely defaced, the locked church of blackened brick and the war-zone pubs that were for the home fans and away fans, and the scruffy park with the tramps where the shrubbery was full of bottles and dirty needles and plastic bags and French letters . . . The tramps, winos and junkies were men and women, but you couldn't tell the difference under the layers of dirty clothing. Poverty and addiction neutralized people. They were just creatures. He couldn't feel sorry for them because he was afraid of what they represented – the black hole on the edge of which his own life teetered.

He turned into the newsagent's, for no particular reason except that Mr Raj could be relied upon for a friendly and civil welcome.

'Hello, young man, and how are you today? Do you have an afternoon off school?'

'Yes.'

'That's nice, all right for some!' Mr Raj was unfailingly cheerful. He was one of the nicest people Nick knew, and he hated himself for the small deception he was about to practise on him.

'I forgot my rucksack. Can I have some crisps and pay you back?'

'Honestly, you can have some and not worry about it,' said Mr Raj, who was well-disposed to lads in school uniform – his own son was studying dentistry in London. 'Choose, choose.'

Nick studied the crisps, as another man came in and went to the counter. He took a packet of salt and vinegar and stood near the other customer. When the man had paid and was leaving, Mr Raj said, 'No need to hang about, that's perfectly fine.'

'And I forgot, can I have some Number Six for my dad?'

Mr Raj peered at him. 'For your father? Or for you?'

'For him. I'll bring the money tomorrow.'

'Yes if you please.' Mr Raj took down a packet of ten from the display behind him, and waggled them in front of Nick's face. 'These I shall write down. If you smoke them, my lad, I shall know, and that will be that.'

He was the softest touch in the world. Nick took the cigarettes and left.

In the churchyard he went round to the far side of the church and sat on the big stone box that housed the remains of someone called Horace Barton and his wife Sarah. He pulled off his tie and stuffed it in his pocket, rolled back his cuffs and lit a fag. Horace and Sarah and their three children (two dead in infancy, another at three years old), all unawares, had afforded him safe harbour on many occasions. From here you could look across the scrubby marshes, littered with caravans and discarded household furniture and neglected horses, towards the estuary. That, at least, was shiny and (at this distance) unspoilt, sliding out into the North Sea between the gleaming mud flats.

The angry energy that had propelled him out of the school building drained away. He had jettisoned the one place where he was safe, in exchange for a job he had been railroaded into and where he'd be the lowest form of life. All for a moment's peace – well, you couldn't call it peace; a moment's reprieve. He had just to keep going, moving forward to freedom.

As he watched, one of the horses, a brown and white one with a long mane, lifted its head and began suddenly to gallop, the others joining in until they were all racing away, kicking their heels and tossing their heads, manes and tails streaming, mud and water spraying up from under their hooves. It looked for a moment as if they might run straight into the estuary, but there was a spindly wire fence before that, scarcely visible to the naked eye but enough to make them career off to the west, rocking, stretching their necks and kicking as they almost ricocheted off one another. Now, instead of the open water, the forbidding tower of the giant gasometer loomed up in front of the horses, dwarfing them like the fortification of a hostile army. One at a time they slowed, then stopped, heads nodding, steam jetting from their nostrils and rising in soft clouds from their flanks.

Nick squashed out his cigarette on the top of the Bartons' tomb, and then brushed it off. The galloping horses had momentarily lifted his spirits; now his apprehension returned.

'Nick!' The voice came from behind him, from the road he'd been walking along. Someone on the corner would just be able to see him sitting here. 'Nick, is that you?'

He stood up, his heart stumbling nervously, his skin prickling, a schoolboy reflex kicking in. The fag, the place, the time of day – none of it looked good. He saw a figure moving out of sight beyond the church wall, and heard the clank of the gate. Whoever it was, they were coming in. He decided to brazen it out. But she was walking much quicker than him, and had cut across the churchyard so that she effectively cut him off at the pass, near the tower with its leprous, licheny gargoyles.

'Hello there. I thought it was you.'

It was her, Mrs Mayfield, the woman from across the road. Regarded by most people with suspicion. In spite of being tall, thin and posh she was a redhead and a knock-out. His father can't have failed to notice those things, but that didn't mean he liked her. His attitude to women was complicated. Nick was a beginner in the field, but it seemed the more Billy Sanders fancied someone the less he liked her.

Nick was always rather tongue-tied in her presence. He hoped she didn't think he was thick.

'Hi.'

'Having a quick gasper?'

She wasn't ticking him off, but she wasn't smiling or joking either. This was just the way she talked. God, he loved it! And the way she dressed, it wasn't exactly fashionable, but it was stylish. In the late sixties even women of a certain age were raising their hemlines, but Mrs Mayfield's remained elegantly on the knee. Sheer stockings, shoes with a small, fine heel. A silky shirt loosely tucked in. A look Nick found almost intolerably sexy.

'Don't worry,' she said, 'I might have one myself.'

She opened her brown crocodile-skin handbag and took out a silver cigarette case and a green leather lighter with a silver trim. 'Want to join me?'

'Oh thanks, no, that's all right . . .'

'Go on.' She gave the case a little shake. 'There's a seat, why don't we . . .'

The black cast-iron bench stood in the right-angle of the church porch, facing the road. He felt horribly conspicuous sitting there with her, but she was composed, lighting his Benson and Hedges (King Size!) and then her own, and crossing her long, languid legs with a whisper of nylon. Nick leaned forward, arms on knees to relieve the tension.

'Not in school?' she asked, gazing around as though the topic were of only passing interest.

'I've left school.' This was the first time he'd said as much, and it felt pretty good. He hoped he made it sound as though he'd left some time ago, but that didn't work.

'Did you? What, this very day? I saw you trudging off this morning.'

Because he knew instinctively that she wasn't going to either criticize or tell on him, he said, 'I left an hour ago. And I'm not going back.'

'Well!' She took a drag, two long, elegant fingers holding the filter-tip to her lips for a moment, then wafted away, as if blowing a kiss. 'That's fighting talk.'

'I want to be earning,' he explained.

'Is that your idea?'

He hesitated. 'Partly.'

'Mostly?'

Suddenly, he desperately didn't want to lie to her. 'I wouldn't say that.'

She didn't comment on this, but said musingly, 'Mind you, I had an expensive education and it never got me anywhere. I might have been better off leaving school at sixteen and working somewhere like Jordan's.' She referred to the grand, old-fashioned department store in the centre of town. 'I always thought I would be good at selling, especially clothes.'

'I'm sure you would have been,' said Nick enthusiastically. She laughed, a proper laugh, warm and happy. He was over-joyed to have been the cause of that laugh.

'It would have involved lots of stroking people's egos and I'm good at that. Flattery's nine-tenths of the job.' She tapped ash on to the grass next to her, turning her wrist so that he could see the blue veins under the thin white skin beneath the wide, mannish leather watch strap. She glanced at him. 'What do you reckon?'

'Maybe. Yes, that might be difficult.'

'What I do now is something similar,' she said.

'What do you do?' he asked, because it would have been rude not to.

'I'm a wardrobe consultant to women with time to fill and money to fill it with.' She glanced at him mischievously. 'I made it up! All word of mouth and it keeps me very comfortable.'

She could see from his face that he couldn't begin to imagine this job, and rescued him. 'So anyway, what's your plan? Where will you work?'

'Dawson's.'

'The electrical place, near Boots?'

'That's it. Behind the counter to start, but they've got a training scheme.'

'He always seems a nice man. I bought my little bedroom radio from him.' Nick shifted again, his mind shifting as well in response to the 'bedroom' reference, so the next question took him by surprise.

'What do your parents think of all this?'

'They're OK.'

'They'd like you to be earning too?'

'Yes.'

He had the distinct feeling, rather as he had in the Head's office, that Mrs Mayfield had a pretty good understanding of the situation without it needing to be spelled out. Though of course there were some things she could – *must* never know because they were too horrible and too humiliating. If he'd thought for a single second that she had even an inkling of how things really were he could never have looked her in the eye again. It was pretty hard as it was.

'One thing's for sure, Nico,' she said, 'ten years from now you'll wonder what all the fuss was about.'

Nico!

He swallowed, cleared his throat. 'I hope so.'

'Take my word for it. If you decide you want more education, you can go and get it. That's what people do nowadays, they reinvent themselves all the time. Why not you?'

'Exactly!' All his explosive joy over that 'Nico' – sweeter and more intimate than any term of endearment – was in the exclamation. 'Why not?'

'That's the spirit!' She laughed again, her eyes on his face, before bending to stub out her cigarette beneath the bench. 'Look at us, puffing away on holy ground. I should go home and bake a pie.' She saw his expression. 'I am joking. I'm going to put my feet up and look at a magazine. Want to keep me company as we're both going in the same direction?'

He didn't know how that would work, but it worked fine. Her stride and his matched perfectly. When they needed to cross the road by the bookie's she tucked her hand lightly into the crook of his arm, and he could feel the smooth convex wall of her breast through the silk blouse. Under that shiny carapace of sophistication there was a delicious softness. When they reached the far side she kept her hand there for a moment, as though it were the most natural thing in the world, only letting it fall when her heel caught momentarily between paving stones. Even the way she dealt with this small accident was – well – cool was the only word for it. She laughed. 'Damn! Drunk again . . .' And she stood quite composedly on one leg, her hand on a lamp post, allowing him to retrieve the shoe and put it in front of her so she could slip it back on. There was something personal and chivalrous in doing her this service, and he couldn't fail to notice the admiring gleam from a passing bloke.

Palatine Road was a road with an identity crisis, a mixture of pre-war villas and turn of the century terraces, the former mostly run-down, the latter on the up. A terraced cottage with a tiny garden front and back represented a practical purchase and a good investment for the rising class of smart young professionals whose weekends were spent hunting the junk shops and salvage yards for tiles, fireplaces, newel posts and Edwardian light fittings.

Mrs Mayfield had moved into one of these about a year ago. Despite handle and wedding ring (the tiniest, thinnest one Nick had ever seen) she was on her own, a woman of mystery. There wasn't much of a local community in Palatine Road and what there was the Sanders were not part of, but it was impossible not to be aware of the frisson of suspicion and interest generated by an attractive single woman. She did her shopping, occasionally worked in the garden, was always well turned out and charming without giving anything away. She had been seen in the library, the Italian deli and in Jordan's. Her little black car was always pristine, and she went out in it a lot, daytimes and evenings. With a flash of pleasure, Nick realized that as of now he was one of the few people who knew what Mrs Mayfield did.

They were on her side of the road, the Sanders' house was just before hers but on the other side. They stopped opposite their gap-toothed wall with its pointless broken gate.

'I shall let you go,' she said confidingly. 'We don't want people talking.' She must have noticed his reluctance, because she added, 'I do hope everything goes well for you. Will you let me know?' He nodded. 'Feel free to drop in, number twenty-three, the one with the peacock over the door. If I'm there I'd love to see you; if I'm not, try another time.'

'All right – thank you.'

'*Au revoir* then, Nico. All the best.'

Nico. No-one else called him that. It was her name for him.

Watching her walk away he felt bereft – smaller somehow, and cold. He hardly knew her, and yet she had seemed on some instinctive level to know *him*, and that had been, well – fantastic. He waited until she reached her house; she must have known he was still there because she waved before going in.

He heard the shouting as he walked up the path. Nothing unusual in that, but it prompted the familiar misery and dread. And the physical reaction, too – queasiness, and a shuddering through all his muscles as he tensed for what was to come.

Before he even reached the front door it flew open and his father appeared, dragging his jacket up one arm and snarling over his shoulder.

'Fucking mad bitch! I'm off, I'm going, you can sort this one out yourself! Stinking bitch!'

But she was on him, wearing that flat, stony expression that Nick most dreaded, grabbing Billy's hair with both hands and pulling him back into the hall, ramming his head against the wall. Nick heard his father scream with pain, he raised a knee and jerked it into her stomach. Nick leapt inside and closed

the door after him. This must never be seen! Never guessed
at – especially by her!

'Stop it, please – come on! Both of you, please!'

The kick had made her step back; she turned her cold
eyes on Nick like a searchlight. Billy staggered away from
the wall. His hard, red face was wet with snot, sweat, saliva,
and furious tears of shame and pain, his teeth bared in a
grimace.

'Don't take it, don't take it from her, son! Get the hell out,
that's what I'm going to do! She'll kill someone soon and it's
not going to be me. Ah!' She lunged at him, her arm darting
like a striking snake at his eyes, but this time he was too quick
and was out of the door, crashing it shut so violently that it
seemed to bounce on its hinges.

Nick knew the drill, he knew what he had to do. The only
sound in the hall now was her breathing – the hiss in, and the
thick rustle out . . . She stood perfectly still now, looking at
him as though trying to make out who, or what, he was.

'Hello Mum.'

He stepped forward and kissed her cheek, the skin clammy,
the flesh beneath solid and fish-like, sour-smelling under his
lips. Remembering Mrs Mayfield's breast warm against his
arm, and her elegant foot reaching for the shoe, he had to
stifle a sob – like the outsiders, she mustn't hear, she mustn't
ever guess. He kept his voice very low, and even.

'Come on. I'm going to make us some toast.'

He walked away from her, down the hall to the kitchen.
There was a conservatory across the whole width of the house
at the back, but its peeling paint and smeary glass edged with
mould afforded little extra light. Slimy blackened leaves
spotted the roof, and the floor with its khaki cushioned lino
(it reminded Nick of the skin of some giant amphibian) was
barely visible under the piles of rubbish. Not junk – not the
friendly disorganized clutter of a home – but the disgusting
banked-up detritus of desperation: broken boxes, damp newspaper, rags and stained cloths and bedding, broken china, much
of it crusted with food, filthy bits of clothing, some stiff and
twisted with bodily dirt, books ripped and gaping, an ancient
hamster cage (he remembered the hamster episode as if it were

yesterday) the saturated sawdust rank with droppings and
pellets. The droppings were relatively fresh: at night the
conservatory twitched and rustled with mice.

The kitchen, or what passed for the kitchen, was against
the wall, as if huddling away from the banked-up rubbish, but
it wasn't much better. The stove was black with hardened
grease, the fridge iced-up and freckled with mildew because
it was impossible fully to close. There was one large cupboard
with a lop-sided door, and a bookcase on which stood tins,
open packets, and butter and speckled dripping in bowls. A
sink with a cracked plastic draining board (both overflowing)
was in the corner near the door.

The toaster and the sliced loaf stood on a yellow Formica
table next to the shelves. Nick put in a couple of slices, took
down butter and jam and rescued a couple of plates from
the sticky landslide in the sink.

There was no movement in the hall. He knew she'd be
standing in the same place, her desolate blank moon of a face
turned his way. Outside his father, free but still fulminating,
would be closing on the Wellington Arms, preparing to dive
into several hours of oblivion, no doubt already re-casting
himself as some kind of noble carer sticking by his troubled
wife because that was what a decent husband should do. Which,
to be fair, he did.

All this was pretty routine to Nick, as he stood waiting for
the toast to pop up. But things were about to change, he reminded
himself. Tomorrow he'd go to Dawson's and say he was ready
to start whenever they wanted him. The process of escape would
have begun.

The toast popped up.

He spread the two slices with butter and the peculiar pink,
jelly-like jam that advertised itself as raspberry but bore no
relation to any known fruit. Then he carried them out of the
kitchen and into the sitting room, knowing she would follow.

'You sit down,' he said. 'Sit down and eat your toast.'

Obedient now, she lowered herself heavily into the brown
velour armchair. A hint of colour showed in her sallow cheeks,
her breathing was no longer audible. Her eyes took in the
toast, her hands reached for the plate. The small familiar ritual

was already working. By tiny increments, nanoseconds, his mother was returning to herself.

It hadn't always been so bad. Nick could remember a time when his father got up from the breakfast table and went to work in a suit like a father in a Ladybird book, and his mother helped him get ready and walked him to school, and even passed the time of day with other mothers at the school gate. He hadn't appreciated it at the time, but she'd been a striking woman. Old snapshots showed her like an Amazon princess, statuesque, with big, sculpted, uncompromising features and fierce deep-set eyes like coals in a hearth, her coarse shock of red-brown curly hair trapped by two combs above her ears, then springing out in an enormous bush that waved and bounced behind her head as she walked. In those first years of school he didn't reflect on her at all, she was simply there, her giant hand enfolding his, her stride encompassing two of his own, her voice deeper than those of the other mothers and less animated.

He was about nine when he began to notice the differences, and to see that they mattered – that there was something about his mother that other people didn't like, or that they found unsettling. The school gate exchanges were rare. Other mothers stood in twos and threes while their children ran around, confident in their sameness, their ordinariness. He stood by his mother, his hand trapped in her meaty fist, caught inside the force field of her bigness, her oddness, her not-the-sameness. Sometimes he could hear her breathing, far above – dragon breathing, heavy and deep, he could actually picture fire inside her, red hot coals shimmering. He became self-conscious, possessed by a gnarly mixture of protectiveness and resentment. If other people would only cross the space, be more friendly, then perhaps she would be less strange. And if she, his mother, could try a bit harder to be like them, they would find it easier to do that.

Around the time he moved on to Collerton College every-thing took a turn for the worse. The breathing, the staring, the unreachable moods. And the attacks – not him, though she could land a heavy smack from time to time. No, it was his father she attacked. After one particularly bad evening of glaring silences he went up to bed and lay there, listening to his father's voice, at first wheedling, then staccato as his temper rose, and then an explosion of movement, things crashing to the ground and hitting the walls, his father swearing violently, yelping and snarling like a dog.

After a minute or two Nick got out of bed and went to the top of the stairs. There were no voices now, just a kind of muted turbulence punctuated by grunts and gasps and the crunch of breakages underfoot. His father appeared in the hallway, stooped over like a hunchback, one hand against the wall, his face dripping, he was spitting and gagging. Nick stepped back just as his mother appeared, walking quite normally. When she flew at his father it was like a snake striking, almost too quick for the eye to take in, her clawed hands coming down on his head and driving him to the ground.

Nick let out a scream of terror, which made his mother look up and that was just long enough for his father to stumble out of the front door and slam it shut behind him. The air as well as the door seemed to shiver in the wake of that slam. Nick's mother stared up at him as if she didn't know who, or what, she was looking at. He would have liked to escape, but if he went back into his room and into his bed, how would he know that she wasn't coming slowly up the stairs after him? At least here on the landing he wasn't completely trapped; he had room for manoeuvre. The strip of carpet under his feet was greasy and cold. Still staring, his mother moved to the foot of the stairs, one hand on the banister, and now he could hear her breathing – long, deliberate breaths as though each one required an effort of concentration. The moment seemed to stretch and hold them like a web, or a bad spell, which he both wanted and feared to break.

'Mum . . .?'

His tiny scrape of a voice, and the word itself, were like a bad joke. However weird his mother had been, he had never before been scared of her. Embarrassed, yes, and even a little ashamed of her giant strangeness, but never, as now, terrified. He felt his smallness, and also a brittle hollowness that contained only fear, roiling inside him. All the energy that had got him out of bed, the energy that had made him scream, was gone. If she chose to come up the stairs and spring on him he would be able to do nothing.

Still there was only the slow, deliberate hiss of her breathing.
'Mum – are you all right?'

Something happened then. He wasn't quite sure what, but
somewhere behind her face, deep inside her head, something
shifted. At that moment he was too far away, too young and
far too frightened to identify the change, but later he came to
recognize that it was the pupils of her eyes dilating – coming
back from the pinpricks which gave her eyes that blank, whit-
ened look, and seeing her surroundings, and him, once more.

Now the breathing got quieter, her shoulders softened, her
hand slipped off the banister and brushed absent-mindedly at
the front of her skirt. Her head moved from side to side as if
she were wondering where she was. Though Nick was still
trembling, some deep instinct told him that the best thing to do
was to go down there, do something, anything, to make things
seem normal, to keep his mother in the here and now. Slowly
and carefully he went down the stairs, feeling her eyes on him.
At the bottom he didn't pause but stepped round her and went
through to the kitchen, picking his way between the breakages,
and righting a couple of fallen chairs. There was a broom in
the corner behind the Hoover (neither of which got much use)
and he swept the shards of china and glass into a pile by the
wall. A full jar of jam had crashed off the shelf, a glutinous red
cowpat studded with glass, but he didn't know where to begin
with that and left it where it was: at least the jam was holding
the sharp pieces in one place. He propped the broom in front
of the sweepings and got a couple of smeary glasses off the shelf.
He poured some orange squash into each of them before filling
them from the tap and carrying them back to where she was still
standing in the hall, and held one out.

'There you are, Mum.'

She stared down at the glass while he held his breath. Then
she took it from him and clasped it between both her hands.
The hands had his father's blood on them, little parallel streaks
like marks left by a paint brush, where she had torn at his hair.

'Night night,' he said. She didn't reply, but she did raise
her glass to her lips and he heard her take a massive gulp,
then more and more, chugging it down as he went back up
the stairs.

As he crossed the landing he heard her say in her deep voice but very quietly: 'Thank you, Nicky.'

Back in bed he cried, stuffing a fistful of rolled sheet into his mouth which made him gag but stifled the worst of the sobs. For some reason he believed she wouldn't come up, or not straight away, and he was right. After a short while he heard her moving about down there . . . shuffle, clump, clump . . . what was she doing? He tensed as the steps came back into the hall, but the next thing he heard was the sound of the television, the bleepy music that heralded the nine o'clock news. Ordinary, everyday sounds that millions and millions of people, some better, some (though it was hard to imagine) worse, were also hearing.

He thought he wouldn't sleep – that he might never sleep again – but he did. What woke him was the sound of the front door. His father? Surely not his father? But it was, because then there were voices; his mother's low and deep, intermittent, his father's higher and harsher, whiney. The pitch of the exchange was just below the point where he could make out what was being said, but that was a good sign. Then one of them, he wasn't sure which, began to cry.

Not many weeks after that Nick's mother went into hospital.

'They've taken her in,' was how his father put it when he got back from school. 'Best place for her.'

He didn't need to ask why she'd gone, but his father was going to tell him anyway. 'She went mad again. Berserk – you saw what it's like. Only this time I saw it coming.'

'What did she do?'

'She went for me – you saw. That's what she does. She's not a well woman. Here . . .' His father held out an arm, flapping his fingers in invitation, he was in a strikingly good mood. 'Poor old Nick, eh, not something you want going on at home. Don't worry, son, your mother's in good hands.'

Nick pretended not to notice the invitation but his father flung an arm across his shoulders anyway and subjected to him to a cringingly awkward sideways squeeze.

From then on, that was how it went – periods of relative normality ranging from a few months to a year, building to the inevitable crises, which were followed by hospital treatment. When she first came back from hospital his mother would be docile and sedated, and supplied with many boxes of pills. To begin with Billy would administer these, but would always reach a point where he was bored, or over-confident and became lax, leaving Nick to take over as best he could. His mother would start to feel better in herself – whatever horrors drove and plagued her receded, and she too got blasé. So after the deep peace of the hospital, and the subsequent honeymoon period, the whole cycle would begin again. Home became a dark secret, and a no-go area for everyone but the three of them.

That was why Billy had suggested Nick leave the College and get a job, and why Nick had agreed, just like that. The school with its drip-drip of notes, and enquiries, and options and invitations, got on Billy's nerves. He had enough to deal with without fending off the whingeing bloody teachers. He wanted things cut and dried, with Nick bringing in some money. He knew his son was considered bright, and was therefore rather surprised by how readily he'd agreed.

'You sure, son?'

'I'm sick of school.'

'All right then! They're hiring at Dawson's – you could drop in and ask.'

Nick didn't say he'd already had a word at the shop. 'OK,' he said, 'I'll do that.'

'Better tell them at school.'

'Sure,' he said. 'Shouldn't be a problem. What can they do anyway?'

And that's what had led to today, with him standing uneasily by the window while his mother ate her slice of toast in that delib- erate, chomping way she had, and his father – well, his father out there somewhere, likely to come back god-knows-when, ready to start all over again.

He couldn't have eaten the other slice of toast, it would have choked him. Instead he put it down next to her and turned on the television. It was a children's programme with clean-cut presenters and a dog: her eyes locked on to it and stayed there. She was calm, content, back down from wherever she'd been.

He left her sitting there, mesmerized, watching them make

a pirate ship out of a plastic bottle and some lolly sticks, and went out of the front door.

It had been surprisingly easy at Dawson's. Old Dawson needed someone and didn't ask questions except the obvious ones about hours and reliability, and whether he was prepared to do more or less anything to begin with. Nick could tell he liked him, liked his look and his way of speaking, and was perhaps pleasantly surprised by both after talking to Billy. He offered Nick a trial, beginning the following Monday, pay forty quid a month in arrears. A fortune!

He didn't quite know what he was going to do with himself over the next couple of days and the weekend. His father didn't reappear until Saturday morning and in the interim everything was quiet. His mother didn't sleep much, but she did that thing of going through the motions of domesticity – carrying things from room to room, heating things up on the stove, wiping a duster back and forth on the windows.

He was always relieved when, against all expectation, Billy returned, but this time he could scarcely believe it. Whatever his father's failings, he was the one who suffered directly and who, as far as Nick could tell, never retaliated. Admittedly he was smaller and lighter than his wife, but he was agile. He never even tried to defend himself. Nick was driven to the conclusion that whatever names he called her, however foul his language and humiliating his treatment at her hands, his father loved his wife – or had loved her once – and kept a memory of happier times that was just strong enough to keep him coming back. Billy was weak, but he wasn't wicked. And that was just as well, because the thought of ever being left alone and in charge was one that was quite terrifying to Nick.

That late summer and autumn of 1969, though he didn't know it, they were all – Nick, his parents, Mrs Mayfield – entering one of those dreamlike golden periods that seem to exist in parenthesis to the general flow of life, and which in retrospect is only the precursor to a defining crisis. But at the time it seemed like very heaven.

His mother was well, or at any rate well enough that they got the house cleared up and a bit cleaner. There were no explosions, and they were polite to one another. With help, she managed everyday chores, even going to the shops and simple cooking. If she seemed a little drowsy and distant, that was no bad thing. With Billy's help she was washed, and so were her clothes – he got her some Cusson's Lily-of-the-Valley talc and toilet water so she smelled fresh and nice. Billy arranged for her to go to the hairdresser's on the corner and get her wild mane cut to a more manageable jaw-length bob, which would have passed for a Mary Quant cut if her hair hadn't been so bushy. She enjoyed television, and puzzle books, and talking about those things, and commenting on anything else that was right here and now – the weather, goings-on on TV (Vietnam, Mohammad Ali, the Beatles, though she was bad at names), food, what any of them was wearing. Once – it only happened once, but that was enough to last Nick for ages – she put her hand on his cheek and for a second there was a connection between them. In that moment he knew that she could see him even if she couldn't understand him. There had been these periods of calm, or remission, in the past, but this one extended well beyond the normal span, and had a different quality to it which neither he nor his father mentioned, for fear of jinxing it.

There seemed a real possibility that the three of them could have a normal life. But that scarcely mattered to Nick, because there was something else – something so tremendous, seismic and unexpected that everything else became of secondary importance.

EIGHTEEN

The feelings began as a teenage crush – what an apposite word, with its connotations of bulging, and squeezing, and sweet juice. But she always treated him as an adult, without indulgence, or pity or patronage, so the almost unbelievable fact of their lovemaking became just that: from the delirium of secret sex, love was made.

The courtship period, if you could call it that, was brief.

Zinny (he still called her Mrs Mayfield then) came into Dawson's not long after he started there.

'Hello. Believe it or not I genuinely need some batteries. And here you are – what a nice surprise.'

He found her the batteries, watched her face and her hands as she studied them. She was perfectly dressed as usual, wearing navy slacks and a brilliant green jumper, a little blue and green scarf tied jauntily at the neck, flat blue pumps on her bare feet; always the thin silver band, rounded like a curtain ring, on her left hand. There to justify the 'Mrs', he assumed, though he was aware of the rumours about her ('no better than she ought to be' – wasn't being as good as you ought to be good enough?) which seemed to be borne out by the gleam in old Dawson's eye as he advanced.

'Is our new recruit looking after you?'

'Perfectly, thank you.'

'Anything else I can help you with? Years of experience; I know my way around.'

Without looking up she gave a small, closed smile, intended more for Nick than for Dawson. 'No, just these . . .' She handed the larger pack to Nick. 'I'll take them, might as well have a supply.'

Dawson hovered, watching as Nick took the money and gave change. Just then the bell on the door chimed and he was obliged to move away. Mrs Mayfield put the batteries in her handbag, then raised a hand, remembering something.

'As a matter of fact, there's a record I'm after.'

Nick said quickly, 'We have records in the next-door shop.'

'I thought so. Is that something you can do? I'd like to listen.'

'Yes of course.'

With Dawson's beady eye following him, he led her through into the small sister shop, which sold transistors, record players and an assortment of albums and hit singles in a partitioned display stand.

This part of the shop faced on to a side road, and was quieter. Two listening booths stood against the left-hand wall. A Brylcreemed young man in his twenties, Leslie Drax, was nominally in charge of this branch of the Dawson empire, his chief qualification being that he was a reformed teddy boy, likely to know about today's pop music. Nick could sense Leslie's territorial hackles stirring, but Mrs Mayfield was up to it.

'Hello there, I've asked your new recruit to help me, is that all right?'

'Carry on.'

'Are you sure we shan't be stepping on your toes?'

'All part of the training,' said Leslie to underline his superior status.

'That's quite true.'

'I'll be here if you need me.'

Nick sensed Leslie's quandary. His jealously guarded musical empire was under attack, but he was susceptible to Mrs Mayfield's charm. The latter won, and he stood aside with a reasonably good grace.

'Let me know if you want any help.'

'Thank you.' She flashed him an enchanting smile. Nick realized he had better go through the motions, for Leslie's benefit at least.

'Do you know what you're looking for?'

'I do actually. It's a Bob Dylan album.' She was full of surprises.

'The new one?' He was hoping for a clue.

'I think it has a country and western theme . . .' She ran a finger over the stacked albums. Suddenly – there was a God! – the name came to him, via a remembered conversation at school in which another boy, a Dylan fan, had derided the singer for 'selling out'.

'Not *Nashville Skyline*?'

'That's it!' She raised a triumphant finger. Nick could feel Leslie's irritation at this minor coup, which might not play well for him later; for now, he basked.

'We've definitely got that.'

Leslie said, 'It's under Country,' at the very moment Nick located the album and pulled it out for her inspection.

'Oh, marvellous,' she exclaimed. 'I'm pretty certain I'm going to treat myself, but there are a couple of tracks I'd like to listen to.'

'Certainly.' He was beginning to enjoy himself. 'Just tell me which ones.'

'Let's see . . .' Her slim finger with its perfect carmine nail ran down the list on the back of the sleeve. 'This one, and . . . this one.'

As she handed him the album she looked very directly into his face which he feared might be actually radiating heat.

'And now I'll park myself over here and wait for the music. I don't need headphones these days, do I?'

Leslie and Nick said 'No' at exactly the same time. He did wish Leslie would stay out of it. Fortunately at that moment Mr Dawson appeared in the doorway.

'We need another on the counter in here – don't mind who, but make it snappy.'

Nick focussed his attention on the record and the turntable and after a split second's tension Leslie went through into hardware.

He had been shown what to do, and had anyway seen the procedure often enough, but his hand was trembling for quite different reasons as he lowered the needle head.

Lay lady lay . . . lay across my big brass bed . . .

Mrs Mayfield leaned against the side of the booth with her arms folded, looking at him as the track began to play, her green-gold eyes wide as a summer sky.

It was in bed that she told him. Not a big brass bed but one with a woven headboard in the shape of a peacock's tail, smooth white sheets with white embroidered flowers along the hem. Her house was not much more than half the size of the Sanders' home, but seemed to have more space. This, he realized, was what a house was like when it was cherished. All was calm and order and simplicity, pale colours and comfort. He couldn't get enough of it, and he could never, ever get enough of her. Her long, smooth, pale limbs, and her slim torso that bore breasts like fruit, twin pears, firm and sweet . . . her hands that guided and caressed him . . . her clear, curved mouth that during lovemaking lost its precision and became swollen and smudged pink as if stained by berries . . . and those watchful feline eyes that only closed for one moment, as her lips opened and her neck arched. He was drunk on her. Zinnia – Zinny as she told him to call her.

First came the weeks of astonishment, that this could be happening at all – he could never wait, never slow down or hold back, was ecstatically helpless in the face of his good fortune. But gradually there came the time of learning, and luxuriating, of being able to ride the wave of desire and even extend it, of realizing that he could give her pleasure too, which was incredibly, unbelievably wonderful and which added immeasurably to his own delight. His fear that his own background would disgust her and put her off proved groundless. When he tried to touch on it, she brushed him aside.

'Stop,' she said, 'I don't care. Not when you and I can make each other so happy.'

He had never heard an older person talk like that; it was intoxicating.

When Leslie Drax asked him insinuatingly what he was up to, he broke out in goose pimples.

'How's life then, Nick? You're looking very chipper these days – got an old lady?'

He was afraid that for a second he looked quite wild, caught out – but the turn of phrase had only been a joke, one of Leslie's rocker expressions.

Still, it was a reminder that they were on thin ice.

As the days began to shorten, so they started to talk. Something about the end of the summer, the closing-in of the year, made them realize that things could never stay just like this. The level of deception and secrecy and downright animal cunning required to conduct their liaison was intense and unceasing. It could only be a matter of time before someone caught a whiff of what was going on. When he mentioned this one late afternoon after work (he was officially 'having a coffee' with some unnamed people from his class at school), that was when she told him. He hadn't been all that serious, just commenting that they'd been lucky up to now, and their luck might not hold. It had been a sort of joke. They were lying on the peacock bed, the light off as always, and they were still joined, though as she began to speak she slipped away from him, and leaned up on her elbow.

'Yes. I need to tell you something, Nico.'

'That sounds ominous.' He put up a hand to touch her face, but she caught his wrist and pressed it gently but firmly down.

'Listen, please.'

'All right.'

'Two things actually.'

'Does that mean good-news-bad-news?'

'No.'

'Which one isn't it? Just so I can prepare myself.'

She pulled herself up against the peacock's tail, the sheet chastely tucked under her arms. Nothing could have more definitely signalled a serious moment.

'Neither, it's just necessary information.'

He tried snuggling up against her, his head on her shoulder, one hand on her breast, but she shrugged him off, the first time she had ever done such a thing. In mitigation she ruffled his hair, clutching it with her long fingers and giving it a gentle shake.

'I'm sorry, Nico, but you need to pay attention.'

This was also the first time she had treated him not exactly as a child, but as someone over whom she could pull rank. Nettled, he felt for his trousers, got hold of his cigarettes and matches and slouched next to her, lighting up. He was being slightly rude and, yes, childish, but she chose to ignore this.

'You felt you wanted to explain about your home circumstances – your parents and so on—'

'Yes, and you told me not to bother.'

'That's right. I didn't want you to put yourself through all that when you didn't need to. I live nearly opposite, remember, I have eyes and ears . . . Nico?'

'OK.' He was embarrassed, scorching, just imagining what she had observed, why he hadn't needed to tell her anything. The shame made him surly. 'Go ahead.'

'Good.' She allowed a pause to stretch, and he knew she was looking down at him in that fond but thoughtful way of hers, but he wasn't going to meet her eyes. Let her spit it out, whatever it was. When she did speak she sounded brisk and businesslike.

'The first thing is about my work. I'm sure people talk, and speculate – have you heard anything?'

He shook his head. There was no gossip in his house for the simple reason that they didn't mix with other people, but he wasn't going to say that.

'Well you might, so I want to be sure that you know first, then there will be no surprises, unpleasant or otherwise. I do quite well as you can see – I love this little house and it's just the way I want it.' Her voice softened a little as she said this and then became brisk again. 'What I told you before, about my job, wasn't the whole truth. In fact it wasn't the truth at all. I lied because that was the best thing to do.'

Nick put his cigarette to his lips to cover the dread he suddenly felt. His face was cold and his stomach heavy.

'I don't help women with their wardrobes. It's men I help.' He felt her glance down again. 'Do you understand? Men pay me, for an hour or two of fun and happiness. Their happiness, not mine – it's business to me, pure and simple.'

His throat filled with tears, he could taste them in his mouth. Then suddenly he knew that it wasn't only tears he could taste, and only just made the bathroom in time. She left him to it, getting out of bed, moving about the room behind him, picking up his discarded cigarette, putting on her dressing gown, drawing the bathroom door to, to shield him as he knelt gagging and spitting over the lavatory bowl. After a few minutes, when there was nothing left to heave and he was sitting white-faced with his back against the bath, she came in and flushed the lavatory a second time. Then she leaned across him to turn on the taps, adding some dark green bubble mixture as she did so. She sat on the edge of the bath while it ran, her legs next to his shoulder but not touching him, occasionally giving the scented water a stir. The steam rose around them. When it was full she turned the taps off and went out on to the landing, coming back with a thick white towel from the airing cupboard.

'Look,' she said, as she turned off the taps. 'I told you, and we're both still here. Hop in and have a soak while it's hot. I'll bring us some tea.'

She didn't wait, or say anything more, but went out and pulled the door to behind her. He could hear her downstairs, the clink of crockery and the hiss of the kitchen tap. The telephone rang in the hall but she didn't answer it. That often happened when he was here – the phone would ring and she would ignore it, even when they weren't in each other's arms. He had assumed that she had plenty of friends as well as a successful business (he'd been right there!), but that she didn't want to part from him for even a moment. When he was in any fit state to think, it was rather flattering to hear the phone ring out . . .

Not now. He remained slumped on the floor, his mouth still tasting of sick, his hands and face clammy. Nothing that had happened in his own house had ever shocked him as much as this, perhaps because it had never been preceded by such happiness.

I've been sleeping with a prostitute. He made himself think it.

I've been sleeping with a prostitute, but she hasn't been charging me because I'm a kid. Because she can afford to.

He remembered something he'd read, or heard about, somewhere. Prostitutes didn't kiss clients on the lips. But she kissed him, didn't she, all the time? Now that her secret was out, would she ever again do that, put her lips on his?

He heard her coming up the stairs, her step light and quick. He didn't want her to find him still sitting there, so he scrambled to his feet. She shouldered open the door and came in with a cup and saucer in one hand and a mug in the other. She put the mug down on the corner of the bath, and the cup on the vanity unit next to the washbasin.

'Drink up, Nico. You'll feel better.'

Her hand was on his arm and he got in, to escape her as much as anything, and to hide beneath the quilt of fragrant bubbles.

'That's the way.' She handed him the tea. 'Here.'

Another wave of disgust and shock hit him and tears poured down his cheeks. Rattled by a sob, his teeth clinked on the edge of the mug. His humiliation felt complete but he took some more gulps of the tea – which was very sweet – in an attempt to cover the crying. She sat on the lavatory seat with her hair and skin damp from the steam, legs crossed, slipper swinging, holding her cup. Her eyes rested on him with that look – thoughtful, speculative, not quite a smile.

'I didn't tell you the second thing.'

He shook his head. Now he felt stupid holding the mug and stretched his arm over the side to put it on the floor. She flicked her fingers in the water and gave the hot tap a couple of turns, before adding: 'Don't you want to hear it?'

'No.' It was the first time he'd spoken since her revelation and his voice was thick.

'Well if you don't mind I'm going to tell you anyway.'

He clutched his nose and sank down under the water. When he came up, she'd gone, taking the cup and mug with her, and closing the door behind her, and he heard her moving about in the bedroom this time. Now he wanted only to escape, to recover some sort of composure. He pulled out the plug and got out, scrubbing himself with the towel, pulling on his clothes which stuck because he wasn't quite dry. The softness of the towel and the scented cosiness of the bathroom mocked him – all this was probably professional. How many others?

She was waiting at the bottom of the stairs, dressed in tan slacks and a white jumper, her hair in a ponytail. She didn't move to touch or kiss him, but her eyes were soft.

'Come back if you want to hear the rest of it, won't you?'

They had a system – he left by the back door and along the snicket behind the terrace (he could go either way, for variety) to the corner, then back along the road to his own house. The light would be off in the kitchen so he could slip out unnoticed.

Walking home, shoulders hunched, he felt as if he were holding a balloon that bobbed along just behind his head – a golden lighted balloon that was Zinny and the peacock bed, and ecstasy and happiness, now there purely to mock him as he trudged back to who knew what.

I could see what it was costing my father to tell me this. At this moment he looked just as I imagined he must have looked then – pale, reduced, wretched. Nothing I could say was going to be any good, and besides I was trying to process all this myself. This was my mother he was telling me about. My mother who, apparently, had been a prostitute.

'Dad . . . How awful, I'm so sorry.'

'Don't be, Floss. It's all history. In the past.'

'Not for me,' I reminded him. 'This is all new.'

'And anyway, it's me that should be sorry.'

We sat in silence for a while, unable to connect over the turmoil of memories, of revelations. The letter – the cause of all this – had drifted to the floor. My father's head was slightly turned away but his cheek gleamed. I thought he might be crying. I would have liked that, to weep, but there was no such relief: I was dry as a bone. I had never known anything much about my parents' past, and hadn't much minded. That was how it was with us. As a child, like all children, inasmuch as I thought about the situation at all, I accepted it. A bit later when I realized through my friends that other families had hinterlands and shared histories, I'd constructed a fable about my parents, a story in which they were perfect, and perfectly romantic, sprung just as they were into life with no need for the mess and muddle of antecedents. Over the years I'd come to recognize this for what it was, a protective fantasy, and then to feel a mildly cynical detachment: if they didn't want to tell me, who cared? I cared for nobody, no, not I and nobody cared . . .

Suddenly I thought of Edwin, who did care for me. Who loved me, and had taught me to love him. Who had taught me to love, full stop. I could not begin to imagine telling him any of this. Did I have to? Did it matter? Perhaps not in the practical sense, but as a newcomer to the realm of love, I felt instinctively that there should be no secrets, especially dark ones.

The room itself was getting dark. Zinny was sick, in hospital. My father must have been worried sick himself, and now he was having to tell me this.

And it wasn't over.

'I did go back, of course,' he said. 'Because we'd fallen in love. That was the mysterious second thing, that she'd fallen in love with me. All through that autumn we fought, and fucked, and found our way to some sort of resolution. And what we resolved was that we couldn't live without each other.

We planned to go just after Christmas – not that that meant much to either of us, but it's the turning point of the year, isn't it?'

I was shocked to hear him use the f-word. Because neither he nor Zinny swore, or only in the mildest way, the word given its proper meaning had a striking special force. He read my expression correctly.

'Sorry, Floss. But that's how it was.'

I nodded.

'We decided to use Zinny's name, Mayfield. And of course she stopped . . . that line of work. She'd already stopped when she told me about it. She had some savings, but we were basically skint. It was all pretty desperate, and desperately romantic, you might think.'

By this stage I just might have thought that. I might have . . . but for one thing.

'What about this?' I asked, prodding the note with my foot. 'What about the signature?'

'That was the thing,' he said. 'We were all set to leave, and you came along.'

NINETEEN
1969: Nico

He would always remember the day, because it was December 21st. The solstice. Short, dark and brutally cold. A thin stinging sleet in the air, rubbish scuttling across the pavements, freezing dirty water racing in the gutters, the glaring shop windows and skimpy municipal lights shaking a pathetic fist at winter's mean black heart.

The earth was turning back to the light, but you'd never have known it.

They'd made their decision and laid their plans. Zinny had drawn her savings and the house would go on the market the day they left: December 27th. They were going to take off, marry by special licence, and head down to the west country. Zinny had no-one to worry about and Nico, now an adult at eighteen, couldn't wait to escape. Just now things at home weren't too bad – his mother was placid, unusually so, and his father was visibly enjoying the respite, his face less pinched, his shoulders less hunched. He and Nico had done some clearing up – you wouldn't have called the house clean, but it was no longer chaotic. So they would be all right and besides, Nico told himself, they weren't his responsibility, nor he theirs. Not anymore.

After work, which had been busy, but cheerful (Mr Dawson had dispensed tiny glasses of sticky sweet sherry at twelve o'clock), Nico didn't go to Zinny's, but straight home. Just for once they could afford to postpone gratification, because soon they would have all the time in the world together. Perhaps because he was going to leave it, the house felt quite nice, almost welcoming. The hall was warm, the small silver tree Billy had bought in Woolworths twinkled gamely in the living room, and the tranny was on in the kitchen: he could hear The Who's 'Christmas'. And there was a faint, appetizing smell of curry. Had the old man splashed out and got a takeaway? It was almost possible to imagine missing home.

But then he heard it. The crying.

He'd occasionally seen stories in the more fruity papers of women having babies when they didn't even know they were expecting. Athletic women, old women, exceptionally large women – every so often it happened and you thought *But how could it? That's impossible! How stupid would you have to be . . .?*

But there it was, audible over The Who, and a great deal more insistent, cutting across Roger Daltrey, the thumping bass and ringing guitars: the fierce insistent squawking of a newborn baby. Nico had never heard one before, but some atavistic response left him in no doubt. He stood in the hall caught between worlds – the dark, damp bustle of outside, the relative cheeriness of the downstairs rooms and that extraordinary alien sound, emanating from somewhere beyond the landing.

As he stood there a door opened and the crying grew louder.

His father appeared at the top of the stairs, with a baby held out in front of him on his forearms like a butler carrying an expensive coat. The baby was loosely, ineffectually wrapped in a towel, beneath which its tiny limbs spasmed and writhed quite strongly; minute red buds, fists and feet, thrust their way out. Its head appeared purplish, and seemed, even from where Nico was standing, to vibrate with the strength of its screams. Above this miniature fury Billy's face was distorted by shock, his eyes and mouth like holes.

Nico gawped, his own face mirroring that of his father.

'What's going on?' he asked stupidly.

His father began walking down the stairs with his enraged burden. 'She's had a baby, that's what.'

'Who?'

'Who the bleeding hell do you think? Jessie! Your mother!'

'But surely . . . how . . .?' Nico couldn't formulate the question he needed to ask.

'Don't ask me! Here—' Billy thrust the baby at Nico. 'Hold on. Hold on, I said!'

'OK . . .' Nico took the skinny bawling creature and tried to gather the towel round its limbs to make it more manageable. He'd never been near a baby, let alone held one, and if he thought about it at all he imagined an infant would be round and cuddly, like a breathing teddy bear. But this creature was a miniature fury, both angular as a clockwork monkey and slippery as a fish.

Billy backed away, holding his hands up. His eyes were wild, wilder even than those times when his wife had attacked him.

'Got her? Got her, got a hold of her, have you?'

'I suppose . . .'

'Well have you? I need to call a doctor!'

'Yes, I've got her!'

So it was a *her*.

'What about . . . Is Mum . . .?'

'I'm going to call the doctor! Take her in there!'

Nico went into the front room and Billy shut the door behind him. In here the small silver tree twinkled bravely and beyond the uncurtained window were the street lamps, and cars, and a festoon of red and green fairy lights between the trees opposite. For whatever reason – the calmer atmosphere, the lights, Nico himself – the baby's crying sputtered to a halt, like a car running out of petrol.

Nico went to stand next to the tree where he could see out into the road. Life was continuing out there while in here . . . *this* had happened. He looked down at the baby, noticing for the first time that she wasn't clean, but scabbed and draggled like the bits of flotsam he'd seen washed up in the estuary. He parted the towel gingerly and what he saw made him jump – his father had told him this was a girl, so what was this alarmingly long slippery rope of bloodstained flesh? Below, it was girl-like – a tiny unripe version of what he saw between Zinny's thighs – but as he looked a squirt of dark matter, black as tar with a tinge of green, came firing out from behind and he only just managed to gather up the towel in time to stop it going all over him.

Such was his agitation that he didn't at once notice that the baby had stopped crying. When he did, he peered down at her with a rush of fear, in case she'd simply given up, and died. There was so little of her, this blotchy rag of life – might she just have withdrawn, unwanted, into oblivion?

Absolutely not.

She was staring back at him, fiercely intent. The whites of her eyes were a fragile near-blue, the irises dark and opaque. Her fingers were pressed together under her chin, and her mouth pouted forward as if offering a kiss. The top of her head under its slick of damp dark hair pulsed gently. Nico experienced a surge of emotion more powerful than anything he'd ever felt – more powerful even than what he felt for Zinny, because this came out of nowhere and ambushed him where he stood. Overwhelming, incomprehensible. And then it came to him.

This is my sister. My little sister.

The door banged open and Billy came back into the room, pushing his fingers back through his hair, feeling in his pockets, twitching with agitation.

'They're coming. Ambulance is coming. I've been up to her, she's all right.'

'What about the baby?'

'They'll take her too, make sure she's fed and that.'

'She doesn't have to go.'

'What?' Billy pulled a face of furious disbelief. 'Of course she bloody does! Her – up there – your mother – she's a sick woman, Nick. Mad!' He made a screwing movement with his forefinger at his temple. 'She didn't even know she was pregnant!' The screwing motion had been so hard it left a mark.

'Then we can look after her – the baby.'

'No we can't, and I'll tell you why!' Billy came so close that Nico took a step back, clutching the baby close. She began to cry again and he could feel something hot and damp on his sleeve, the black stuff oozing out. 'I'm not stopping – not after this. I kid you not, I'm going, and not before time.'

'But this is your daughter!' whispered Nico. He was about to cry – from fear, from sadness, from sheer love.

'Who knows?' snapped Billy. 'I don't. Could be anybody's. She doesn't know the time of day. She's never been bothered who she gives it out to, I've always known that. Any randy bastard who gives her the glad eye.'

Suddenly, Nico knew there was something he should do. He walked past his father, turning his shoulder away as he did so to shield the mewing baby, not from any violence, but from that searing blast of indifference.

'Where are you going?'

'To see Mum.'

'Don't bother, son, she won't know you!' Nico was going up the stairs. 'Let the medics take care of it, for Christ's sake!'

He kept going, though he was terrified. He dreaded going into the bedroom, and what he might find there, but the baby was like a talisman in his arms. Nothing bad would happen while he held her. They were each other's shield and protector.

His mother was sitting on the side of the bed, facing the window that looked out over the back garden. The bedding was rumpled and the pillows disordered, but that was all. She was wearing a dress she often wore, a sort of green and yellow patterned sack, with a grey cardigan over the top. Her great cloudburst of hair prevented Nico from seeing her face. Everything looked surprisingly normal – he had prepared himself for blood, smell, the shocking disorder of a crime scene, a violent assault on the senses. This unnatural calm was if anything even more disconcerting.

She appeared not to have noticed him come in but as he moved, with excruciating caution, round the end of the bed she turned her head a little and looked at him. Her expression was that of a child caught with its hand in the sweet jar – sly and self-satisfied but in her case also abstracted. She may have been looking at Nico, but she wasn't seeing him, or either of them; her eyes were heavy-lidded and her mouth drooped in a slack smile. His mother was in some unimaginable world of her own.

The baby was yelling again, shuddering with the violence of its own voice, and he jiggled her up and down, but there was no change in his mother's expression.

When he was able to, what he saw was this: the skirt of the dress was runkled up above her knees and her tights and knickers were round her ankles. The underwear, her slippered feet and the cheap bedside rug beneath them were soaked in blood, more than Nico had ever seen before in his life, some of it containing shreds of darker matter. He had to swallow hard. The rest of his mother seemed separate, as if every part of her body above the waist had had nothing to do with the upheaval below.

'Mum?'

For a long couple of seconds she continued to look in his direction, but without any sign of having heard, or even seen him. The baby's cries subsided to little exhausted, choking tremors. Nico had come up here with the half-formed intention of reuniting mother and baby, of closing the circle, but he could see now that was hopeless. From outside came the yelp of the ambulance, abruptly cut off, and the sound of the front door opening, voices on the doorstep . . .

'Mum!' He had to try one more time. 'Do you want to see your baby?'

But she was swaying slightly now in time to a tune in her

head, fingering the hem of her dress, and the voices were louder, there were brisk footsteps coming up the stairs.

He had made the offer, and it had been refused. As the first of the ambulance men appeared in the doorway the only certainty in Nico's life was in his arms, against his heart. And he was never going to let her go.

'And I didn't,' said this man I'd always known as my father – whom I couldn't yet think of, let alone call, anything else. 'And I never have.'

I couldn't speak, even if I'd been able to think of something to say. I was stone dumb. Petrified.

'I told Zinny,' he went on, 'that I couldn't go with her unless we took you. She didn't hesitate, not for a second.'

There was something insistent in his tone now. Was I supposed to admire this selflessness of his and Zinny's, and perhaps be grateful? That was still far, far beyond me. I got up, a shade too quickly, and my head swam. Nico got up too. I wonder if I looked as terrible as he did. We were like two ghosts.

'Where are you going?'

'I don't know, out somewhere.' I headed for the door.

I swear he wrung his hands. All his debonair confidence had deserted him, and I despised him for it. He said, 'I shall be going back to see Zinny soon. Would you like to come?'

In all I'd learned in the past hour, I'd almost forgotten Zinny was in hospital. Were we supposed just to carry on as normal, then? Play happy families? I shook my head.

'I don't know if I really made it clear, she's very unwell.'

'I'm sorry,' I said.

'Ironic really,' he went on almost frantically, 'that she gave up all those years ago – because we had you – but I never bothered, and now she's the one who's . . . who's ill.'

'I'm sorry,' I said again, 'but I can't come.'

Didn't he realize that he had just taken the whole of my life to date and thrown it up in the air, letting it fall down around me in shreds like the sordid lie it was? He seemed to think, as usual, that it was all about him and Zinny, and their selfless rescuing of me.

'Can I at least give her your love?' he asked. It was merely an expression, a form of words, but at that moment it hurt, and I chose to take it literally and throw it back at him, to hurt him too.

'Do whatever you like, Nico.'

He made a little sound and ducked his head as though I'd punched him in the stomach. 'Oh, Floss!'

I went into the hall and snatched my coat off the chair. He followed me.

'Will you be here when I get back?'

'I don't know.'

'Please do stay. You brought the note, we need to talk about it.'

'Not any more. You've explained the whole thing, haven't you?'

He scrubbed fiercely at his head, leaving his hand there for a moment, his arm over his face protectively. 'I don't know about explained. I've told you what happened.'

'At last! Finally! Because you had to, because there was no alternative!'

'I suppose that's true, but—'

'Nico, I'm going.'

'But you will be back?'

'Some time.'

'What does that mean? Floss?'

'It means I need to be away from here for a while.'

I heard him say something else as I closed the door.

'From us, you mean . . .' I think it was. And he was right.

TWENTY
1999

I should never have been behind the wheel. I was a danger to myself and others. For the first hour I drove much too fast and on autopilot. I couldn't remember making a single conscious decision: how I avoided a collision I'll never know. Then, in the space of a few hundred yards I was poleaxed by exhaustion, and had to weave unsteadily along the A-road, hugging the verge, until I reached a lay-by, where I'd barely switched off the engine before I fell asleep.

I woke up with a sort of psychological hangover, dry-mouthed and disorientated. For a moment I didn't know where I was or what had gone before, then everything rushed back over me, bringing with it an attack of nausea. I opened the car door and leaned out just in time.

Walking up and down the verge to settle my stomach also cleared my head. I had about eighty miles to go – just under two hours on the road if I was lucky, but that felt far too much. I recognized, now that it was too late, that for every imaginable reason I should have stayed. Seen it through. Allowed the worst of the shock to pass. Allowed for Nico's pain as well as mine. Spared a thought for Zinny, sick and in hospital . . .

I hadn't even brought the note with me. The note from 'Dadder' – Billy, who had walked out on everyone and now had the nerve to try and insinuate himself back into my life. According to Nico, back then Billy wouldn't even accept paternity. She'd give it out to 'whichever randy sod was around', that's what he'd said.

Dadder! How dare he?

I think that's when I realized how much I loved Nico, the man who had been there all through my life. And that was why he was so hard to forgive.

I got back in the car and drove on, away from Nico and Zinny, away from disgusting 'Dadder'. Back to the place which, even if it wasn't home, provided me with some sense of who I was.

The light was blinking on the telephone and the small screen registered three messages, but I hadn't the heart or the energy to play them. I dragged off my clothes and crawled under the duvet like a stray dog, diving at once into a deep, black sleep.

I woke up as I had in the car, with, for a couple of seconds, no idea of the time or place. Then I recognized the outlines of my room, and checked my watch to find it was only half past midnight: it had been before seven when I'd arrived home and passed out.

I got up, put on dressing gown and slippers and made myself some tea. Being in my little kitchen calmed me – this was after all my place, under my control. Back in the living room I pressed the button on the answering machine and sat down to listen.

The first call began with a long rustling silence, and I thought at first it was a wrong number, but then I heard Nico's voice, broken and distracted, saying something barely audible. I played it again, with my head close to the speaker, and now I could make out two words '. . . the Prof . . .' Zinny's phrase for Edwin, and the very last words I expected to hear. There was something eerie about hearing them in my father's – in Nico's – mouth, and now, when I was still lurching in the wake of all the revelations about my past. I couldn't catch the rest of what he said, and it wasn't much, so I moved on to the next one.

Edwin.

'Hello, my love. I'm afraid I'm guilty of having called your parents' number in the hope of finding out how you were, the journey and so on, but a bit concerned to hear from the chap on the other end – your papa? He didn't say – that you'd already been and gone. He was pretty short with me. I do hope everything's all right. I don't like the thought of you haring all the way back on the same day, possibly after some sort of difficulty . . . Anyway, that's not my business. Do ring me when you're safe home. I miss you and worry about you. Can't wait to see you. Bye . . . I love you, Flora my darling . . . Bye.'

For the first time since the conversation with Nico, I cried. The straightforward heartfelt love in Edwin's voice was over-whelming. That love was all I wanted and what I most needed – but at the moment I felt so depleted, so stained and ashamed, that I could not imagine deserving it. Who was I, after all, to be loved at all, by anyone, let alone a man like Edwin? I no longer knew. Nico had been right: he'd told me what happened, but that still left me well short of understanding.

Still in tears, I pressed the machine again, and again it was Edwin.

'Just wondered if you were back yet . . . Let me know when
you are. Or actually, you know what, I'll stop being a fusspot
and assume no news is good news. Get in touch in your own
good time. We have invitations— anyway, that's not important.
Speak soon my darling . . . Bye.'

He had made an effort to be brisk and practical, and I loved
him even more for it. I wanted to be the woman he loved, but
I was no longer sure that woman existed. She'd been taken
from me, and so from him.

Jesus, was I sorry for myself!

What with the self-hatred and the even worse self-pity, I
sat up until nearly three and fell asleep on the sofa. The next
time I woke up it was a light, bright, freezing morning and I
was foul-tempered, always a sign of incipient recovery. When
a couple of kids rushed past me on the stairs, bumping me on
the way, I snapped at them quite nastily and they exchanged
a look that was part fearful and part mocking – what a grumpy
cow!

I decided to walk to Edwin's. This was partly to settle my
head so I could talk to him sensibly, and partly the very opposite of deferred gratification, to put the moment off. I knew I
couldn't *not* tell him. At the very least I needed to account
for my unexplained disappearance, and for worrying him. Also,
more importantly, I recognized that telling him was at least a
step on the way to my own rehabilitation – an acknowledgement of the past, and the violent re-ordering of the present.

I paused just before I reached the cathedral precinct, and
made a detour on a narrow footpath that would take me right
round to the south side. A wall ran along on one side of the
path which increased my sense of scurrying secrecy.

How would he react? Edwin, with his ordered, cultured life,
his successful portmanteau career, his charming friends. Might
it all be just too distasteful, too plain nasty? I wouldn't have
blamed him if he'd backed off in horror and alarm, wondering
what on earth was this succubus he'd taken into his life . . .
That was how I myself felt, but then *I* had no alternative other
than to wear it.

When I was the far side of the close I was moved to turn
right, cross the greensward and enter the cathedral through

the small north door. To my confused and jaundiced eye its soaring bulk was like a mother ship exerting a pull over lost seafarers like me, which was I suppose the idea. A tall Christmas tree stood near the pulpit, ablaze with white lights, a nice conjunction of sacred and secular. There weren't many people in here today, and only the softest susurration of voices floated up into the vast space, the visitors drifted, paused, peered, looked up. Here and there a person sat in one of the pews, studying a leaflet or simply gazing inward in whatever passed for prayer.

For the first time in, oh, ten years, I thought of the couple I'd encountered that time in Paris – the louche, engaging rogue and his sweet-faced partner with the rose on her beret. They had made a profound impression on me then, and now that I called them to mind their images were as bright and poignant on my mental retina as if the meeting had been yesterday. I remembered thinking even then that there was something significant about it, that the crossing of our paths had not been simply random. I was pleased to have met them and to witness, in a small way, the complex balance of their autumnal love. He had seemed to hold all the power – his the careless, prac-tised exercise of charm, the ease, the chat, the bold presumption of intimacy; hers the yielding tolerance, the patience, the soft stoicism . . . And yet I'd known instinctively that the real strength was also hers, even if, as I suspected, it had been hard won. When I'd spotted them later in Notre Dame they had not been on show, and these differences were quietly, plainly evident in his haggard restlessness and her serenity.

Standing now in the cathedral, I didn't analyse or re-examine any of this. The couple, with their accompanying cloud of impressions, simply came to mind. And, for some reason, comfortingly.

'Flora?'

Rachel was wearing her on-duty clothes – black trousers and a grey tunic, a soft, bleached blue cotton scarf draped anyhow over her shoulders in a way that would never have stayed in place if I had done it. Her hair was up and she was wearing her glasses.

'How nice to see you. It's my day on.'

I said hello though I couldn't pretend I was pleased to see her. But if there was anything in my manner she didn't appear to notice.

'Is all well? I dropped in on Edwin a little while ago and he was rather worried. What am I saying – he was *very* worried.'

She was being kind, not critical. I said, 'Everything's fine. I had a family crisis to attend to.'

She held up her hands in apology. 'Oh dear, I'm so very sorry.'

'Unfortunately I didn't have time to explain to Edwin.'

'He'll understand.' She smiled, and I saw her attention veer off to the side. 'I spy a question bearing down. I'm so glad you're back, Flora, and that I spotted you.'

I left by the north door, the one where an orchestra of angels lined the arch, and two broken-nosed gargoyles known locally as Bill and Ben leered down between obscenely drawn-up knees. Edwin's house was exactly opposite. As I walked towards it I remembered vividly coming here, to the close, that first morning with no idea what to expect or who I was to meet. Forces at work, surely. And now in a way the roles were reversed: Edwin could never imagine what I was about to bring over his threshold.

I had come out without a bag, and consequently without my key. Perhaps I wouldn't have used it anyway – it felt right to knock, to wait, to take nothing for granted. When he didn't come I remembered that in the middle of the morning he might well be working, out in the shed. Again, I could have walked down the side of the house but instead I pulled on the rod marked 'Garden Bell' – I wasn't aware that anyone ever used this – and waited again. This ritual, this small, self-imposed torture was bracing: if I assumed nothing I was less likely to get hurt.

In the event he surprised me by coming not through the house but up the path at the side and so that I heard his voice and felt his hands on my shoulders at almost the same time.

'There you are!'

He turned me round so I was in his arms, and then kissed me vigorously and unashamedly, in full view of the whole close.

'God, how wonderful. Come in at once!' He pushed at the door, but of course he didn't have a key either, so he grabbed my hand and towed me purposefully back along the path into the garden.

'Come,' he said, 'sit down here with me.'

We sat on the bench where Rachel and I had had our first conversation. Edwin had my hand in both of his now, and was perched on the edge of the seat so he could look into my face. The bench wasn't large, so we were very close. I had no option but to stare back into his face, that bony, idiosyncratic face with its long, lined cheeks and the mobile mouth with its downturned smile. His hair was disarrayed as ever, and behind his specs his eyes were slightly hooded at the outer corners. He was not a handsome man, as I knew my— as I recognized Nico to be, but I had never met anyone whose face so brimmed with quietly energetic thought and interest. A face in which the human and the humane were so vividly *present* and open to receive.

Sensing something, he lifted my hand, gave it a brief kiss and returned it to me.

'Is this OK?' he asked.

The simplest possible question, and yet I had the weight of it. He knew I had things to say, and he was making sure the circumstances were right. I was under no pressure; he was ready when I was.

'Perhaps,' I said, 'we could go in?'

'Let's do that.'

He got up and moved towards the house, but I had a sudden thought. 'No.' He looked at me. 'Can we go into your study?'

'The shed? Of course.' He smiled ruefully. 'So long as you remember it's a while since it was subjected to your ministrations. What's the expression? Cut me some slack.'

I followed him down the path. The door of the shed was open, and the inside as he'd left it when he heard the garden bell – the chair pushed back from the desk, the screensaver of planets gently passing and re-passing in dark space, the biro on the spiral notebook, the coffee mug with the name and logo of a literary festival. But there was no pile of paper on the armchair.

'Thanks to your ministrations, there is at least a seat I can offer you.'

'Thank you.' I sat, and he pulled round the chair from behind the desk. The door remained open and it was nice to be in this unfussy, secluded space, but still to be able to see the pale afternoon light, the tussocky lawn and the languorous sprawl of the clematis on the wall opposite.

'You're right,' he said. 'It's lovely to have you here, where no-one else comes.'

But now I'd stipulated my conditions, and had them fulfilled, I had to speak.

'Don't worry,' he said. 'How about the cup that cheers?'

He didn't wait but put water in the kettle from a large tartan thermos, and switched it on. He retrieved the lit-fest mug from the desk and set it alongside one of the William Morris ones that had been a present from Rachel. It occurred to me that I hadn't yet given him a present – there had been no occasion to.

'How was your journey, anyway?' he asked over his shoulder. 'Should I say journeys? You must be shattered.'

'I'm OK.' I wanted to say that if I was shattered it wasn't because of that. Instead I added, 'I don't mind driving.'

'That's one of the differences of age. I used to love it, but not so much now. You'll be able to take over.' He glanced at me, a hot, narrow glance with a grin. 'Didn't Dr Johnson have some quip about a fast carriage driven by a smart woman? That'll be us.'

I did love him. The soft patter of his words was like manna. It was not so much that he knew what to say but that he knew what not to – and knew not to elicit anything from me. Now he handed me the mug and sat down with his. The desk chair was higher, and he had his back to the window, so his face was in shadow. He realized this and moved slightly to one side, his head turned to look out, away from me.

'The garden's a little shaggy.'

'It looks nice. You don't want it too manicured.'

'Good grief no, I'd never be able to live up to it.'

'Edwin.' I took a deep breath, quite audibly, but to his eternal credit he didn't turn round. 'Edwin, I owe you an apology.'

'I don't think so.' He looked down at his tea, lacing his long fingers carefully around the mug.

'Well, I took off without explanation, and I didn't return your calls.'

'Don't give it a thought. I knew you'd have your reasons.'

'I did, and I want to tell you. Or at least, I don't exactly want to, but—'

'Flora, you don't have to. I don't believe in all that no-secrets business. Everyone's entitled to his or her quota of secrets. And,' he leaned a little towards me, teasing, 'I have complete faith in you.'

He may have been teasing, but I knew that was true. With Edwin's love came his trust, his discretion and his respect however (as it seemed to me at that moment) undeserved. My heart contracted and pushed a lump into my throat, so that my voice, when I found it, wavered dangerously.

'I'm not sure what you're going to think . . .'

'Nor me,' he said. 'Try me.'

You hear people say they 'don't know where to begin', but in my case that was literally true. Having screwed up my courage, I found myself tongue-tied and overwhelmed, but Edwin understood and came to my rescue.

'Why not start with why you had to go home? Are your parents all right?'

I said 'Yes' before I remembered that wasn't true, and added, 'Actually Zinny's not well. She's in hospital.'

'Zinny's your mother, yes? I'm so sorry to hear that. How is she?'

'I don't really know . . . That's not why I went . . .'

It was horribly shaming to admit it, and I wavered. Edwin passed me a handkerchief.

'Don't worry,' he said, quietly and seriously. 'Just keep going.'

What a rare gift it is to be a good listener. Edwin, it turned out, had a genius for listening, and just as well. Heaven knows how he followed the story I had to tell him. It was already complicated and what with that, and the fact that I had barely digested it myself, and so was recounting it out of sequence and in emotional fits and starts with frequent digressions, and backtracking, it must have been far from easy. At no point did he express shock, or horror. His expression throughout remained intent, calm and concentrated. Occasionally he'd nod, but he didn't speak, or touch me.

He was right not to. I had to find my own way through. As I spoke, there were so many other things that bobbed up from my memory which made shocking sense. My childish hand touching that other, older hand on the window frame . . . my parents' secrecy, the conversations that stopped as I appeared . . . the sense I developed of my having, uniquely, no past . . . the visit to Jessie and those half-heard words – *The children* – the hard-faced man glimpsed at her funeral, the *Dadder* of that creepy note.

The netted tangle of hair in the fusty, haunted spare bedroom. Oh, yes., it was all coming together in my mind.

I can't say how long it took me, but by the time I slowed and ground to a halt the sun had moved over so that it fell across the garden, and the wall opposite cast a short shadow.

For a moment Edwin said nothing, but let the blessed silence rise and lap and wash over us. He rubbed his hand over his face, and I mopped mine with his hankie and tucked it in my jacket pocket – it was in no fit state to hand back. Then he got up and stretched, the normal, everyday stretch of a tall man who'd been sitting down for too long.

'Thank you . . . I could never have made that up. Come on.' He stood in the doorway and held out an encouraging hand. 'Let's have a stiff drink.' He caught my reflexive glance at my watch. 'I don't care what time it is.'

I followed him, like a child, and he closed the door of the shed behind us. He stretched again, opening his shoulders and tilting his face to the sun.

'Turned out nice again.'

We walked side by side back to the house. Something in his manner made me feel less like a child. More myself. He had said nothing yet about what I'd told him, but now that it was out there, and the world had not imploded, some sort of perspective was slowly returning.

In the kitchen he opened the bottle cupboard and took out whisky in one hand, brandy in the other, plonking them on the table and adding two tumblers.

'Don't say "neither", this is the moment for strong liquor.'

'Brandy then.'

'Good choice.' He poured us each a third of a glass. 'In or out?'

'In, it's too cold.'

'I'm glad you said that.' He nodded in the direction of the darkening garden. 'I need to do some more work out there,' he observed. He wasn't going to return to the subject independently, not yet. 'Make time for it before I get into the next book. I think I could enjoy gardening given half a chance . . .'

'We could . . .' I began, and then told myself to spit it out. 'So what do you think?'

'About what, specifically?'

I took a large gulp of my drink, such that my eyes watered. 'What should I do?'

I saw at once that was the right question. I had his attention and was assured, this time, of a reply. He spoke quickly and incisively as if he'd been longing to say something like this, and just waiting for an opportunity. But his answer still surprised me.

'Nothing. Do nothing.'

He saw how lost and confounded I was, and leaned into me removing his glasses so that his face was bare and vulnerable, before placing a kiss on my mouth. It may sound strange, but that gesture, the removal of the specs, made my heart beat faster. It was his way of showing that he was no longer interested in what could be seen, or heard, only in what could be felt – the prelude, usually, to lovemaking. And the kiss was not brief and placatory, a sop to my anxiety, but ardent and warm.

'Nothing, my darling Flora,' he added. 'Except this . . .'

Because so much had happened and (for me at least) changed, it felt like a long time since we had made love, though it can only have been a few days. I'd like to say that it was perfect, but it wasn't. I was still too uncertain of myself. But being wrapped together, skin on skin, in Edwin's room where we had watched the light change and the seasons roll round on the cathedral spire, assured me of his certainty, and that of our love. Afterwards, I fell asleep in his arms.

When I woke he was sitting in a chair by the window, the curtains still open, reading beneath a lamp. He'd pulled on his clothes but the cotton sweatshirt was inside out and his feet were bare. He didn't realize I was awake and there was an immense sense of peace in watching him as he turned the page, absorbed in the text.

'Hello.'

'Oh, hello,' he said, closing the book, smiling across at me. 'You're back.'

That evening we talked some more, about everything. We discussed the TV series, and his new book, and Rachel, who was seeing someone (I was genuinely pleased to hear this and not only for selfish reasons). Edwin was also keen that as soon as work allowed we should go away together.

'Somewhere where it's just us standing side by side looking at beautiful things,' was how he put it, and I didn't argue. Nor did he when I said I was going to go back to my flat that night.

'Of course,' he said. 'You need to make it feel right again.'

Just before I left I voiced the nagging fear that was still there.

'What if he turns up?'

'The note-writer? He won't.'

'But he knows where I am. And I can't reply, because I don't know where he is! What if he just appears?'

We were standing on the path that ran between the garden and the close. Behind us the front door stood open, but Edwin's face was in shadow and unreadable as he said: 'What if you were somewhere else?'

I didn't realize then that I'd been proposed to. He only waited for a moment before adding, 'No-one should let the sun go down on their wrath. It's not good for the health. Speak to Nico and Zinny, and when you're ready, let's go down there. You because you must, and I because I want to meet them.'

TWENTY-ONE

I t was strange – more than strange, a shock – to hear their names in Edwin's mouth. All my life I had been accustomed to the vacuum that surrounded us. No past, no extended family, few friends and no close ones – just me, Nico and Zinny in our tacit and, to me, mysterious conspiracy of secrecy. That was what I was used to, and the reason why Nico's revelations, startling enough in themselves, had given me something like vertigo.

But now Edwin knew, and the sky had not fallen in, nor the earth opened up. When he spoke their names they became more real, more normal – two fully comprehensible people who had made the best of the hand they'd been dealt.

He had given them back to me.

That didn't stop me feeling nervous when, a week later, Edwin drove us down. The last time I had made this journey I had been fuelled by rage and horror. I hadn't needed to screw up my courage, I wanted only to say my piece, to throw the note in their faces and demand an explanation.

Now, I had the explanation, and the freedom to make of it what I would. 'Grown-up time', as Elsa had said to me after she'd listened.

'So you've got a man there who not only adores you, but who's wise and generous too,' she said. 'Please don't tell me he can bake a pie as well, or I'll have to divorce Brian.'

'I do know I'm lucky,' I confessed.

'So go with him to Devon, and face your demons.'

'They're not demons.'

'You know what I mean. You owe it to Edwin, as well as yourself, to get over it. Stiffen those sinews, girl. And now,' she raised her glass, 'the toast is: To you, and all who sail in you!'

We clinked, she laughed, and I prayed.

*   *   *

But now we were nearly there and I had butterflies. We drove down into Salting for a pub lunch and – for me anyway – some Dutch courage.

On the phone, Nico had sounded more like his old self and it was soon apparent why.

'We'll both be here. I picked Zinny up yesterday, time off for good behaviour.'

'How is she?'

'Oh . . .' I could picture him taking a quick covert drag; he must be outside. 'You know Zinny.'

For a stupid moment I wanted to say that I didn't, and I never had, but I squashed the impulse instantly.

'She's very chuffed about meeting the Prof. I'm in charge of supper – does he eat fish and chips?'

'He eats anything. And by the way, we won't be needing a bed, we're booked in at a B&B.'

'You sure?' I could tell this hadn't crossed his mind.

'Quite sure.'

'OK.' After a short pause, his tone changed. 'We're awfully glad you're coming, Floss. Honestly. I thought I might have frightened you away with all – you know, all that.'

'No,' I said. 'You didn't. We'll be with you some time in the afternoon.'

As we walked up the high street from the car park to the Hat and Feathers, Edwin said, 'I knew the name rang a bell – I've been here before.'

'Really? Why?' It would have been more normal to ask 'When', but his visiting Salting seemed so unlikely.

'They started rather a nice literary festival here about ten years ago, and I came to speak at the very first one. My venue was the library . . . Is that still going strong?'

'The library certainly is. Zinny would know about the literary festival, she's a fan of yours.'

'Is that so? Excellent, it's always good to meet a satisfied customer.'

In the pub I drank my glass of white too quickly and could only pick at my food while Edwin talked about his previous visit.

'They were a charming and receptive audience, I remember. Average age rather older than I was then, about sixty? But all keen readers and widely read; there were plenty of questions. I was put up in considerable comfort by a couple in a lovely Georgian house just up the hill . . .'

He was keeping me amused, trying to divert me from my anxiety, and I was only listening with half an ear, but even so his thumbnail sketch of Salting in all its well-read, prosperous respectability served to remind me of what I was taking him to – the place of the outsiders, the non-belongers, the misfits – and my stomach churned. I prayed he didn't imagine that I – that we – had been part of this.

'. . . a delightful town,' he was saying, 'typical of lots of others especially around the south coast. The best place in the world to retire to, if that's what you're after. But—' he leaned forward and lowered his voice – 'I confess it would send me round the bend in short order!'

As we walked back to the car, I reflected that while nothing he said or did seemed calculated, it was so often exactly what I needed to hear. Just as I was in danger of feeling alienated, he'd pulled me back, and aligned himself with me, reminding me that I was not alone.

I took the wheel for the last few miles, out of Salting and up on to the coast road. This afternoon – the short afternoon of the solstice – was hard, clear, perfect, the sea below like a millpond and the sky an intense blue, fading to a wintry dove grey on the horizon. The road was so high here that gulls wheeling in the sunshine at the cliff top were level with the car window so we seemed almost to be flying too.

'It's so beautiful here,' said Edwin. 'What a place to be brought up.'

I wondered if he was imagining an Enid Blyton childhood, full of madcap adventures in the great outdoors, boating and hiking and picnics with lashings of ginger beer. This made me remember something I had kept buried for years.

'I had a dog,' I said. 'Towser. He was a runaway who adopted us and I pressured them into keeping him.'

'Your very own dog, lucky girl. I wasn't allowed. My parents weren't in favour of pets, they reckoned they'd wind up looking after whatever it was and I bet they were right: I was an idle so-and-so. Did you look after Towser?'

'Yes. But when he got run over by a car they were secretly relieved. I heard them talking.'

He said matter–of-factly, 'How awful that you heard them. But good that they let him stay.'

We came to the fork in the road where we turned down towards the bay, and in a moment there was our roof, like an upturned boat below the swell of the hill. I pulled over and put the car in neutral.

'That's us.' I realized what I had said, the odd turn of phrase, but Edwin was gazing down.

'I'd say it's idyllic but in stormy weather it must be fearsome.'

'Edwin . . .'

'Come on, driver.'

'I'm not sure . . .'

'It'll be dark if you hang about much longer. And anyway, how do you think I feel, the man in your life about to meet your parents for the first time?'

'They're not my parents.'

'Whoah.' He put his hand, dry and warm, on the back of my neck. 'Don't say that. Never let me hear you say that.'

'But it's true.'

'They are the people who brought you up, and cared for you and loved you, and made sacrifices for you – yes, they did that. I'd call that being parents, good ones. All that's happened is that you've found out something new about them, and yourself. You've found exactly how much they *did* love you. Especially Nico.' He pushed his fingers up into my hair. 'Flora? Yes?'

'I suppose.'

He removed his hand. 'Come on then, or I'll walk and be there before you.'

We pulled in behind a car I hadn't seen before – a gleaming silver convertible with a sleek, almost sinuous appearance as if made not from metal but some more pliable substance. Edwin's eyes widened in admiration as he got out.

'By George, a classic Lotus Elan!' He breathed reverently. 'You never said they had a car like this.'

'They didn't. It must be span new.'

He was walking round it. 'Not span new, no. But a lovely, lovely thing.'

The car was spectacular, but too sudden, too much. For some reason it bothered me. I heard a tapping and looked up: Nico was on the verandah. He sent me a wave and beckoned, stepping away to meet us at the door.

A moment later I thanked God for the car because it made the meeting between Nico and Edwin almost normal. Once they had shaken hands it acted as a lightning conductor, and they went outside to admire it, though I was sure Edwin was no connoisseur. Just as well there was this distraction, because seeing the two of them together was overwhelming. They were so different in appearance, and I'd calculated that Edwin was at least ten years older, but the vital spark seemed far more evident in him. Nico looked tired and puffy, his boyish handsomeness tarnished. Zinny's illness (and other things, I imagined) had taken its toll.

The moment he was outside the door he lit a cigarette, and broke off from car talk ('1969 model . . .') to say over his shoulder: 'Go on in, Floss, she's expecting you.'

As soon as I saw Zinny, I could tell how things were. And how much it meant to me, because my heart plummeted. She was sitting on one of the basket chairs, with her feet on a small footstool, and made no move to get up, though she did extend a hand, which I took briefly.

'Hello, stranger.' The voice was firm, but the hand in mine was insubstantial, silky and loose-skinned.

'Hello Zinny. How are you?'

'Faded,' she said caustically. 'No point in pretending, you can see for yourself. What have you done with the Prof?'

'He'll be in shortly. Nico's telling him about the car.'

She murmured without rancour, 'Stupid thing, complete madness,' and craned her neck a little to see out into the garden. She was almost transparently thin, and her hair had lost its lustre. Perhaps most shockingly she was wearing a pale blue tracksuit – Zinny, in a tracksuit! But elegance is not all to do with presentation; it's innate, a gift, and Zinny still had it. She was still looking out of the window when she added in the flat voice she reserved for the expression of extreme emotion, 'I can't tell you how glad we both are that you're here.'

'And we're glad to be here, Zinny.'

Not much of an exchange you might think but one which established, simply and irrefutably, the truth: that there wasn't much time.

The men stepped down on to the drive to take a closer look at the car. I guessed they were being tactful, allowing us this moment. Zinny turned back, spreading her fingers on her knees and looking down as she twiddled her loose ring, the plain gold band Nico had given her.

'I understand you heard from Billy.'

'Yes.'

'I used to think him a ghastly man, and a coward.' She tilted her head slightly both reflecting and, I thought, taking a deep breath. 'But now I'm not so sure. He had much to contend with, and he stuck it out till the last.' Her pale hazel eyes lifted to mine. 'Almost the last.'

I wasn't going to lie. The injury was still raw.

'You mean till I arrived.'

'No, not that. You weren't you then, you were something that happened to him, and he couldn't cope any more. He knew you'd be cared for.'

'All right,' I said neutrally. I wasn't going to argue. There was strength in her frailty, and we both knew it. There was only so much energy she could give to this.

'You weren't happy to get his note.' I shook my head. 'I don't blame you. But don't feel too badly about him, or your mother. I've been pretty uncharitable about her, too, in the past. Certainly nothing was her fault, she was appallingly ill. He wrote to you for the right reasons. Have you replied?'

'There was no address, but I wouldn't anyway.'

Again, Zinny's little gesture with her ring. 'She was here once.'

'I know,' I said. 'I guessed.'

She went on as though I hadn't spoken. 'Nico always felt terrible about her being in hospital and then in that place, so we had her to stay for a while when you were away. And then you came back early.' She gave me a cold, sad smile. 'You must have been terrified.'

'I was.'

'You poor thing. We took her back that night.'

I wanted to ask *Did she know it was me?* But it was all so long, long ago.

Edwin and Nico were visible again now, looking out over the bay, Nico pointing. Zinny said very quietly: 'I understand, Flora. But really we should be grateful. He's done us all a favour.'

The men turned towards the house, hunched with the cold. Edwin was smiling at something Nico had said. I felt a tiny beat of something unexpected but irrepressible, like hope.

'Perhaps,' I said. 'Maybe.'

We stayed for not much more than an hour; it was clear Zinny couldn't have managed much longer. With Edwin in the room she bloomed and sparkled, and I could see he was enchanted. Watching them I reflected that maybe that accounted for her reserve, amounting almost to chilliness, much of the time: before Nico she had needed all her vivacity and charm for those other men, the clients. She had formed a habit of dignified control in the rest of her life, a protective coloration.

I don't know to this day whether she knew Nico had told me about all of that. If she did, she had the wisdom not to mention it. The four of us talked about the future – about Edwin's books and our plans to go away together, this house (they feared they'd have to sell it) and the beauty of the surroundings, Salting (Zinny had been to Edwin's talk) . . . And the symbolism of that car.

'I was telling Edwin,' said Nico. 'A flash motor's always been a dream of ours, and I woke up one morning thinking "Now's the moment", and why not?'

Of course we knew what he meant, though Edwin and I could never have guessed at the full implications.

Edwin said, 'Well, perhaps now is my moment to confess I want to marry your daughter.'

Zinny let out a little cry, which I shall never forget – a sound of pure happiness – and Nico's eyes shone bright.

'Blow me, that's great – does she know? Floss?'

'Yes,' I said. 'I know.'

So it was that we said goodbye on this joyful note. It was clear they didn't want to discuss Zinny's illness, or how the treatment was going, preferring to let Edwin and me take centre stage. I found the swirl of emotion quite overpowering, and I was sure Nico and Zinny did too, but the habit of covering up and carrying on was ingrained. When, on the doorstep, we assured them that we would be back very soon, they didn't react. It was as if they were too pleased with our other news to hear – something I was to remember later.

It was too dark to walk then, but the next day we came back, at Edwin's insistence, before hitting the road. The forecast was changeable, but for now the morning light was lovely, with that poignancy that comes with a low winter sun. We moved our car to the cliff top lay-by and went for a walk on the beach. We had the bay to ourselves. The tide was on the turn, still far out but gently licking its way in. The sand faded from shiny copper where it was speckled with fine shingle, to pewter, to a creamy gold near the top, where the path met the beach.

We walked side by side, eastward, my gloved hand tucked into his arm, for a while anyway – we didn't feel the need for that. And to begin with we didn't talk, either. I believe we were both thinking of Nico and Zinny up there in the house, doing whatever they were doing. I imagined Nico helping Zinny to walk, the two of them bowed and slow, solicitous of one another, and found I was crying, openly, uncaringly, my sobs small in the wide sea air, my tears drying as they flowed.

We had reached the end of the beach and Edwin put his arm across my shoulders.

'I know . . . I know . . . Here.' He steered me to a rock

where we could both sit down. 'What we need is the sun on our faces.'

The tall rocks at the far, western end looked like a castle with the sunlight on its towers. Gulls glinted white in the dark shade below them. The house was somewhere up there to our right, but invisible now beyond the edge of the cliff, the hill behind it billowing up like a soft green sail. The small waves crept silkily towards us, spreading then trailing a delicate edging of watery lace on the hard sand. The first of the clouds trailed shadows over us. Edwin cupped my chin and turned my face to his, wiping my tears with his other hand, and kissing me.

'I love you,' he said. 'Was that a "Yes" in there? Yesterday?'

'Yes, it was.'

'Thank God for that. I risked looking three kinds of idiot otherwise.'

'They liked you so much.'

'And I liked them.' He kissed me again, this time on the forehead, and turned his own face back to the sun. 'Actually, I more than liked them. They're truly wonderful, Flora.'

I looked at him in surprise, but he was gazing not so much at the view now as into his mind's eye.

'It's not given to many to have parents who are truly still in love, the way they are – I mean the romance still undimmed like that. Or to know, as you do, that you were chosen. That you were so important to Nico that he risked losing the love of his life for you – no, listen – and that she risked freedom and happiness so that you could be together . . .' Still thinking, he brushed his hand on mine. 'They are beautiful, and I don't mean just handsome, which they are undoubtedly are. They're beautiful, and graceful – and heroic.'

We sat together for another minute or two, and then he rose, and held out his hand, taking me with him back over the sand as a chilly wind chivvied us on our way.

'Like you,' he said.

TWENTY-TWO
2000

T he next time we were there, in that very place, was late spring, that breathlessly lovely time when the English countryside has a bridal air, the trees with blossom in their hair, the air sweetly green-smelling, the grass studded with daisies and the cliff ledges with thrift, the little waves frisky in the bay.

We parked in the same place as before. There was one other car there, a well-used Japanese hatchback with two child seats in the back. Down on the beach, at the tip of the western rocks, we could see two figures – a child running in wide, excited circles and a woman with what looked like a rucksack on her back, which we then realized was a papoose.

Edwin insisted on going ahead of me and I followed him carefully down the rickety steps, holding my posy, and the paper bag of seeds. At the bottom he stood aside, touching my back gently with his hand as I did so. He didn't follow, and when I glanced over my shoulder I saw him starting to walk slowly across the sand towards the water's edge. The man I loved had abandoned his shoes and was barefoot, an instinct common to all ages.

I too walked slowly, held by the spell of the perfect day. I'd imagined this – both this visit and what had happened – so often, that it held no horrors for me. When I reached the flat rock where Edwin and I had sat before I paused, to look around and orient myself.

From the cliff top lay-by I ran my eye along to the point where I knew the narrow downhill road turned away from the sea to run past our house. That was the place, that bend – even with spring growth you could still make out the red earth graze on the lip of the cliff, and the hurtling path they'd taken after that. I clutched the flowers and seeds in one hand and set off over the rocks, taking long, careful strides, my free arm held out wide to steady myself. I was ungainly by now but I moved surprisingly surely, buoyed up by my purpose.

The exact place wasn't hard to find. The ground was scarred and the gorse bushes broken and flattened. The authorities had done a good job tidying up though: there was no debris – or almost none. I felt something under my sandal, and when I picked it up I found it was a tiny shard of blackened metal no bigger than my thumbnail, the broken edge razor sharp. Hopefully, full of excitement, I rubbed the smooth side with the hem of my dress, and in no time the silver shone through.

This, then, was where they had ended their story, Nico and Zinny. Where they had flown in the Lotus, their gleaming chariot. No accident, whatever the coroner might say, but their last escape, together as always.

The first stumble of rocks was behind me, but here there was hard turf beneath my feet, laid bare by the car's impact. I kneeled down and, using the tiny piece of metal, scraped and gouged until I was sweating, and had succeeded in roughening the surface so I could see loose earth. I opened the paper bag and sprinkled the seeds, trickling water over them from my drinking bottle. Then I laid the bunch of pink and blue flowers (love-in-a-mist, the man in Salting had assured me) on the ground alongside my makeshift border. Finally, I said my farewells.

Getting to my feet was awkward – I hadn't allowed for it. I had to go on hands and knees to the nearest rock and haul myself up by easy stages.

The woman in the distance was sitting down now, her baby next to her, the little boy paddling crazily, feet stamping, water flying. Edwin had been watching me, and began unhurriedly walking towards me over the sand.

As we drew closer, I felt our baby push at my walls, eager for life.